950

BENEVOLENCE

Also by Cynthia Holz

Home Again
Onlyville
The Other Side
Semi Detached
A Good Man

BENEVOLENCE

CYNTHIA HOLZ

To Mark & Rebecca —
Good to chat with
you!

Cynthia Holz

ALFRED A. KNOPF CANADA

PUBLISHED BY ALFRED A. KNOPF CANADA

Copyright © 2011 Cynthia Holz

All rights reserved under International and Pan-American Copyright
Conventions. No part of this book may be reproduced in any form or by any
electronic or mechanical means, including information storage and retrieval
systems, without permission in writing from the publisher, except by a reviewer,
who may quote brief passages in a review. Published in 2011 by Alfred A. Knopf
Canada, a division of Random House of Canada Limited. Distributed by Random
House of Canada Limited, Toronto.

Knopf Canada and colophon are trademarks.

www.randomhouse.ca

The poem quoted on page 165 is from *Short Journey Upriver Toward Ōishida*, by
Roo Borson © 2004, published by McClelland & Stewart Ltd. Reproduced with
permission of the author and the publisher.

Library and Archives Canada Cataloguing in Publication
Holz, Cynthia, 1950–
Benevolence / Cynthia Holz.

Issued also in an electronic format.

ISBN 978-0-307-39889-5

I. Title.

PS8565.O649B46 2011   C813'.54   C2010-904221-2

Text design: Jennifer Lum

First Edition

Printed and bound in the United States of America

1 3 5 7 9 8 6 4 2

For Leo Murphy

Everything that is fine and beautiful

Has been created for the one with eyes to see.

—Rumi, the *Masnavi*

CHAPTER 1

"The temperature dropped," Stella said, "and snow was coming down hard—no, not up or down, more horizontal—and snow was blowing up from the tracks. Sometimes it was so thick all I could see was my reflection in the window, but every once in a while, when the wind changed direction, flakes stopped and scattered like they were, I don't know, confused, and there would be an opening, a slot, a sort of peephole, and I could spot a telephone pole, a tree, a roof, a parked car.

"We were passing by a small town, going very fast, I think, the train rocking and trembling, the wheels jiggling the way they do—you know, a kind of chattering—and I felt it right through me. It cheered me up a bit to see lit-up houses shining through the dark after miles and miles of greyness and nothing to distract me from it, no one talking or touching my hand.

"Grant was sitting next to me, our arms slightly apart, and his chair was back, his eyes closed, but I don't think he was sleeping. His lips were pressed together and his jaw was too tight and still, his face not moving at all, not even his nostrils, and his earlobes were red, the way they get when he's angry. We were going to Montreal for his mother's birthday, which I was excited about, never having met his parents even though we'd been together more than three years.

"But we weren't getting along that day, we'd had an argument earlier when we were still in Union Station waiting to board the train. It wasn't about much at first, just a little thing, which is usually how it goes with us, but then it got bigger. All I said was we should talk more in the evening. He was always coming home tired and then he watched TV or turned on the computer and barely spoke to me. And he said it wasn't his job to entertain me—he worked hard all day and wanted to relax at night, and if I was bored I should go back to school or find something else to do. But that wasn't it at all! I was only looking for a way for us to be closer, which is what I said next, but that got him steamed up. We kept on bickering and people in the station were giving us dirty looks like we were ruining the fun they were having standing in line, but nothing I told him could make him see it my way, and by the time we got on board both of us were feeling wronged.

"So there we were on the train together, sitting side by side without touching or speaking, worse even than strangers. It wasn't a big enough argument to end our relationship, but the way he was being so mean made me wonder why I bothered to stick it out.

"You probably want me to get to the point already," Stella

said, "but I think it's important that you know what I was thinking when the train ran past the town—because of what happened next—how mad I was, and sad too . . . the train rolling
as it went so that I was swaying in my seat, looking out at spots
of light and listening to train sounds, hearing that whoosh and
a sort of clicking like teeth coming together hard. When the
wind slowed down a bit I saw the flashing lights of a crossing
ahead and the horn sounded four times, two longs, a short, a
long, and then I heard warning bells, the noise exploding like
fireworks, then fading away to nothing. Next to me Grant was
still turned away toward the aisle, our shoulders almost meeting, his left leg over the right, his eyelids shivering at the sound
of hoots and ringing but still stubbornly shut tight.

"By then I was feeling sorry for myself and decided to
rattle him, to make him wake up and move, so I shook his arm
and told him that he had to get up now, I needed to go to the
bathroom—and actually I did, except it wasn't urgent and I
could've waited till later, but I wasn't exactly lying. Generally
I try to tell the truth about things because it's easier that way,
but this time I stretched it a bit. I guess I just wanted him to
know I was still there.

"So he sat up, blinking straight ahead without looking at
me, and I climbed over his stuck-out legs and walked to the
back of the car. I slid open a bathroom door and stepped into
the tiny room, locked the door behind me and squinted at the
mirror. As I watched myself, frowning and pale, a single tear
crept down my cheek like a worm, and I felt all alone in the
world, which made me a little sick, and I leaned over the sink

to spit my heartache into the small bowl. It was like I knew what was coming next, how sorrow and loneliness were going to mangle me, how I would bleed and dry up and hurt would stick to me like a scab.

"But here's what I'm getting at, the action part," Stella said, "where things suddenly blow apart . . . how first I heard a thunderclap and everything was shuddering, and the room jerked and flew up and so did I, hitting my head on the.ceiling. I tripped from one wall to the next with things punching into me—a handrail, the counter, the door, floor, spears of glass— while all around the room was heaving, snapping into pieces, and it was clear that something really awful was happening. I was dizzy, breathing fast, bruised and weak all over, and what I heard from the other side of the bathroom wall was the groaning and grinding of metal on metal and a roar and crunch like gravel spilling from a dump truck. I knew the train had jumped the track and all I could think of was to cross my arms over my head, crouch down and curl up small.

"Then there was a pause, just a blink or two of stillness, and I was glad I hadn't been peeing when the train crashed because I wouldn't want to be found like that, my panties around my knees. I mean, the things you think of during a crisis don't make sense, they seem so silly afterward . . .

"The car scraped and squealed and finally stopped with a big jolt, and then I heard shouting and the panicky sounds of people in pain—all that screaming and weeping—and I tried to get out of the bathroom but the door was stuck in its frame and shoving hardly moved it, so I had to work a long time using a piece of broken pipe to wedge it open just enough for me to flatten and slip through. By then I was starting to hurt too—my arms sore, my nose bleeding, pain up and down my spine— but I kept going anyway, trying to get back to Grant.

"The car was totally off the rails, leaning to the right and ripped open like a can, a long gash in its left side and a wall torn into strips that looked like—I don't know what—metal tongues, I suppose, with broken glass and slices of this and that everywhere. At least the car wasn't completely on its side— though what I saw made me want to run back to the bathroom and hide. There was plastic and twisted scraps of metal all over the place, smashed windows, crushed seats, hats and coats and luggage that had flown out of the overhead bins—some of the bags split apart with clothes hanging out—a coffee pot spilled in a corner and empty shoes.

"There were worse things, if you want to know—people pinned under seats, a woman screwed up with her legs bent backward, and bloody lumps of flesh like what a lion might have chewed on and spat out.

"There were phones and laptops and something rolled under a seat I couldn't put a name to, a football or volleyball— no, not exactly—but I only looked for an instant.

"The last thing I saw was an almost familiar shirt, tattered and stained red, on a nearly whole body that was flopped across the lap of a bawling passenger, her arms overhead like this was a holdup . . . and then I turned my face away, I'd seen enough.

"We're no better than melons, I thought—thin rinds and squishy inside, so easily sliced up. Growing, ripening, rotting, then we end up a heap of mush oozing back into the ground. Nothing we can do about it, people are dying all the time, but it scares us stupid anyway.

"And then I sort of crossed my eyes to make them un-focus and stopped seeing everything except what was in my mind. I was picturing a snowman with coal eyes, a button nose and corncob mouth who was melting into a puddle, and I started thinking of how you make a snowman from a fist of snow, rolling it and rolling it, the strength it takes, the patience, and how you have to heave the middle snowball onto the bottom one, and then the head onto that . . . and thought of all the snow songs my mother used to sing to me—'Jingle Bells,' 'Sleigh Ride,' 'Winter Wonderland' and other ones you'd know too.

"My mother was a quiet woman, so small and light on her feet that when she walked around the house you wouldn't even know she was there, but when she sang her voice was loud and strong as a diva's. When my father still lived with us he'd tell her to shut up, she was giving him a headache, and then she'd drop her voice and whisper songs so only I could hear, which made them very special.

"I guess I'm off topic here but wanted you to know that about her," Stella said. "It's something I never said before, but I want you to understand how beautifully my mother sang and how much it meant to me, how important that was . . .

"Well, after that my thoughts turned and I stopped think-ing about her and thought about Grant again, wishing we hadn't argued while waiting in the station. I wished he was still next to me with his eyes closed and his ears red so I could apologize and say how much I loved him and how we shouldn't fight about unimportant matters but talk things out instead . . . then everything would be okay between us, like before. No—better than before.

"I wished it hadn't snowed and the roads weren't icy, so the truck that couldn't stop and skidded through the crossing gates and was hit by the moving train—its front part, the cab part, smashed by the locomotive and its trailer torn free and spinning into the side of our car and the next one—that never would've happened. I wished that the driver got tied up earlier while making a delivery and never even reached the crossing till the train passed, or that we'd sat in different seats, or that I'd never got up to go to the bathroom and Grant wasn't the only one killed on the train but me too, dead in his arms. That would've been the end of it, and I wouldn't have to keep seeing and hearing what I saw and heard, and later I wouldn't still be dreaming about it, having all these feelings . . .

"So I stopped partway down the aisle, sat on the floor and spoke to him, to the ball that had rolled half under the seat with its eyes still open, whispering so no one would hear. I said his name and that he ought to close his eyes and rest now and told him I was all right—though I wasn't really sure of that— just a little banged up with smears on my dress from my bloody nose, cuts and scrapes, but nothing to worry about.

"Sitting there, I thought that Grant didn't answer because my voice was too low or maybe there was something wrong with his ears because of the accident, because of how loud it was, or else that he was still mad and didn't want to talk to me, which would've been the worst thing.

"I wasn't thinking he was dead.

"I just waited for him to speak and say he wasn't angry and soon we'd be in Montreal and I could finally meet his folks, but then I couldn't wait anymore—my eardrums hurt like the tips of knives were jabbing them, and I slapped my hands over my ears to stop the commotion that was getting worse around me. My arms ached when I reached up so I had to put them down again, and then the noise of everything filled me to bursting—I felt like a cooked sausage breaking out of its skin—and people kept shouting for help, calling to their loved ones, praying at the top of their lungs so you'd think God would answer them, *Calm down, I hear you*, and all that time the train was hissing, creaking and grunting, and sirens in the background were getting loud and louder still.

"Pain was beating hard in my neck and chest and shoulders, and my back was hurting so bad I couldn't sit up straight anymore and had to lie flat on the floor and not move another inch, waiting for someone to come along and tell me what to do next.

"I smelled smoke, blood too, and then there were emergency crews with ladders and torches. Two firemen put me on a stretcher and carried me off through a pushed-out window, and I saw a fleet of ambulances and pieces of broken truck littering the snowy track.

"They wrapped me in a blanket and moved me to a farmer's field somewhere behind the wreck, and snow was falling over me, wet and icy on my face—startling because after riding the train I'd forgotten how cold it was outside—and then a man with kind eyes and a calm way of speaking asked me how I was, and I can't remember all I said but something about the way that snow feels on your skin . . . and then the firemen lifted me and put me in an ambulance and drove me far away from the train, and I felt a headache starting.

"The next time I saw him, Grant was lying in his coffin in the funeral home, and that's where I finally got to meet his parents, who were shocked and didn't say much. His hair was clean and combed back in a way he never wore it, his nose sharp, cheeks rouged, his eyes closed, round as bulbs, and his shirt collar buttoned high, though he hated doing it up like that, and I thought what a handsome guy he was, even-featured, dignified, except for his mouth that didn't look right anymore, it was orange coloured and too small.

"So then I bent over him and kissed his wide forehead that was cool and smooth as a seashell, kissed his bulging eyelids, his pink cheeks and painted lips, and I whispered I was sorry— Do you understand how sorry I was? Sorrier than he could know."

"I'm afraid we have to stop now," Renata said to Stella. "I'll see you again on Monday."

CHAPTER 2

Renata Moon looked out the street-facing window of her second-floor office. Snow was falling steadily and everything seemed to be covered with fur. The only tree, a maple with uplifted branches and a tangle of Christmas lights, was sugar-coated, shining. Icicles hung from roofs and awnings, snow softened the shapes of cars, and footpaths and tire tracks marked the sheet of white road like strokes drawn with charcoal.

Her ten o'clock was late again, but soon she would turn a corner and enter Renata's field of vision. Stella would come along the street and, if nothing alarmed her, would shoot across the intersection, then drop out of sight again until she came through the office door. Getting here was risky, but at least she lived close by.

Ah, there she was now. From up here it looked as if she were tottering past the stores across the street like a wind-up doll. Her arms were straight, her chin held down and to one side, close to her shoulder. She was wearing her usual flared coat, short brown boots and a tuque pulled low on her head. Though she hated the attention, passersby glanced at her, perhaps because of her awkwardness.

Renata kept watching.

Her sessions with Stella Wolnik had always been challenging. It hadn't been Stella's idea to start treatment a year ago when she quit university because of panic disorder; the insistence of her partner Grant had moved her to get help. And yet, despite her initial reluctance, they'd developed a good relationship and made progress over time. If not for the accident, she might have gone back to school after Christmas . . . but that was out of the question now.

It wasn't just trains that triggered her flashbacks. All sorts of vehicles—cars, buses, streetcars, taxis and motorbikes— and all sorts of street sounds—honking horns, clanging bells, revving engines, and even people hollering—reminded her of the crash and made her panicky outdoors. At first she wouldn't leave her apartment to shop for food but had it delivered to her door, and she kept her windows firmly shut against intrusive noises. Now she was able to go out alone for short stretches, though it still took all her courage to get as far as Renata's office.

They had started desensitization with train pictures and videos, and after a while she could look at different images without trembling or turning away. Then they moved on to Stella holding a toy train, and after that, to her imagining being on board while Renata played a CD of bells and horns, the drone of a locomotive or the rush of wheels on steel rails. The sounds were especially upsetting to Stella, and the exercises had to be repeated many times, but minor setbacks were to be expected, and overall things had gone well. The next step, today's session, would be to walk as far as the railway tracks, to see what would happen.

Nothing bad, Renata hoped.

None of her other clients moved her in quite the same way. She was drawn to Stella, childish and difficult as she was. Renata liked to think of her as an unknown sea creature, tightly curled, spiky, and possibly poisonous—yet one she was curious to touch and see unfold in spite of the danger.

But also there were moments she was rattled in Stella's presence and needed to back off. At times, after their hour together, Renata would be left drained, light-headed, and shivering, a blunt sadness in her chest because she'd failed to keep her professional distance and had moved too close to Stella's pain. Pacing the room, it was all she could do to compose herself before the next person arrived.

Stella had now reached the crossing in front of the office, but didn't rush across. In a blink Renata saw, and heard, what was the matter. A parked car was trying unsuccessfully to pull away from the snow-choked curb, its wheels spinning and spattering slush, making a high-decibel whine. Stella put her hands over her ears and backed away from the curb, elbows high and pointed as if she were trying to take off. She pressed against a storefront and turned her head away sharply when anyone walked by. Seeing her on the street like that, Renata had to fight the urge to rush down, scoop her up and carry her into the office.

Then she lost sight of her. Had she made it across the street, only to stop at the entrance below, frozen in a nightmare of frightening images of the crash?

Several minutes went by before she heard Stella bumping around the waiting room and went out to greet her. She was already hunched in a chair, her fingers clamping the armrests. Her hat and coat, wet in places, were hooked on a rack, and her boots stood alone in a puddle on a rubber tray. Renata invited her to come into the office and watched as Stella got up slowly and clumsily, banging her shin on a table. A magazine slipped to the floor and opened to a colourful spread of fat and glossy vegetables. Stella's hand shook as she picked up the magazine and put it back on the table. She made it to the end of the room before stopping to lean against the door frame and draw air.

After a moment, Stella walked into the office, sat on a folding chair she moved to the centre of the room and proceeded to inch back, so that if she stretched her arm she could touch the door behind her. There were more comfortable chairs or a long, plump sofa close to Renata's desk she might have picked instead, but she never chose those.

Renata followed her in, shut the door and sat in her swivel chair, a birthday gift from her husband, ergonomically shaped to protect her tender lower back. Smart gift, that chair was, a gift to remind her of him every time she sat down. Not a thing to be left on a shelf but one that was bulky and practical, always in view. There'd been other smaller, more whimsical gifts over the years, like silver rings, figurines or pearly seashells, but lately his choices were large and impersonal. The bigger his presents got, the less she enjoyed them, and one day soon, she feared, he'd buy her a fridge.

She rolled her chair from behind her desk and slowly forward to partly close the distance between her and Stella.

"How are you today?" she asked.

"I almost didn't make it." Stella's eyes were downcast.

"Worse than before?"

"I was sweaty and my chest hurt. I thought I couldn't breathe and was having a heart attack. I thought I was dying."

"But you weren't really dying, you were having a panic attack that made you uncomfortable. How did you handle it? What did you do this time to help yourself keep going?"

Stella paused to undo the top button of her shirt. Her eyes half closed as she breathed in through her nose, out slowly from her mouth. A pretty girl, Renata thought, especially so because of her short, beaked nose and the chipped corner of a front tooth that she hadn't crowned. Renata found physical flaws appealing and had never had her own crooked front teeth straightened.

"I thought about a still lake and soft sand," Stella said, "no one near me, no one around, and walking barefoot by the shore, the sun going through me and shooting out my fingers and toes—like when I was a girl and we used to go to Sandbanks off-season in the fall when the beach was almost empty, and sometimes on a warm day the sun would feel strong on your face and you could take your sweater off and roll up your pants and your arms would be burning and the lake twinkling, full of jewels. So every step I took outside, I tried to see water and sand."

"That was a good thing to do. You used calming imagery to help yourself relax and were able to get here."

Stella's shoulders dropped. "But it only worked for a short time. Not when I had to cross the street."

"Tell me about that."

"I didn't see any cars at first and started across, but then I heard an engine and wheels turning round and round, not going anywhere."

"How did that make you feel?"

"Afraid."

"What did you think would happen?"

Her shoulders rose as she clasped her hands between her knees. "I thought the wheels would roll up and over me, pinning me, and things would cut me—metal things—and then I'd hurt and start to bleed."

Metal things, Renata thought. A memory flashed of herself on a table with her legs bent, knees apart, and she felt pain in her abdomen. She took a moment before she said, "That was a painful fantasy."

Stella turned in her seat and groped for a Kleenex, and although Renata slid forward she resisted the urge to hand her one. Boxes were strategically placed next to all the office chairs, and there was one on her desk too. Renata reached for a tissue herself and balled it in her fist.

Stella flattened a hand on her rising and falling belly. "My stomach hurts," she said, "and my chest too. I can't breathe."

"You're hyperventilating. Drop your head between your knees and focus on your breathing. Remember what we practised: in–two–three–four, hold–two–three–four, out to the count of eight. Close your eyes and think about that quiet beach you imagined, the sand hot on your bare feet, the sun shining, filling you with warm, healing, yellow light."

Stella lowered her head and spoke in a muffled voice: "I'm dizzy now. It's getting worse."

"These are just temporary symptoms you're having. I want you to keep your head down and breathe as I tell you to. Inhale, hold it, hold it . . . exhale three–four–five–six–seven–eight." Renata switched to a softer voice. "See if you can do it again. Close your eyes and count the numbers very slowly to yourself. Do it till you feel calm."

She watched Stella's heaving chest. Since the train accident, their sessions always went like this: the difficult walk to the office; fear, pain and dizziness. Despite signs to the contrary, it was hard at times like this to believe she was improving.

Renata pushed her aching back into the chair. Was she helping her enough? Should she send Stella to someone else?

Give it time, Ben would say. Some patients are harder than others.

Some doctors are less skilled.

Stella slowly sat up and rubbed her hands over her face. "I'm better now."

"Good!" Too enthusiastic. Renata said more quietly,

"Remember we talked about going to the tracks today? Are you ready for the next step?"

Stella glanced at the window. "You mean outside in the snow?"

"The exposure would do you good."

"The sidewalks are slippery."

"I'll be right beside you and it's not far. You walked here, didn't you? And later you'll be walking home. You've made good progress. Why not challenge yourself and go a few blocks more?"

"I don't know. It sounds bad."

"We've been preparing and I think you can do this. Facing a scary situation will help you learn to deal with it. Avoidance won't."

"How far do we have to go?"

"That's up to you, of course."

She crinkled her nose. "Two blocks?"

Renata had a moment of doubt. Was Stella really ready for this? What if she made things worse by pushing her client too far?

In the end it was a judgment call, and that's what she was trained to do: judge the situation and act. But always she suffered this blink of hesitation, a fear her decision might be wrong. Ben didn't second-guess himself the way she did. He made choices and followed through, no matter what the outcome, and she admired his confidence.

Stella pushed herself to a standing position and dropped her eyes. "You won't leave me alone, will you?"

"I'll be there the whole time."

Stella left the office, and Renata kneaded her lower back discreetly as she got up, strode across the room and pulled her coat from the closet. She put it on and buttoned it, found a pair of gloves in the pockets, tugged on a felt hat and exchanged her heels for ankle boots. When she emerged, Stella was already waiting in the anteroom, dressed again for outdoors. Renata locked up, then led the way downstairs to the lobby and out.

The road was clogged with traffic, and stores on one side of the street and homes on the other were trimmed with Christmas lights. People stepped carefully on the icy sidewalks, their heads down, collars up, faces half covered with scarves. A woman brushed snow from her sleeves. A man recklessly chased his hat wheeling away in a sudden blast. Renata tried to focus on the pleasures of the season: decorations, turkey dinners, chocolate and presents. Otherwise, her mood might turn as miserable as the weather.

Stella walked on the inside, past a row of houses and a winter-crisp front yard with blown-up figures of Santa and his reindeer. Her head was tipped to the right, her breath a white spurt pulled away by the wind.

Snow blew diagonally into their faces and stung Renata's lips like so many pinpricks. Like Ben's quick kisses as he tripped out the door to work, or later at night before he rolled away from her in bed wearily and fell asleep. When was the last time he'd kissed her slowly and deeply? When was the last time they'd spoken about the loveliness of icicles and snowflakes? The delicacy of winter light? They used to walk in High Park after a blizzard and find beauty in everything—blowing drifts, humped curbs, the snow-heavy branches of trees, or a frozen pond. Even now she could hear his laugh and feel the press of wet lips.

They used to laugh a lot more.

She moved closer to Stella. "How are you doing?" she said, but didn't get an answer.

Slowly they made their way toward the corner. When someone approached, Stella would freeze, her chin against her shoulder like an Egyptian bas-relief, and every time she came to a halt, Renata did the same. The sudden starts and stops left Renata feeling unbalanced, as if she were wearing skates.

Which made her remember the long-ago December morning Ben tried to teach her to skate as she teetered around an ice rink—only to give up and trip into his waiting arms. His breath on her face had been steamy-warm, still scented with pancakes and coffee from breakfast.

At last they reached the end of the block. Renata grappled with her collar. She was starting to feel cold now. Wind slipping down her neck was like an icy necklace lying on her breastbone. Her face was dripping melted snow; her toes and fingers tingled. Stella must be cold too and would probably wind up cursing her for taking her out in a snowstorm. She was hunched against the weather now, staring at the crossing ahead.

Renata asked softly, "Are you cold? Have you had enough? We can go back if you like."

"I want to tell you something."

Renata had to bend toward Stella's mouth to hear her. "What is it?"

"I'm pregnant."

"You're . . . pregnant?"

She nodded.

"How long have you known?"

"Not long."

She squinted at the midsection of Stella's coat. "How many weeks?"

"Ten."

Renata kept her face still, her eyes fixed on the woman's middle, where something was alive and growing.

"I'm going to keep the baby. My sister wants to move in with me for a while and that'll make it easier."

"These are big decisions, ones that need"—Renata faltered—"ones we should sit and talk about . . ."

Stella interrupted her by suddenly stepping onto the road. Renata yelled at her to wait, to look both ways first—be extra careful now because of the baby!—but Stella didn't hesitate.

The only cars in sight were parked in a line at the curb. Stella raced across and Renata followed closely, her arms raised as if she might catch her if need be. But Stella made it safely to the other side and kept going.

She was moving quickly now. Renata had to speed up to keep pace, until, minutes later, Stella stopped short and said she was light-headed.

As if drawing a sled over the snow-thickened sidewalk, Renata took her arm and pulled her into a nearby bus shelter.

Stella dropped onto the bench and cupped her belly with mittened hands.

"It's like there's a knife in me."

"A panic attack," Renata said. "What are you supposed to do to help yourself when you feel like that?"

"Breathe slowly," Stella said, "and focus on my special place." Rounding her back, she bent over and carefully sipped air.

Renata breathed along with her, inwardly counting in fours and eights. A duet, she was thinking: so many shaky breaths to the bar. A silent performance in two voices. Two women trying to feel confident and stay calm.

Except it wasn't working. Thinking about babies, Renata was feeling queasy herself and wanted to turn around and go back. But when she suggested they return to the office, Stella wordlessly stood up, left the shelter and started toward an intersection just ahead.

They had to cross a four-lane road. On the other side, the street they were on turned left and continued. A path ran beside the street and overlooked the train tracks stretching east and west into the distance. Just beyond the rails was the whining expressway and then Lake Ontario spreading to the horizon.

Hands on her ears, Stella stood at the curb and watched. Traffic was heavy and fast. Cars sped by like bobsleds, and the road was rough with tire tracks and dark ridges of snow and slush. They waited for the light to change, a complicated business of arrows and signals. When at last it turned green, Stella fixed her eyes on her boots and, without looking up, dashed across. Renata flew after her recklessly, not even checking for cars.

On the far side of the intersection, Stella was triumphant. "I knew I could—I knew it!"

"Yes, but you need to be more careful crossing the road." Renata was panting. "We'll go to the tracks another time. Now we have to get back."

"No, this time," Stella said.

Cold air circled Renata's wrists above her gloves, and her nose was runny, her fingers numb. Everything was off-kilter, suddenly moving too fast. Things had gone wrong somehow.

She touched Stella's shoulder. "We've already gone two blocks, as much as you wanted to do. That's enough for one day. Let's go back to the office and talk."

"Look!" Stella pointed at the lake ahead. "We can't stop, we're almost there."

Renata couldn't leave Stella alone on the street, but couldn't force her to turn back either. Blinking snow from her lashes, she saw the green swells of the lake and buckled slabs of grey ice and felt that she too had become a frozen-solid block, unable to move or think. Ben would make a decision and act . . . but she could only stand still.

"You're always saying how important it is to get well. Now it's not just for me, it's for the baby," Stella said. "I want to take her outdoors to parks and playgrounds and don't want her growing up scared to death of everything."

Just then the wind let up and the snow changed to flurries. A sunbeam parted the clouds, and lit-up snowflakes flitted about like fireflies. Renata took this as a sign.

"All right, we'll keep going—but only if I hold your arm."

She hooked Stella's elbow. A line of snow collected in the creases of their coat sleeves, connecting them as if they were fastened with white glue. Linked together, they walked on.

Renata matched her step to Stella's, the swinging of the young woman's hips to her own hips. She squirmed under her coat as she thought about the fetus wriggling inside Stella in its solitary, aqueous world. About an inch long, she imagined, already flexing its fingers and toes. Its head would be tucked, its tiny arms and legs curled.

Back in university, she'd studied a medical book with pictures and descriptions until she knew exactly the features of the fetus she'd briefly carried inside her: the thing she got rid of because she was young, a serious student, and knew the father fleetingly and only by his first name.

She never told Ben because it had happened before she met him and had nothing to do with him. That's not why she couldn't conceive: they'd done all the tests and there was no particular reason. And even now she was hopeful. If she had done it once, she could do it again. She wanted a family of her own. She longed to be part of something warm and intimate— a family nothing like the one she'd grown up in.

Her mother had never had any trouble getting pregnant, though Renata was the only child who survived. A brother with a faulty heart died the day he was born, and her sister June died in her crib before her first birthday. Then there were the miscarriages, one after another, blood in the toilet, blood on the sheets.

The third time, they took her away and Renata thought she'd bleed to death, she'd never see her mom again. She was relieved when her dad brought her home from the hospital in a taxi, but after that her mother rarely spoke. Inconsolable, she stared at herself in mirrors, combing her brittle hair, sighing her loneliness through the day. At night she would pace the rooms, crooning to her dead children, so that Renata learned to sleep with her head under a blanket.

Lying rigidly in bed, Renata dreamed of yellow-eyed, part-human monsters with claws instead of fingers, rats' tails and webbed feet, and would wake up whimpering, determined not to fall back to sleep. But to wake from a bad dream and hear her mother's keening was another kind of nightmare, another terror deeply felt: the horror of babies lost. Throughout her girlhood, there didn't seem to be a day she wasn't half dumb with fear.

It was cancer that finally killed her mother. Cancer and the weight of grief.

A grief that became her own, filling the empty space inside.

Renata put a hand over her stomach now and pressed hard. Sometimes she was glad that nothing was growing there.

They turned east and onto the path beside the railway. Between the trail and the tracks below was a chain-link fence, then a border of bare trees and a steep embankment. At the very bottom, the steel rails. On the south side of the tracks was a blur of cars on the highway, and beyond that, in the background, a thin fog of frozen vapour hovered above the lake.

Stella dropped Renata's arm and put her hands on the fence, her multicoloured mittens conspicuous against the links. Her tuque, clotted with ice pellets, sagged to one side as she pulled her chin to her collar, then bent and straightened her arms as if doing a set of push-ups. Finally she arched her back, looked up and grew still.

"What are you doing?" said Renata.

"Waiting for a train."

"How anxious do you feel?"

Stella only stared ahead. The grid of tracks was brushed white, four pairs on the rail bed, and looked like rows of fallen logs in a snowy woods.

We can't just stand here, Renata thought. They didn't know the schedules and could end up waiting hours before Stella gave up.

But then, as if conjured, two bright marbles appeared on the horizon. Soon they saw the yellow cones of oncoming headlights and heard the eerie blast of a horn, the melancholy clamour of bells. The air began to vibrate. Stella pulled her mittens off, curled her fingers around the links and pressed herself against the fence.

Renata moved toward her.

The train was clearly visible now, an engine and three cars. It sped westward on its track, snow spuming out from the side of the cowcatcher, streaming past the coach windows, twisting and billowing.

Stella started shaking the fence.

"What is it?" Renata asked. "What are you remembering? Is it like one of your nightmares?"

Stella continued to joggle the links as the train slid by with a loud exhalation—the long, deep ocean sound of waves rubbing against the shore—and moments later it was gone, leaving curls of powder in its wake and bare, shiny tracks that seemed to have been licked clean.

"Talk to me," Renata said.

Stella turned around. Her back to the fence, she doubled over suddenly, hugging her middle, and began to pant. "Something hurts."

"What hurts?"

She pointed to her stomach, and Renata grabbed her arm. "Are you bleeding?"

"Just pain."

"A lot?"

Stella swayed on her feet. "I have to lie down."

"You can't lie down in the snow." Renata unbuttoned her coat, pulled off a glove with her teeth and groped for her cell phone. "I'll call a cab—an ambulance—and get you to a hospital."

"I think I'm . . . going to faint."

Reflexively Renata opened her arms and Stella fell against her, hugging her waist.

"Don't let me fall," Stella said.

"You can't— I have to call for help!"

She tried to loosen Stella's arms, but even though she was taller she couldn't break the woman's hold. As they stood body to body, Renata began to sweat. Her stomach hardened and her inner thighs seemed wet.

Looking past Stella, she focused on the white snow, smelled the odour of diesel fumes and listened to the traffic for several moments, until she felt calmer.

"Let go," she said at last. "Let go or we'll both fall."

Stella drew back and touched her belly. "The pain's gone."

"You're okay?"

"I think so."

"Can you walk?"

She took a step and nodded.

Now it was Renata's turn to lean against the tall fence. It bowed under her weight as she slumped against it, shivering.

Stella stretched her neck out and peered into Renata's face. "You don't look so good," she said.

Whereupon, Renata Moon sat down in the snow and wept.

CHAPTER 3

Ben got upset when he heard what his wife had done. "You took a pregnant woman for a walk in a snowstorm?"

"She didn't say she was pregnant till later."

"What if she fell and lost the baby?"

"I told you, I didn't know."

"What if she was hit by a car? She could've been traumatized, even killed! What were you thinking?"

"I was trying to help her."

They were seated at the table in the kitchen of their townhouse, eating takeout Thai food straight from the containers, neither one of them having had the energy to fetch plates. Last night, it was two-for-one falafels and tabbouleh; the night before, rotis. They never seemed to cook anymore.

Ben dropped a slippery chunk of green pepper on his lap and rescued it with his fingers. The conversation wasn't going anywhere good and he wanted it to be over. He wanted to be long past this part of the evening, to retire to his study and finish his poem "A Day Off." He knew how to end it now and wanted to jot down the lines before he forgot and they disappeared forever.

Stirring a container of mango chicken, Renata regretted her decision to tell him about her day. He wasn't really listening and was making her feel worse. One encouraging word would have brightened her mood considerably. If a perfect stranger wishing her good morning could do that, why couldn't her husband?

I wake with nowhere to go today, Ben repeated the opening stanza, safely planted in his brain. *No office door to open, no one waiting to see me: I stay in bed and stare at the taut sheet of the ceiling.* He wasn't sure where to break the lines.

"Anyway, it wasn't stormy," Renata insisted, "just windy with flurries."

She lifted a knob of chicken with her chopsticks, slid it between her lips and angled herself toward a partly frosted-over window. The panes were black and brittle with night. A cold draft blew across her knees and made her shiver. All right, it might've been a bad call, she allowed, but surely her intent was good. Why couldn't he see that? To try and understand someone—to give your full attention—was a greater act of love, she thought, than holding hands, exchanging looks or mouthing affectionate words.

"Who'd be responsible if anything had gone wrong? Who'd be faced with charges?"

She turned to meet his look. "You're making me feel awful. I'm sorry I brought it up."

He glanced at her changeable violet eyes—a pleading expression now—and felt a little kinder. "Anyhow, it's over and nothing happened. We all make mistakes sometimes," he tried to wrap up.

Renata didn't reply. She looked past him, out the window, chopsticks in her right hand, her left fingers twisting her hair.

Ben returned to his poem. *At first, silence. Stillness. An idea of thirst and a memory of appetite.* Then what? What comes next? For a second he couldn't remember. Did he lose the rest? No, wait . . . *But then something rattles in the dull emptiness of my chest: a waking shake of hunger.*

Renata finally spoke up. "Going outdoors was important for her treatment."

"So how did it end?" he said, hurrying her along.

"We went back."

My stomach closes like a mouth around a bite of fear and swallows it whole.

When Ben didn't press, Renata offered nothing more. He really didn't need to know the rest, she decided. Imagine what he'd say if she told him that she broke down and cried in front of a client.

Ben poked at his dinner in its cardboard container, tried unsuccessfully to scoop up rice with his chopsticks, then gave up and used a fork. Fact is, he didn't like the way that his wife worked: bringing props into the office—snakes, spiders, rats in cages—and taking patients outdoors. The closeness and iffy-ness. The unnecessary risks. What was wrong with the talking cure?

"Still, you have to admit it was a risky thing to do—"

"The woman's pregnant," Renata interrupted, "not disabled. We took a walk and came back and later she said she felt better."

"What about how you felt?"

She smoothed her hair behind one ear. "What are you getting at?"

"You've never worked with a pregnant woman before, have you?"

"So what?"

"Maybe that had something to do with your taking her out in a blizzard."

"Don't you ever listen to me?" She slapped down her chopsticks. "It wasn't a blizzard and I told you twice already that I didn't know she was pregnant—and when I asked her to turn around and go back, she refused!"

He reminded himself it wasn't important to have the last word but kept talking anyway. "Isn't it possible you might've had feelings you weren't aware of?"

"You think I meant to hurt her? You think I'm irresponsible because I'm not a mother? I can't believe I'm hearing this!"

"I meant that if it had been me—"

Renata pushed her food aside and stood up, a sign that dinner was over and the conversation ended. She flicked her wrist at the morning's dirty dishes in the kitchen sink, the clutter of bags on the counter, the scraps and stains on the stove. "I'm going to bed now. You can clean up all this crap."

As soon as she was gone he dropped what was left of their supper into the garbage, loaded the dishwasher with the cups and bowls that had been piled in the sink and scrubbed an expensive pot glazed with dried oatmeal. Quickly he cleaned the counter, swiped at the stove with a sponge and wiped up spills on the table. As he worked he pictured the desk in his study, his pens, papers and books, and his handwritten poem on a lined yellow notepad, waiting for an ending. Dismissing from his mind the argument with his wife, he rushed out of the kitchen thinking, *What is left, What is left . . .*

His chilly room on the top floor seemed colder and gloomier tonight than usual. An old sweater hung on the back of a chair, and he pulled it on, sat at his desk and scribbled the line about his stomach closing. Then he wrote, *What is left*, but couldn't think of the next bit.

No, it's there, the words are there. Hear them. Concentrate.

He got up and paced a figure-eight on the rug with its dizzying pattern of vines and leaves. Renata's choice, not his. A solid colour would've been more to his liking, a grey mat under his feet instead of tangled greenery, but she was so keen on this particular carpet he had backed down.

He stopped, threw back his head and squinted at the ceiling as if he might find the words to his unfinished poem there. It wasn't uniformly white but slightly varied in hue, and as he gazed he saw a pair of eyes and a mouth: like finding a face in the moon. Renata had once wanted to paint the ceiling a dark shade or cover it with embossed tiles to give his study character, but that's where he drew the line. It had to be white and smooth. Anything else would've felt like a hand pressing down on his skull as he tried to think.

Pay attention! Think of those lines.

But what he continued to think about was his wife. In the next room, he imagined, she was curled on the edge of their bed, facing out the way she did, the blanket pulled up to her mouth. Probably wide awake. Even though he disapproved of her brand of therapy, he should've been more careful in what he said over dinner—at least in how he said it—and stopped talking sooner. Renata was very sensitive and now he'd hurt her feelings, which she wouldn't easily forget. Angry, she'd hardly sleep, would be a wreck in the morning and drag herself through the day, and that would be his doing. He put an ear to the wall as if he might actually hear her breathing through the plaster, but heard only silence.

How could he focus on his poem when she was fuming? Arguing had been a mistake, had ruined his reflective mood. Such a stupid thing to do. Exhausted, he had overreacted to what she said. It wasn't her fault that he'd had an especially hard day. Not her fault he had to tell a mentally unstable woman she wasn't a suitable candidate for a liver transplant—and couldn't stop thinking about what his decision meant.

Report that to the team and the patient would be passed over, left to die. No one would overrule him if the issue was psychological. Yes or no; life or death: his call.

But some must be left to die. They couldn't all get on the list when there weren't enough organs to go round.

Screening was part of the job. Who was going to benefit most? Who was most deserving? Who would be cooperative and best able to care for a new liver or kidney? Who should he recommend? Who should he fight for?

Some people would get organs and others wouldn't. The team relied on his judgment. But his negative verdicts were driving him mad.

A sharp and familiar pain pushed through his ribs, and he stopped pacing and sat down again, waiting for it to pass. No, not a heart attack: tightness in the chest wall. Nothing to worry about. He got regular checkups and worked out twice a week—

Stop this!

He shut his eyes and slowed his breath, feeling his rib cage expanding and shrinking, until his chest relaxed somewhat and he became lost in a pothole in his brain. No wife or patients here. No livers, kidneys, lungs, and no imagined children . . .

Then out from behind his thoughts, the words he'd been searching for theatrically appeared. *What is left in me now that can grow in this cavity? Where is my heart?*

As he wrote down the lines the ache in his chest returned, moved up to his shoulders and down to his belly and feet. He buttoned his sweater and sank into it, all of him cold and trembling.

Where, where? looped in his brain.

He cupped his hands over his ears until the song grew faint. Worn out, he lowered his head; could easily have fallen asleep on his folded arms. But no, no, not yet. Not until he read it through. Not until he looked at his poem in its entirety. He shook himself alert again, sat up and recited "A Day Off" from start to finish.

His pulse throbbed in his temple as he read it again. Good? Bad? He couldn't tell. Sincere and original, or trite and sentimental? A worthy subject poorly handled? Done before and done better by any number of gifted poets, living or dead?

Fifty-three years gone and nothing to show for his efforts but a poem here, a poem there printed in unknown, unread journals, and not enough satisfactory work to make a collection he might want to publish: a book to send to a small press run by a grad student or self-important English prof, someone inattentive or too swayed by current fads to recognize a good piece, who'd leave it in a stack for months with hundreds of other submissions and then return his manuscript without having read past the first poem. Nevertheless, the rejection would stick. Without encouragement he'd continue to doubt himself, doubt that he was exceptional. And if his was only a mediocre talent, why even bother to write? Worse than no talent at all.

He dropped his pen and clenched his fingers together until they reddened. His body was hot now; his thoughts darkening, sliding away. A lousy end to a lousy day. Sleep would be impossible. He saw himself in bed with his wife, both of them wide-eyed and hopelessly restless as the black minutes ticked by.

Only a few years ago he wrote a short piece about setting aside sixty minutes at night to make love to her. The last stanza wasn't bad: *This is your hour, / my life, / ticking by.* A better way to spend time than lying anxiously awake . . . though now when they had sex it took only twenty minutes. Like everything else in their busy lives, it went by too fast.

Enough already! The pressure in his head and pounding of his heart had become unbearable. He reached for the phone and speed-dialed Mel's number. Better than a sleepless night of ruthless self-appraisal was a drink and good company. His brother lived close by and could sometimes be talked into going out for a nightcap.

Ben was in luck tonight. Mel was awake too—he wasn't getting along with his wife either—and glad to escape the house.

———

They met in the bar of a down-at-the-heels hotel that had changed hands recently and was undergoing a facelift intended to attract a better clientele. Ben's choice. White sheets nailed to the walls partly concealed reconstruction in progress. Wherever visible, the exposed wires, bare bulbs, ductwork and lathing were perversely comforting, as if the building itself were as vulnerable as he was. But with or without renovations, it wasn't Mel's kind of place. His brother preferred downtown bars with track lighting, Arborite tables, wall art and patios. Nevertheless, the place was conveniently located halfway between their homes, so Mel didn't kick up a fuss.

Ben arrived first. The only other customer was a man in a cloth coat slouched at a back table, cleaning his ear with a finger. Ben sat on a counter stool with a torn vinyl cover. He smiled at the frowning female bartender, who seemed to disapprove of him, and asked for a draft. Looking up, he winced at his reflection in a long mirror framed with blinking Christmas lights. He didn't like what he saw: a head of receding hair, more grey than brown now; a long, creased, mournful face; an off-centre nose and wrinkled neck. He seemed to have aged all at once. Within months his hair had thinned, his skin had slackened, his vision had changed; he'd put on pounds around the middle, and his head hung for no reason except maybe his neck was tired of holding up a brain weighed down with thoughts of mortality. Only his eyes, like a pair of chocolate truffles—not at all suited to a weary, meditative man—belied his decay. Though Renata liked his eyes, she preferred his flawed, crooked nose to any other feature.

She herself had many perfect parts he could choose from—Liz Taylor-ish plummy eyes and an all-around great bod which, though it excited him at the moment to think of it, was unavailable tonight.

This is your hour, / sixty minutes in which to reimagine your / hair, teeth, tongue, bones . . .

His mother, God bless her soul, had frequently and loudly warned him not to marry a shiksa, especially a pretty one—by which she meant "desirable." *They think about themselves first, not about their husbands. She'll never make you a proper home. She'll give you goyishe children!* She was off base on that last point, but it gave him no pleasure to prove her wrong.

He'd nearly finished his beer when his brother finally walked in, his boots smacking the rough wooden floor with authority. He was shorter than Ben by seven inches—five-foot-eight standing tall—which always made Ben smile when his baby brother entered a room. Balder than him too, but more athletically built.

"What took so long?"

Mel sat on the next stool. He wasn't wearing his customary suit, tie and dark shirt—blue lagoon, rain-forest green or Mafia purple—but still looked formally dressed in a leather jacket, black turtleneck, stiff cords and suede boots. The boots alone, Ben reflected, probably cost more than your average worker makes in a week.

"I was too mad to drive right over," said his brother, "so I sat in the Audi in the garage and swore until I lost my voice and hit the wheel till I hurt myself." He spread his hands above the counter to show his red knuckles to anyone who cared to see. The bartender, bent over a sink of soapy water, didn't even look up. Mel called out to her and ordered a rum-and-Coke for himself, another beer for Ben.

"So what's wrong?"

"Libby refuses to see Mama tomorrow evening and I'll have to go myself. She says she won't eat there again and won't let me take the kids . . . and next week is Chanukah."

"But you're the good son who brings his family to see her Friday nights."

"Not anymore I'm not." He rubbed his eyes with his fingertips. "Last week the kids were bored and got a little rowdy. They crawled under the velvet rope and jumped on Mama's sofa."

"They touched her plastic-covered couch no one's allowed to use except for shiva and Yom Kippur?" Ben slapped his cheek and moaned, "*Gott in Himmel!* What were they thinking? And why didn't you and Libby stop the little hoodlums before they destroyed the room? You're lucky Mama didn't faint."

"She said it broke her heart to see her grandkids acting like juvenile delinquents, but if they didn't know to respect a person's property that was their parents' fault. So Libby got in a huff too and told her she was fed up—a couch was meant to be sat on, not roped off like something in a museum—and maybe it was better if we didn't come there anymore but met in a restaurant."

"At least she didn't write her off completely. That's something."

"Mama hates restaurants."

"'Why spend good money on something you can cook yourself?'"

"'And cook better also!'" Mel rolled his eyes. "Yesterday she called to see if we were coming tomorrow, like nothing happened. I said I'll be there alone, the family wants to stay home . . . and we've been fighting ever since—me and Mama, me and Libby. Everything is my fault."

"Human interactions are always complicated. People are hard work."

"That's all you've got to say?"

"I hope she won't want to see more of me and Renata now."

"It wouldn't hurt for the two of you to visit her once in a blue moon, especially on a holiday. She's always asking why you're too busy to see her."

"We're too busy for everything . . . and also tired of hearing how Renata should convert and have a dozen Yiddishe babies."

"Tell her you're impotent."

"She'd never believe it. No son of hers has trouble with his putz."

The bartender nudged Mel's drink across the counter, and he turned his attention to her, appraising her slack, puffy features with a professional eye. Ben knew the look well, had often been inspected in the same way. It meant that Mel was picturing how eyelid surgery, a brow lift or Botox could wipe away twenty years of hard-won wrinkles.

But then he swivelled to face Ben. "You're not actually having trouble——well, you know . . . getting it up?"

"What, are you serious? You want to hide under the bed and hear Renata howl with glee?"

"I'm your brother, I can ask. Don't get so excited." He turned back to his drink and had a long sip. "I'll tell you a secret . . . I wish I made Libby shout. She whines a little when she comes, then she cries her eyes out."

"What's she got to cry about?"

"Women are indecipherable, completely ruled by hormones. It's not for us to understand. I put in my pecker and give her a shtup, the rest is her business. Count your blessings you got a screamer. Lots of guys would fall on their knees and thank God for a wife like that."

"Except she can't get pregnant."

Mel glanced at him sidelong and stirred the ice cubes in his glass with his index finger. "You're not going to talk about that again, are you?"

"It's probably too late now anyway." Ben shrugged. "Her best baby-making years are behind her."

"What about IVF?"

"It's such an ordeal, and she doesn't want to put herself through that with no guarantees—especially at her age."

"You should've started sooner."

"We didn't expect this. We thought we could wait."

"So why not adopt? The planet's full of orphans looking for good homes."

Ben took a swallow of beer. "I know this sounds selfish, but I want to have a son or daughter with my genes."

"You've spent time with my two, you know what a pain-in-the-ass they can be, and still you want to reproduce? You think your genes are so terrific the world can't do without them?"

"When I die, that's it, the end of a lineage—not counting you, of course, and what you managed to pass on to David and Chloe."

"All the short, bald genes."

Ben eyed his reflection in the long, winking mirror. "What's wrong with wanting a kid who looks like his old man?"

"My two take after Libby. The only thing I recognize as mine is Davey's pecker. And tell me, where did you come from? Who do you look like? No one I can think of."

"Who's going to carry my DNA into the future? Who will remember me when I'm gone?"

"If you're dead, what do you care?"

"I don't just want to disappear. I want to leave something behind."

"What about your poetry?"

"Something more important."

"So go out and discover something. Write a bunch of articles."

"I'm not exactly a giant in the field of psychiatry. No one's going to name a new mental illness after me or give me a lifetime achievement award."

Mel drank some rum-and-Coke. "What about your job? Doesn't that count for anything? Isn't it enough to make life-and-death decisions, to say who does or doesn't get an organ and a second chance?"

"It's not all up to me."

"One way or another, you're going to be remembered by a shitload of patients."

"Love me or hate me, they probably forget me once I've given my verdict to the team." Ben finished the rest of his beer. "I'm just one of many docs and nurses they have to deal with and don't want to think about after they leave the hospital."

"You help people cheat death. You're like the Almighty himself! Me, I do tummy tucks, I lift tits and asses, suck out fat, tighten thighs, fix chins and noses, I rejuvenate the faces of the vain, shallow and insecure."

"I know what you do, Mel."

"So tell me, what's my contribution? Who am I helping?"

"You tell me."

"Myself, that's who, to the tune of hundreds of thousands of dollars—"

"Never miss a chance to mention your fabulous wealth, do you."

"—and a bunch of sorry has-beens who think they'll find happiness at the end of a scalpel." Mel shook his head. "At least we can agree that your patients are dealing with more urgent matters."

Ben played with his empty mug. "You want to know something? After a while you can't tell one patient from the next, they're all humble and desperate. They all say the same things, pleading for their lives with a doctor they hardly know. Their fear fills the office. It smells sort of like burnt hair. And I take notes instead of helping them to face death."

"Here's what your problem is—the problem is you're morbid. Instead of thinking about what every husband thinks about—car payments, mortgages, how to keep the wife happy— you think about kids you don't have and other useless stuff like death and immortality." Mel inspected his hand, then ran it over his thinning scalp. "You know what I worry about? I worry about my blood pressure, I worry about lawsuits. Do I worry about the substance of my life and its reason? Do I give a shit who will remember me when I'm in my grave or how I'm improving humankind beyond making it prettier? No, I do not."

"That's you."

"I'll tell you another thing. If I were Renata I'd slip a little Prozac into your coffee every morning. But meanwhile I'll buy you a beer—though personally I think you should have something stronger." He called to the bartender, "Sweet-heart, a couple more," and when she brought their drinks over, peered at her and grimaced.

He bent close to Ben's ear. "I could do something about her eyes."

"Yeah, and it would only cost her pain, swelling, blurred vision, maybe even blindness, and a quarter of her annual pay."

"You exaggerate, as usual. It's a simple operation. Besides, everyone plays the odds—your patients, my patients.

Everyone wants to be a little better off than the next guy. It makes life exciting."

Ben leaned away from him. "Mine only want to live."

"Even at the cost of somebody else's life."

"They're not causing anyone's death."

"Just keeping their fingers crossed."

"They're good people with good intentions."

"Who'd lie or promise anything in order to get their names on a list for an organ."

"You're making me tired," Ben said. "I'm going home now to curl up on the sofa."

"Barred from the bedroom?" Mel sniggered. "What was it this time? The baby business stuff, right?"

"Nothing to do with that."

"You should learn to keep your mouth shut."

"And maybe you should open yours. Tell Libby it's her duty to bring David and Chloe to Mama's for Chanukah."

Mel pulled at his turtleneck. "What's she care about duty?"

"Then tell her to go for my sake. Tell her if she doesn't go, Renata and I will have to . . . and that would cause a tear in the already threadbare fabric of our marriage."

"Well put," Mel said. "Another Allen Ginsberg. Libby likes your poetry, but even so I don't think she's going to see it your way."

The brothers were silent for a long while after that, concentrating on their drinks, their backs identically rounded, their shoulders equally slumped. Both had knotted foreheads and thick, worried eyebrows pulled close together so that they met in stern furrows ending where their noses began. In a more urbane setting, they might have been mistaken for introverted math professors pondering algorithms or PowerPoint slides, but in this out-of-the-way bar they were no more than brooding husbands nervous about returning home.

It was Mel who spoke first, making chitchat about snow and the benefits of a four-wheel drive. Then he complained about his thickening prostate and how he had to pee all the time, the pain in his knees that prevented him from jogging, his underperforming stocks and the upkeep on his cottage. Ben smirked at the mention of the so-called cottage, a three-storey, stone-and-cedar lakeside house that was regularly featured in glossies. Renata loved to go there, to sun, swim, kayak and play aggressive games of Scrabble late into the evening while music purred from hidden speakers and logs sang in the fireplace. But Ben was miserable in the place. Everything about it, from its wide-plank floors and cathedral ceilings to its hand-carved doorknobs and marble-topped kitchen counter as long as a bowling alley, announced that his kid brother was more successful than he was.

"That's it," Ben interrupted Mel's blather. "I can hardly keep my eyes open." He slid off his wobbly stool and zipped up his parka.

Mel shot out a hand and grabbed Ben's coat sleeve. "Wait a minute, hear me out. I think you should go instead."

"Go where? Instead of what?"

"To Mama's for Chanukah. Light the candles, have a meal . . ."

"Renata and Mama don't get along. They're like oil and water."

"It'll give Libby a chance to cool off. I know her, she just needs time before she comes round."

"It's not going to happen."

"Ask her and see what she says. Tell her it's Chanukah and Mama shouldn't be alone. Tell her it's a good deed, a mitzvah— if she knows the word—that'll get her points in heaven."

"She knows about mitzvoth, for your information, but it won't make a difference."

"Talk to her. What can it hurt? Isn't that what shrinks do—talk things over, work things out?"

"I'm not as good at that as you'd think," Ben admitted. "In my defence, I know certain unmarried or badly married mental health professionals even more clueless about their relationships."

"Very heartening," Mel said. He twisted his brother's sleeve. "Let's keep it simple, then. Tell Renata she can get a good meal at Mama's instead of the usual dreck you eat. That should persuade her."

"How many times do I have to say we don't have time to shop and cook? By the end of the day we're wasted. Anyway, we don't order just anything. We're selective."

Last week, for instance, dinner had been gourmet pizza, delivered free, with sun-dried tomatoes, bocconcini, roasted peppers and grilled zucchini. The thin crust was Renata's idea, the last-minute suggestion of fresh garlic, his. He hadn't been worried about his breath, since clearly they were both too exhausted to make love. In fact, they were too tired even to argue about the toppings and agreed on them after minimal discussion.

When the pizza arrived and he set it in front of her, Renata had opened the box and picked out the smallest slice. She dragged it onto her dinner plate, leaving a colourful track of vegetables on the table. Then she folded her arms, dropped her forehead to her wrist and said, "I can't even eat this. I can't keep my head up."

"You have to eat something," he said, "you're fading away to nothing," so she took the tiniest possible bite.

Ben grabbed a slice too and aimed the tip of it at his mouth. The thin crust gave out, and gobs of cheese and grilled zucchini slid off onto his plate. Chewing the bare crust and picking at the glop on his dish, he'd thought about Mama and the pleasure she used to get from cooking for him when he was still living at home. Those simple, satisfying meals: warm, filling, comforting. Not fancy by a long shot, but made with attention and love.

He shook himself free now from his brother's grip and stepped back. "Okay, I'll speak to her, but don't get your hopes up." Reaching, he punched Mel's rock-hard upper arm and wondered how much time and money had gone into those biceps.

———

When Ben walked into the house, Renata was on the sofa, wearing one of his flannel shirts as she drank herbal tea smelling of almonds and cinnamon. The room was coloured orange from the light of a copper-shaded lamp, the walls deeply shad-owed. Music was playing: Nina Simone.

He shrugged off his parka, yanked off his boots and asked why she wasn't in bed.

"I couldn't sleep."

"Me neither."

"I heard you go out." She stared at her teacup. "Where did you go?"

"The Bald Eagle."

"Alone?"

"With Mel."

"It's such a dump. I can't believe he went there."

"He doesn't mind it once in a while."

"How's he doing?"

"Not bad."

Pulled slowly forward by the magnetism of her voice, he moved up to the sofa, and she rearranged herself, making room for him to sit. Nina sang about love in her pained, husky voice as Renata inched up to him until their knees and shoul-ders touched.

At the press of his arms and thighs, a space opened behind her ribs and hopeful pictures of an energetic night in bed ran like an uplifting movie at the back of her eyes.

"You're not mad anymore?" she asked.

"No."

She put down her cup. He curled his arm around her and felt her soften and sink into him heavily.

Maybe it wasn't the best time to bring up visiting Mama,

but he had her attention now and needed to get it off his chest. He needed to keep talking, to empty his mind as best he could of family and work stuff, the never-ending daily distractions that oppressed him.

"Actually, he was kind of upset. Libby had a fight with Mama and won't see her next week."

Renata widened her eyes at him, nearly black in the dimness, and fluttered her lashes as if she'd just woken up.

"He wants us to go instead, give Libby a chance to calm down and think it over."

Why were they talking about his family? She pulled out of his hold and slid away on the sofa. Loose hair had fallen across her face and she swept it back.

"We haven't been there in ages and she's not getting younger. She won't be around forever, you know. Imagine how I'd feel if she cried on her deathbed that we never came to see her."

She got up and turned off the music, standing with her back to him, his flannel shirt pulled tight across her shoulders. The burning she felt around her eyes was more than disappointment. It was like grief.

He pleaded, "Do me a favour."

"You know how she is," she said. "It's you she wants to be with, so say I've got a headache and go by yourself."

"She'll know that's a lie and think you're being disrespectful."

"I'm not disrespectful."

"She'll know you stayed home because you don't like the way she talks."

That was true, she had to agree, recalling suppers with his family: words speeding round the table as everybody spoke at once, trying to be heard when no one was listening. Wouldn't it be something if they sat still for once and enjoyed each other's company? Or accidentally brushed hands and were suddenly aware of the feel of each other's skin? Renata rubbed her own cold hands together briskly. Then for an evening they might know what bodies know.

The body could be trusted. When a phobic looks at a rodent in a cage and feels her heart pound, her throat constrict, her palms dampen, her terror is undisguised. Over time, as she meets it again and again, her fear becomes familiar, a thing to be observed and examined, like the mouse itself. If she can learn to sit with her uneasiness and let it be, it might lessen someday. And then she will have learned an important truth beyond words.

"Make an effort," Ben said. "We're talking about my mother."

"It's not as if I haven't tried."

"Try again for my sake. I'm not asking much."

"You're asking me to do what I don't like doing." She shook her head decisively. "Maybe when I'm not so busy . . ."

"It's an obligation. Next week is Chanukah and Mama shouldn't be alone."

"Sorry, but I'm just too . . ." Tired, edgy, unmoored? Which adjective would do? Renata wasn't sure, so she left the sentence dangling.

He stood open-mouthed, as if he meant to finish her statement, but then turned sharply away and hurried upstairs, his clopping footsteps an unmistakable reprimand. She heard the telltale croak of the door to his study and knew he'd spend the night in there, his tall body uncomfortably coiled on the daybed, or fall asleep in a chair with his head on his arms on the desk. In the morning he'd be stiff and cold.

A few minutes later, she went upstairs herself and slid into their chilly bed, still wearing Ben's shirt. Despite the heavy flannel, she shivered between the sheets. Dinner with Molly. Was he really asking so much?

Seeing her mother-in-law never got any easier, regardless of how many Fridays she spent with her. As a newlywed, she'd hoped his mom would be a mother to her too; would hug her and joke with her and listen to her secrets. But that hadn't happened. Though Molly was polite, she had never seen Renata as anything but Ben's wife—her son's barren, goyishe wife. And yet, when she begged off, claiming a headache or a crushing workload, the old woman got upset. By some long-standing rule, the family was supposed to visit with fierce regularity. The whole family, she insisted—even, apparently, those who hardly mattered.

She wasn't a bad daughter-in-law. This wasn't about making a stand against Molly, it was more about standing up for herself. After a long week, the last thing she wanted was to be trapped in Molly's kitchen, hearing the prattle of mother and son. She'd rather be with Nina Simone.

Sometimes she thought that she should've studied singing instead of psychology. Her voice wasn't half bad. It had been fun being part of a high school choir once, belting out tremulous notes in the school gym. Later, she liked singing in church, filling the vaulted room with notes richer and more stirring than any she'd sung before. But she lacked the faith for devotional music and it didn't last.

She rolled her head on the pillow, recalling that exuberant sound. If she found time to practise she could join another choir now, just as a hobby. Except there wasn't time, of course. There never was enough time, and more and more there wasn't enough energy either.

How different things might've been if she had married Howard, a singer in the church group who sang so feelingly and promised to devote his life to her happiness. Who finally left in despair when he decided that he loved her more than Mary or Christ himself.

Ben had won her heart in the end. Sexy, smart, distinguished Ben, the man she believed truly saw and understood her. Unlike Howard, whose intense affection seemed to have little to do with her, Ben loved a life-size woman with crooked teeth. He swore he loved her mind, honesty, warmth and sensitivity—but said how could he ignore her breasts, eyes and great legs? Which made her laugh: another plus.

Shaking now, she swung out of bed, pulled on a pair of socks and then dove back in, tucking the quilt around her. Missing the heat of his body, the intimacy of his flesh. People shouldn't sleep alone. And yet here she was again, her husband in the next room. Too many nights he'd nod off in his study or come to bed late, when she was already sleeping. She understood his need to write, but she needed closeness. Skin to skin, heart to heart: wasn't that the stuff of poems?

A long day of phobics, then an evening with Molly . . . only to be dropped into the sea of an empty bed. No, seeing Molly would be too much. He was asking a great deal of her.

She inched to the side of the mattress, the middle being too wide, and faced the bedroom door as if Ben were going to yank it open momentarily, then pulled the quilt over her chin. Her eyes refused to close, and her ears kept waiting for clues that he was next door: throat clearing, nose blowing, the chair squealing across the floor. Footsteps, grunting—anything. Why was he being so still?

Renata rolled onto her back, unbuttoned the flannel shirt and ran a hand over herself, feeling the sharpness of her bones as well as soft hills of flesh. Her slender neck, cool and smooth as a Popsicle, the gully between her breasts. Flat belly, slim thighs . . . Forty wasn't old. She was only just forty and a lot younger than he was. How could he not still find her desirable?

She wanted him. Right now. If he opened the door, walked in, got into bed and asked again, she'd even agree to see his mom. Then she would take his hand, press it here, put it there, and he would touch her all over. No more talking.

But she was alone, the door closed, her eyes stubbornly open. She stared at the clock on the nightstand and the red numbers blinked back: 1:11 . . . 1:12 . . . The house was painfully quiet, and the hand on her body was her own.

CHAPTER 4

G ood morning, Mr. Rae."

"Call me Arthur."

"Please sit down," Ben said, but Arthur paused to look around.

The room was small, scantily furnished, with bare white walls and grey filing cabinets that disappointed those patients hoping for a more personal glimpse of the doctor's life. He didn't have time for decorating and usually left that to his wife, so really it was his own fault if his office was a dull box, his home cluttered and fussy, and neither place reflected him.

He pointed to an armchair behind a low table, waited for Arthur to take a seat, and sat down opposite. "Haven't changed your mind?" he asked with a short laugh. He often used humour to ease the way into a difficult exchange, as much for his own sake as for the patient's.

"Certainly not," said Arthur.

"Well then, let's proceed."

Ben opened a folder on his lap and blinked at the top page. For a moment he seemed to be staring at a to-do list— *dental appointment; call Mama; speak to accountant*—but quickly pulled his mind back.

"Here's the situation. You know by now that the team met on Friday—me and the social worker, transplant coordinator, nurses and nephrologists—some of whom you've already met . . . and your particular case was discussed for a long time. In fact, we spent most of the time talking about you."

When Ben looked up again, Arthur Rae was smiling. He had a soft, wide mouth and cream-coloured, narrow teeth. His thick brows were raised.

"And what did the team say?"

"Everyone agreed that the two of us should meet again to talk things over. The team still has certain questions—certain concerns—because you're not related to the designated recipient. Not even a close friend."

"The tests show our blood and tissue types are compatible. I'm a suitable candidate."

"Yes, from a biological perspective. But there are other issues here, because this isn't about giving an organ to your wife or child, a sibling or good friend. In fact, you hardly know the woman . . ." Ben glanced at the paper on his knee. "Mrs. Stanley. Last week you said she used to show up at meetings of a neighbourhood committee, or else you'd see her on the street. That's all fine, but it doesn't fully explain why you've put yourself forward as a possible donor. In a case like this, the whole team—the other doctors and myself—must be clear about your intentions."

"Isn't it enough that I want to help a dying woman?"

"Well, no, actually not. We have to understand why you want to take this risk . . . the risk of giving a kidney to someone who can best be described as an acquaintance."

"Carol is a neighbour. I knew her husband when he was alive, she knows my wife and children. But I've told you all that before."

The firmness of Arthur's replies was unusual. Ben checked his notes again, fumbling the sheets. A page fell out and he caught it between his knees, slid it back into the file. He knew he was being sized up, and levelled his shoulders, straightened his back.

"You said she lives on your street and is part of your community . . . but after her husband died, and then with her kidney problems, she didn't get around much and dropped out of sight. Is there anything more you'd like to add?"

"Only that no one's forgotten her. We're worried about her situation, which is bad and getting worse." Arthur slid his hands into the pockets of his cardigan and stared over Ben's head. "She's a big-hearted woman. She used to visit seniors to bring them food and rake leaves. Everyone in the neighbourhood talks about her good deeds and what we can do for her. I look in on her sometimes and bring her fresh pineapple, which she's very fond of. She only has her friends and neighbours now to help out." Arthur's eyes met Ben's. "And so I thought, Why not? I have two kidneys and really only need one."

This was reassuring, and Ben relaxed his posture. Nothing would please him more than to end the interview right now, convinced of Arthur's altruism. What a relief it would be to empty his mind of doubt.

But he pressed on. "As I mentioned last time, there are certain medical risks involved—things explained to you earlier. Have you thought more about these challenges?"

"I have."

"And what's your understanding of what could go wrong?"

"From what the nurses told me, I don't foresee any problems."

Ben rubbed his hands together as if rolling his thoughts smooth. "While it's true that generally removing a kidney is a safe operation, each and every surgical procedure has its risks—a bad reaction to the anaesthesia, for instance, or the chance of infection and internal bleeding."

"I'm aware of that."

"Did they tell you it would take several weeks to recover, especially for a man of your age?"

"I don't see myself as old. I'm still in my fifties, in good health, and expect to heal quickly."

Scribbling a few notes, Ben thought how much he himself felt his years. Every night he did a mental body scan, recording the day's aches and pains and other injustices, aware of life creaking forward like a rusty wheel. Arthur, with his cheery outlook, probably went to bed counting his blessings.

He skimmed over the man's chart. According to his test results and personal data, Arthur Rae was fifty-six. With his

straight hair, grey at the temples, neatly parted on the left;
his skinny neck and crumpled eyes; checked tie, tennis shoes
and zip-up cardigan, he looked like the ageless host of a children's show—like the amiable Fred Rogers of "Mister Rogers'
Neighbourhood," a TV show he'd loved as a boy—and also like
Ben's dad, a gentle, resolute man, and someone he missed
even now.

"Have you considered other possibilities?" He glanced at
the file. "You have a wife, children and grandchildren, it says
here, siblings, nieces, nephews . . . a good-size family. What
if one of them needed a new kidney someday and you were a
suitable match? If you give one away now, you won't be able
to help later. Or what if you yourself harmed your one remain-
ing kidney through illness or accident?"

"Those are hypothetical situations, Dr. Wasserman. We're
all healthy now and I don't see the point of fretting about
the future."

"Yes, hypothetical, but isn't that the nature of risk—
considering the downside of what you plan on doing and
deciding if it's worth it? Tell me, have you talked things over
with your family?"

"None of them objects to this. They know how I feel about
helping others. If I were to die suddenly but basically intact,
they'd follow my wishes and donate as many of my organs as
possible to people who needed them."

"I'm glad you spoke to your family and everyone's agreeable. But still, from a medical standpoint, a doctor's first duty
is to do no harm . . . and what you're proposing involves

exposing a healthy man with two functioning kidneys to the risks of surgery and post-operative problems. Exposes this man to harm."

Exposes him to death, was his actual meaning. Tell me how you feel about dying. How do you manage fear?

"I have a right to take those chances."

"It's more complicated than that. It's not just up to you, it's what the doctors and nurses think too. Respect for your autonomy has to be balanced with what you might call a paternalistic attitude—with not wanting to harm you. This is true for any medical procedure, but especially in the case of an organ donor like yourself, and they need to be persuaded that yours is the right decision, medically and ethically. I think you can understand how certain members of the team want to be reassured. They wonder if it's a good idea to take such risks when there's no benefit to you—that is, to your physical self—and worry about the possible emotional fallout if you give a healthy kidney to someone not close to you, genetically speaking. So what I'm getting at . . . what I mean to say is, the team thinks—"

"The team thinks I'm out of my ever-loving mind."

"It's just that your case isn't typical, Arthur. It's not what we usually see." We usually see people who are anxious and frightened. Why aren't you afraid?

But Arthur was basically right: many of Ben's colleagues were uncomfortable with altruism that went beyond offering organs to family and close friends.

At heart, he too was skeptical. Patients sometimes lied to him, or would-be donors revealed dubious motives. Still, he tried to be neutral. Every once in a while a guy like Arthur walks in, and you want to be receptive. Willing to be surprised.

You have to keep an open mind, he imagined arguing with the team. *Even if we doubt his motives, he's offering a valuable gift and deserves respect.*

But more than open-mindedness was needed in a case like this. You needed to have trust in the bigness of a stranger's heart. Was he capable of such audacious optimism?

"Choices like yours aren't simple," Ben continued. "In my experience, they involve many ingredients. For instance, do religious convictions—does your faith—play a role in your decision?"

"Is she a member of my church? Is that what you're asking?"

"Only as an example."

"I see myself as a spiritual man, but not as part of a con-gregation. Carol Stanley matters to me, as every living being does, and if I can save her or help her lead a better life, that's the right thing to do."

A brave thing, Ben thought. How is it that some people always do the decent thing? The skin around his eyes tensed as he peered at Arthur openly, trying to see into him. Hoping, as if by osmosis, to absorb some elusive, essential part of him.

"Have you mentioned this to anyone else? A friend or neighbour? I'm wondering how other people, outside your family, have reacted to your decision."

"I spoke to a few friends. Most of them understand, but one thinks I'm crazy."

"And how did you respond to that?"

"Not everyone will approve." Arthur crossed his arms. "I told him I just don't see it the way he does. In my opinion, many people would do the same."

"Many would *not* do this," Ben insisted. He himself would give an organ only to his mother, to Mel or to a child—if he had one who needed it—and to Renata . . . though honestly, he'd probably want to think about that first.

"I'm wondering if other factors entered into your choice. For instance"—patting the file as if it held the answer—"how do you see things unfolding in the future, when you and Mrs. Stanley have recovered from the surgery?"

"I see us both happy and well."

"Do you think your relationship would change in any way?"

"With Carol? Why should it?"

"Or what if it doesn't change?"

"What are you saying?"

"Sometimes a donor has certain expectations he may not want to bring up or even imagine, but we need to look at them anyway, to talk about these things . . . to make sure you fully understand what you're doing."

"Expectations? Can you be more specific?"

"I'm looking at something I jotted down, another possible factor." He pointed at a scratched note he could barely make out. "As you said last time, Mrs. Stanley is fifty-one and a widow. I wonder if it's possible that after your donation you might wish to know her better."

"Well, I suppose."

"Would you like that?"

"I don't know. I haven't given it much thought."

"Maybe we can talk about it now, if you don't mind."

"All right. Go ahead."

Ben's leg was bouncing and his pants made a breathy sound, as if they were whispering, *Don't disappoint me.*

"How deep is your friendship with her right now?" he asked.

"We're neighbours, I told you."

"But are you aware—do you have a romantic interest in her?"

He flinched. "I'm a married man."

The lines on Arthur's face were suddenly more apparent, and Ben wanted to confide that even a married man can start feeling lonely.

"It's not uncommon for a donor to want to feel closer to someone who's received the gift of his organ. To hope she'll be appreciative and want to express it—that she'll want to feel closer to him too. Would that be important to you?"

"You mean, do I expect her to be grateful for my kidney?"

"Grateful . . . or maybe a stronger emotion."

"Like what?" Edginess in his voice.

"Well, like a deeper friendship or affection. Maybe even love," he said. "Any expectations along those lines?" That she'll love you wholeheartedly, without judgment or reservation. Which is all anyone wants.

Arthur's cheeks darkened. "You don't know my wife, Doctor, what a special person she is. I'd never do anything to hurt or shame her."

"I have to— I'm obliged to ask sensitive questions like these. We have to examine all sorts of possibilities, even those that may not apply in your particular case. People are"—he paused to find a suitable word—"complex, and the obvious reasons for offering an organ are not necessarily the most important ones to discuss. Sometimes there are hidden factors we should have a look at too . . . at anything that might have affected your decision."

"The only thing I want is for Carol to be well again. I don't expect our friendship to change. I love my wife and she loves me, and everything else"—waving his hand—"is irrelevant."

"I don't mean to embarrass you."

"I absolutely disagree with what you're suggesting."

Ben shut his eyes briefly, searching for soothing words, then resumed speaking. "As I've been saying, my job is to explore any possible motives you might have. I don't have an agenda other than to find out as accurately as I can what's going through your head."

He gave him another minute to settle and was reassured when Arthur nodded.

"Good. Let's go on, then. There's something else we need to discuss, another difficult question. Are you at all interested in a monetary reward for the risk you'd be taking?"

"Certainly not."

"But what if, years from now, you have financial problems, or someone close to you does, and you can't raise enough cash to meet your obligations. Suppose—is it possible in five or ten years that you might turn to the person you gave this special gift to and ask for compensation?"

"Would I extort money from her? Is that what you're asking?"

"What I'd like to know"—tapping the arm of his chair—"is what you see happening between the two of you if Mrs. Stanley gets your kidney."

Arthur slid forward, spreading his hands on the table. "I'm retired, as I told you, with a decent pension, and my wife has savings. I don't foresee any problems, but even if we were to experience hard times, the last thing I'd do is demand payment for a gift. That goes against my nature."

In his long career as a staff psychiatrist for the transplant team, Ben had never seen anyone as frank and articulate about his convictions, so willing to risk his health for a virtual stranger. He had to do his job and understand the man's reasons, but there was no denying he was rooting for Arthur. *I want to believe him*, he wrote in the file, his words crooked with soaring loops.

Some people you meet affect you more than others. Some fill you with sorrow, while others awaken you and make you hopeful, more alive. Your heart creaks open.

"What if, before we can organize the transplant . . ." He knotted his fingers under his chin. "What if Mrs. Stanley has a medical event—a stroke, say, or heart attack or even develops cancer—and we can't proceed with the surgery because of the greater risk to her health . . . and suddenly your kidney is no longer needed. What would you do next?"

Arthur pursed his lips briefly, then said, "Go home."

"Do you think you might offer it to another patient who needs one? Is that a possibility, to give your kidney to someone else?"

"I know there are many sick people waiting for organs, but this is about Carol. She's the one I want to help."

Ben pushed his knuckles into the puffy skin under his chin. "Suppose you get your wish," he said, "and we go ahead with the surgery, and by some chance, some bad luck, a problem occurs and the kidney you gave to Mrs. Stanley doesn't take. Suppose, for reasons we can't predict, her immune system rejects the organ despite whatever medical interventions are carried out . . . in which case your sacrifice—your gift—will have been in vain. How would you feel then?"

His face twitched as though he'd been slapped. "Terrible," said Arthur. "She'd be back on dialysis and have a miserable, shortened life."

"And you'd be left with one kidney."

"I'd go back to an active life, but Carol wouldn't. That's the greater tragedy."

Exactly the right response. The one he'd been hoping for.

He closed the file, leaned back and silently counted ceiling tiles to quiet himself down. Straightening up again, he saw Arthur watching him and flushed with embarrassment, as if caught doodling.

"Last week," he resumed, "we talked about your childhood, your parents, brothers and sister, and your life in a small town. From what I heard, I got the sense you didn't have to deal with any losses or traumas in your early years. Do you agree?"

"Mmm."

"Is there anything else you'd like to add? Something I should know about your past you haven't mentioned?"

"Nothing comes to mind."

"Well, good," said Ben. "And I don't think you have—at the risk of oversimplifying—self-esteem problems. Does that seem like an accurate impression?"

"It does."

"That's something we always have to take into consideration because, in certain cases, poor self-esteem can show itself in the need to help others to a great . . . an unhealthy degree."

"That doesn't apply to me."

"Okay, you sound clear on that. But there's still a matter we need to discuss."

Arthur put his hands on his knees and waited quietly with raised eyebrows.

"The matter of the accident . . . and how you reacted. You retired soon after, and I'm wondering just how deeply that affected you."

"I was thinking of retiring anyway," said Arthur.

"But would you have done it just then if not for what happened?"

"No one can be blamed for a random occurrence. I acted correctly, but the collision was unavoidable. There's nothing more I could've done."

"Logically speaking, you can't be faulted for anything. These things happen. But we're emotional beings, and logic doesn't necessarily win the day. I'm asking about your feelings when the vehicles collided, and later, when you found out two people had been killed . . . And right now, right here—I'd like to know that too."

Arthur looked away and Ben sat as still as he could, a spasm pulling his eyelid. Tell me that you don't reproach yourself or feel remorseful. Tell me that you sleep at night.

When Arthur first came here wanting to give up his kidney and said he'd been involved in a crash in which two people died and others were injured, Ben assumed the man had come forward out of guilt. Later, driving home, he considered telling Renata about his new case—which might have led to an interesting conversation about altruism. Every now and then they'd discuss an unusual patient, ask each other for advice or share amusing or poignant stories. It made them feel close and was often very useful.

But when he got home that night there was just a message waiting, the red signal blinking on the phone like a clown's nose. Something or other had come up and she wouldn't be back till ten, her recorded voice said clearly. And after she arrived she was tired and cranky and went to bed.

In the morning there wasn't time. No time that evening or on Wednesday or Thursday either, and then they had that argument about her pregnant patient, and the one about Mama . . . so that now he no longer wanted to tell her anything. The enigma of Arthur Rae, the mystery of his resolve, was something he'd keep to himself. What he thinks about the man sitting before him has become his secret.

Arthur was speaking again, staring down at the table, and Ben realigned his thoughts.

"It's not easy knowing that people died in an accident where you were one of the drivers, but I don't feel guilty, if that's what you're getting at."

"And yet you retired. Can you tell me more about that?"

"I took stress leave, as you know, discovered I enjoyed being home after working for thirty-three years and decided it was time to move on. My wife liked the idea, so I took my pension early and have never regretted that decision for a moment."

Ben chewed a thumbnail, then hid his hands under his thighs. It was only natural to feel awful following an incident in which you were, to some degree, responsible for the deaths of a driver and passenger—even if you did what you could and no one was accusing you. But something still bothered him. What if his original assumption was right and, consciously or otherwise, the man was offering his kidney to a neighbour to make himself feel better—to offset the bad with good?

Was it foolish to believe in selflessness . . . or was he now pathologizing Arthur's brand of altruism that went beyond the more usual "looking after one's own"?

"We were talking about your feelings," said Ben. "Let's get back to that."

Arthur crossed his legs and laced his long fingers, with their clean, carefully clipped nails, around his jutting knee. "How do I feel? Bad. But I don't—I do *not*—feel accountable in any way."

Ben put the file down and nodded sympathetically. Folding his hands in his lap, thumbs free and working, he bowed from the waist and reduced the space between them.

"Sometimes people respond to a tragedy by wanting to make amends. You know, even things up. Counterbalance something bad by doing something good in return. Do you think that might apply here?"

"I don't understand."

"I'm thinking that you might have remembered Mrs. Stanley, who was dying for want of a kidney, and thought that by giving her one you could make up for lives lost. And then you might feel less overloaded somehow. Does that seem right to you? Does that sound plausible?"

"I told you already that I'm not feeling guilty. But even if I was, am I not allowed to offer a life-giving gift to a person in dire need because it would make me feel good? What you're saying doesn't make sense."

Ben rubbed his face, moving the loose skin in circles. "Let's suppose you were feeling bad about the accident and thought that helping a sick woman would lessen your burden . . . and then you had the operation, but after your recovery you felt no better, or even felt worse . . ." What other parts of yourself would you be willing to donate to ease your shame?

He waited for Arthur to consider what he'd said. When the man seemed to have nothing more to say, Ben continued. "There are people I've met who would spend the rest of their lives trying to square things up, who would try to give away a second organ to someone else, and you need to think about whether you'd do the same."

"I talked this over with my wife," Arthur spoke up, "and made a decision based on what I know about myself and Carol Stanley. I don't see how anyone can be expected to do more."

Ben pushed up his left sleeve surreptitiously and eyed his watch: just a few minutes left. Normally he'd reach his conclusions by the end of a first meeting with someone, which is what he was paid for, but this time he was still hesitant after a second round. Though he wanted to believe the man—for who doesn't want to believe in benevolence?—Arthur still eluded him. What was he going to report to the team?

An unusual request, Ben rehearsed silently, *but not necessarily one that points to instability. It's possible—probable—that Mr. Rae is an honest man who has made an informed decision. Let's not dismiss his type of altruism out of hand.*

"I hope you understand that no matter how well I explain your position, mine is only one voice and the team could still say no."

"I know they could finally turn me down, but right now, as I see it, my job is to persuade you to argue in my favour."

Ben pushed his chair back. "Sometimes, in certain cases," he said slowly, "two meetings aren't enough. I think you should come back. I think we should keep talking so I can learn more about . . . all this."

"Okay."

"I'd like to speak to your wife too. How would you feel about her coming in to see me?"

"Fine, if you think it'll help."

"I'd like to meet with her first, if that's all right, and then you can join us. Is there anything you don't want me to ask her or bring up?"

"Talk about whatever you want."

Ben walked to his desk and consulted his appointment book. "I have an opening Wednesday at three, if you're available."

"I'll have to check with Iris."

Arthur stood up, his face pinched, adjusted his collar and fixed his tie. "Meanwhile, Dr. Wasserman, don't forget that while you're puzzling over my mental state, Carol Stanley is dying."

CHAPTER 5

Molly Wasserman wasn't much of a cook by any measure but her boys had never minded, they weren't fussy about food so long as there was plenty of it, and Nathan, God rest his soul, never complained about anything but ate whatever she put on his plate: clear soup with noodles and boiled chicken Friday nights, cheese or tuna casserole Tuesdays and Thursdays, meat and fish the rest of the week—though sometimes they had scrambled eggs—and then he'd burp and rub his belly, a little joke between them, thank her for his supper, get up and go to the basement to read.

Her Nathan was well read and should have been a professor, would've been a professor if he'd stood up to his father and refused to join the family business selling wires and widgets and other things she couldn't name—"component parts," he called them—to companies who needed them to manufacture God-knows-what, and he knew and she knew he wasn't happy doing it but made enough money so his wife didn't have to work, a very important matter to him even though she might've enjoyed being in an office where you got to talk to different people, not just your neighbours like Ida Abramowitz or Ruthie and Phyllis Cohen with nothing to say except for what they read in flyers from the stores and how successful their children are and how much they donated last year to the synagogue, not even knowing they were boring her silly . . . not including Ida's news about her cousin Saul, of course, which perked Molly right up, although she had to pretend she was only barely interested.

But she wasn't thinking about Saul Rosenberg now, she was thinking about Nathan.

It was his idea to start calling her Molly after so many years of just plain Miriam, a name as dull as laundry that never really suited her, because of a character he liked in a book by a famous Irish author, a woman he said reminded him of her, so naturally she was curious and tried to read the novel but never got very far, it was really too impossible with long, twisted sentences and a plot she couldn't follow and the main character talked and talked until you wanted to scold him to close his mouth and let someone else get a word in. But she kept the name anyway, she liked the way it sounded and made her tongue roll up and how she felt like a young, freckled country girl from Ireland every time she heard it, except that her complexion was spotless and rather pale and she was born in Brooklyn, where trees had a hard time, and her parents, may they rest in peace, were Yiddish-speaking Latvians who came here from Riga, and she was too old now and heavy in the legs to be anything but what she was.

Nathan came from a long line of merchants and craftsmen who were also from the Baltics, not a milkmaid among them, who handed down brains and a good head for numbers but also the heart problems that cursed them for generations, which is why he died at sixty, a tender age it seems to her now that she's in her seventies, and his dying words were *Molly, I have always loved you dearly*—and how many wives have a husband as adoring as that?

It was lonely without him, and not just in bed, where she liked lying next to him and would fall asleep to his snoring, as steady as a clock's tick, but also because he was always giving her compliments and bringing flowers and little gifts without any reason, making her heart sing out, though truth to tell he hadn't been as good with the physical stuff even when they were youngsters and such things mattered, having a hesitant nature and therefore unwilling to try things—sexual things— she thought would give her pleasure. Not that she was wanton, but she was five years younger and had a passionate makeup, which accounts for the one-and-only time she ever had an affair, three years into her marriage and before she had Ben, a fact she can now look back on without shame but which she has nevertheless kept secret for fifty years and never felt the need to talk to anyone about, enjoying private memories of all the thrilling things they did, though not even once did she think of leaving Nathan—such a sweet, reliable man, who wouldn't have been able to go on a day without her—especially for a dis- tant cousin of Ida's who was said to have a wife and daughters in Europe, who came here looking for work and disappeared a few months after they became lovers and never got in touch with her since—a nobody in the eyes of the world, but what a prince in the bedroom!

And now he was staying with Ida again. He'd come back last week hard up for money and needing a place to live, so Molly told her neighbour there was plenty of space in her house—that is, if he was interested—what with the boys gone and Nathan in the arms of God eighteen years now, and she wouldn't mind letting a room to someone Ida could vouch for, one of her *mishpokhe*, and Ida said he gets a small pension and is good for the rent, he's quiet, tidy and doesn't smoke, and Molly couldn't keep from blushing, turning her head aside to hide her embarrassment, because of the reckless thing she'd done—inviting an ex-lover she hadn't seen or spoken to in over five decades back into her life again. A man she could still see naked when she closed her eyes.

Sometimes she wondered what her sons would say if they knew she'd been an adulterer, if they knew she even thought about sexual things at her age, and then she'd have to explain that the older you get the more you rely on what you remember to get you through the boredom and trials of your later years. But why should they understand? The young think time is something scratched on a calendar and can't imagine being old.

Now she glanced at the kitchen clock and saw that it was getting late; she ought to start supper if she wanted it to be ready when Ben got here at six thirty, just the two of them tonight, which she was secretly looking forward to even though it was disrespectful of his wife to stay home. She hardly saw him alone anymore, it was mainly with Renata if she saw him at all, and it always shocked her to know he was part of a couple now, that his loyalties had shifted from her to a stranger. She didn't feel the same with Libby, maybe because she saw her so often she was used to her, but also because her other son, dear as he was, wasn't Ben.

Around noon Renata phoned to beg off with a headache, which Molly hadn't believed for a second but wasn't too upset about, not just because she'd have Ben to herself this time but also because he could never get his wife out the door, and when they came late they were always full of excuses—construction or traffic or the lineup at the gas station—and Ben would be tense knowing the chicken would be overcooked, dry as lint, and the vegetables boiled to mud. And now that she thinks of it . . . the last time they came to dinner, so long ago it's hard to remember what for, a birthday or holiday, Her Highness refused to eat, saying she wasn't hungry after a long day of dealing with people's problems, and not eating when someone spends an afternoon cooking for you is just plain rude, in Molly's opinion.

She'll never know what he sees in her. Aside from anything else she's got the body of a boy, not a bit of softness anywhere, which Ben can't be happy about. A man likes to push his fingers deep into a woman's flesh . . . or so her lover once said.

A lover! Imagine! Sometimes she wanted to shout it to everyone, to Ida, Phyllis and Ruthie, to Mel and that Libby with the big mouth and no manners—which is why both her youngsters are juvenile delinquents and Molly will never have the grandchildren she deserves—to Ben and his skinny wife who eats like a guppy and probably doesn't want a baby because it'll ruin her so-called figure. She wanted to tell them all and see the look on their faces when they realized there was part of her they knew nothing about, something wild and unexpected.

When Ben knocked and rang the bell, Molly blew a kiss through the glass panels of the door, let him in, hung up his coat, then hugged him long and hard, her heart pitter-pattering. He was so much taller than Mel that her face was in his armpit. Vitamins, she said when he was young and asked why no one else in the family was his height, and when he wanted to know why they hadn't helped his brother she explained that the genes of his Grandpa Wasserman, a bigger-than-average man, had skipped a generation and reappeared in his grandson, and wasn't he a lucky boy?

Her lover was almost the same size and had a similar narrow and out-of-proportion face, too long in the jaw and with close-together eyes, but there were certainly men on her side of the family who looked like that, and anyway she wasn't going to think about such things, she had to stop thinking them every time she saw Ben because Saul was more or less out of her life by the time she found out she was pregnant. She'd counted the days and months a thousand times over the years without being certain and finally just made up her mind that Nathan was her son's father—why shouldn't that be so? Look how successful he was, how honest and reliable—which only proved he took after Nathan and not Saul.

And really, what's the difference? Would she love him any less if his actual father wasn't the man she was married to? "Love child" was the name for it, a fitting expression because you love a boy like that as much as his so-called legitimate brother—maybe even a little more because of the mystery of his birth. Any child is a blessing. The point of having children is to open your heart no matter what, to make yourself brand new by loving more than you thought you could.

Ben wiggled out of her hold, stepped back and stared at her, sizing her up, his eyes like globs of chocolate pudding. "Is that a new dress?" he asked. "And what's with the makeup? All this just for me?"

Molly didn't answer. It was a new dress, with a fitted waist and scoop neck, a little daring at her age, and yes, she was also wearing lipstick and rouge . . . but no, not just for Ben. Thinking about the past had made her want to look good tonight.

She smiled at him, took his hand and led him into the kitchen. "Come to the table and we'll light the Chanukah candles. It's dark out, we're already late."

Molly gave him matches and together they sang the blessings as Ben lit the shamus and all the other candles . . . and her throat shrank with feeling because she was remembering all the times he stood over the blazing menorah, a boy with flame-bright eyes, and warbled in a bird's voice. Of course it would've been better if the whole family was here tonight, the way it used to happen, but just Ben was good enough, a private celebration. Anyway, her grandchildren lacked the proper spirit and wouldn't play dreidl anymore.

"Sit now, I'll bring the chicken. It's not quite done yet—I bought a big bird because I thought your wife was coming too."

"She has a headache."

"So she said."

"Renata gets migraines, especially when she's over-worked. It has nothing to do with you."

"You wouldn't tell me if it did. But listen, I understand . . . a boy gets married, his mother doesn't count anymore."

"It's not that you don't count, it's more that Renata does. I have to think of her too, like Mel thinks of Libby. You should be happy your sons aren't wimps."

"Sure, I'm happy for you both."

Happy about this, she thought, unhappy about that. How is it a person can have two exactly opposite feelings at the same time?

Molly sat down with her elbows on the table and Ben sat across from her, his hands spread and fingers curled as if he was getting ready to push himself up again. She reached over and flattened his fingers, so long and slender that he might've been a surgeon or concert pianist—less gloomy and much more rewarding, to her mind, than talking to dying people about organs in short supply—and left her hands on his.

"You spoke to your brother?"

"Friday, after he saw you."

"Out the door in forty minutes. He ate like a chicken, peck-peck-peck, hardly touched anything." Molly pursed her lips. "So he told you what went on here a couple of weeks ago?"

"You mean with David and Chloe?"

"Those disrespectful juvenile delinquents Libby raised. They ducked under the velvet rope and ran into the living room, where everyone knows you shouldn't go, and jumped up and down on the couch like clowns on a trampoline—and what do you think their mother said when I hollered and shooed them off? She said a couch is for sitting on, this isn't a museum, and stop being an old fool!"

"Libby called you an old fool?"

"Maybe not in those words—but that was her meaning, there's no mistaking what she meant."

"Libby loves you, Ma, but has to stand up for her children. Remember how you'd get if anyone criticized me or Mel?"

"That's different, I taught you manners. My children never embarrassed me in public."

"We're talking about two kids playing on a sofa. Why is that a big deal?"

"We're talking about trespassing! This is a special room for family gatherings, like on the High Holidays, and this is where we all sat shiva for your father. Your children wouldn't go some-where they're not allowed and purposely break the furniture."

"I don't have children, and if I did, there's no telling what they would or wouldn't do."

Molly sighed and squeezed his hands. "So how's it going with you two?"

"Me and Mel?"

"You and her."

"What kind of question is that?"

"I know you want children," Molly said, "and now she's already forty and should've had them years ago."

"We're still hoping," Ben replied.

"I dream you'll have a son and name him after your father . . . a baby I can look at and remember my Nathan. You can tell that wife of yours that looking after nervous people is well and good, but first she has to look after you and give you a family."

"It's nobody's fault. But you already know that."

"I know you're like me, with a sensitive nature, and it hurts me to look at you and see so much sadness."

"It's not just the baby thing. There's work . . . and other stuff."

"I know how much you want one. I know because I myself long for a child of yours to comfort me in my last years."

"You're already a grandma. You've got all the comfort you need."

"Remember that nice girl from high school?"

"Madeline?"

Pregnant on her sixteenth birthday with Ben's child; unpregnant shortly thereafter, to his relief. He'd paid for the abortion himself with money earned after school and no one ever knew a thing.

Once he'd tried to tell Renata what he'd done at eighteen but couldn't get the words out. Couldn't say he'd squandered his best shot at fatherhood.

"She married one of the Levy boys and now she's a mother of four. I can't help thinking if you had stayed with Maddy . . ."

He yanked his hands free of hers and hid them under the table. "The chicken's ready. I can smell it."

"Sure, don't listen to me. It's just your mother talking."

She got up and crossed the kitchen, bunched a towel in her hands, opened the oven door and pulled out the roaster. Even with the towel she could feel the heat in her fingers, and she swung the pan over to the stove and dropped it with a clang. Then she jiggled the bird's thigh and saw that Ben was right, it was done—probably overdone—but he was used to dry meat, she'd served it often enough, and how could he complain if she said that she'd been listening so hard she lost track of time?

She stopped fussing with the bird and grew as still as a house when she realized he'd begun speaking urgently to her back.

"I do want a child but it's just not happening. The doctor says we need to unwind, take it easy, so we tried relaxation tapes, hot tubs, acupuncture, long vacations, Swedish massage, shiatsu, reiki—nothing works."

Her ears ached to hear his voice thick with misery. She went to him, looped her arms around his shoulders where he sat, chin lowered to his chest, and kissed the thinning crown of his head. "There's still time," Molly said, not believing a word of it, fearing he would never be a father, never know the joy of holding a baby . . . that nothing would relieve his pain spreading in all directions and she would have to witness what she only partly understood—see and endure his suffering till the day she died.

But tonight, at least, she could feed him. There was comfort in a hot meal.

She walked away from the table to cut up the chicken, a leg for Ben, his favourite, and white meat for herself. She served it with kugel and carrots, never mind the gravy, which she didn't have patience for and couldn't make properly even when she tried hard—and who needs the calories? Pepper was good enough and better for you, and naturally she didn't use salt in her food at all, didn't so much as keep a shaker on the table, and Ben should avoid it too because high blood pressure runs in the family and it's never too soon to worry about your health.

She hummed while they ate, though her heart wasn't in it, to add a note of cheeriness and break the heavy silence. Ben didn't like to eat and talk at the same time, a habit she respected because at least he'd never choke on his food, but as for herself, she enjoyed conversation. She had to wait until he finally put down his knife and fork, the chicken and kugel already gone, the carrots scattered on his plate, before he asked what she was humming. She tried but couldn't remember the name, only that it was something she'd first heard from Nathan.

"Something Irish," she said, "that your father sang. He liked Irish books and music."

Ben used his finger to push his carrots into a line. "He had lots of interests aside from work," he said, and Molly had to bite her lip to keep from saying that the one thing Nathan didn't care enough about was what used to interest her most before she got old and literally dried up.

"Your father was a cultured man."

"He loved books, loved to read."

How little Molly knew about her own mother and father, with their broken English and reticence, their fear of strangers, men in uniforms, unfamiliar places. One of the things that had attracted her to Nathan was his beautiful English. His English books.

After Ben finished eating, Molly said she needed him to help move furniture in his old room. She asked as sweetly as she could, knowing that he wouldn't like changing things around in there.

"Can't it wait till next time? I have to get going."

"I can't do it myself," she said, "and who knows when I'll see you again."

"What's wrong with it like it is?"

"The room's too hard to clean, too many things in there. I want more open space."

"You're bored, that's the problem. Why don't you learn bridge?"

She motioned for him to follow her and moved carefully up the stairs, one painful step at a time because her left hip was hurting, and God knows her knees would be aching on the way down. Ben came after without complaint, except for sucking his teeth in irritation, which annoyed her.

She hobbled to his bedroom and leaned against the door frame, hands slowly rubbing her hips, both of which were killing her now, and asked him to push the big dresser closer to the wall. Then she had him rearrange the nightstand, chair and desk. Finally she pointed at the toybox under the window and told him to pick it up and carry it to the basement.

"Why not leave it where it is?" He knelt down in front of the chest.

"No one plays with toys anymore, not you and not my two spoiled-rotten grandkids who only want computer games and electronic *chozzerai*—nothing but garbage!—so why should it take up space? I'll put down a rug instead."

He creaked open the wooden lid on which he'd once carved his initials with a pocket knife, poked around inside and pulled out the pieces of a wooden train. He sat down cross-legged, linked the cars together and dragged the little engine with its smokestack across the floor, never mind about the tracks. His face softened all at once, became fuller and smoother as the wrinkles in his forehead and around his mouth relaxed.

He used to play with his train after supper, she remembered. Down on one knee, he would pull the long chain of cars around the locked-together tracks, puffing pretend smoke, shushing like a boiling kettle, whistling and chugging while Molly and Nathan watched. She predicted he was going to drive a train someday and Nathan laughed, *Now there's a fine profession for a Jewish boy.* Then he squatted, reached out and pulled his son against him, and Molly kissed them both on the tender back part of their necks . . . her Benny burning red like a coal-fired engine, his skin heated up with love.

Now he put the train away and stared into the box with his elbows out and hands on the lid as if he were going to dive in, hung his head and looked hard for God-only-knows-what, until he finally closed it and lugged the chest to the hallway.

When he came back he asked in a boy's voice, "Are we done here?"

Missing his childhood, she thought. Missing Nathan. For one blurry instant she was sorry to have started this.

"That's it, all done. I want to move the pictures too, but that I can do myself."

What made her add that? She grimaced at the wall with the family photos she'd put up after he moved out because they looked nicer than his posters of modern art and girls in bikinis. Why did she have to open her mouth and make him curious?

"You're putting them in your room?"

"There's more than enough in there. I want them in the hall where everyone can see them."

"Can't they see them where they are?"

She didn't have to answer because he had already walked up to the pictures and forgotten all about her. He was staring at the old man with wet-looking eyes and a bushy white beard who was Nathan's grandpa, and he wouldn't have heard her anyway even if she'd thought of a clever lie that made sense. After that, Ben examined the photo of her in-laws—Nathan's *tateh* in spectacles, a bowler and three-piece suit; his mama in her wedding dress, looking into the future and not liking what was there. Farther along he stopped at portraits of Nathan himself: a little boy with short hair, in dark stockings and knickers; a wavy-haired young man; a soldier in uniform, his hair receding like Ben's.

"He looks so gentle."

"A real gentleman," she agreed. Not a perfect gentleman, because of his temper, but Ben already knew that. No need to say more.

The best picture of all, as far as Molly was concerned, was the one of her and Nathan she had hung near Ben's bed, their wedding photograph—and wasn't she a lovely bride! Smooth skin, a high bosom, eyes bright with visions of the marriage bed and tossed sheets, despite her mother's warnings of pain and disappointment.

Sad to say, Mama was right. Nathan's mouth was soft and his body hard and ready, but he did in fact let her down the night of their wedding, left her stunned and miserable. It was all over too soon and she was aching, sticky-wet, the hotel sheets stained red beyond washing, which numbed her with embarrassment. When Nathan hurried into the shower, she bit her lip to keep from shouting, There must be more to it than this! She cried briefly to herself, not wanting to shame him, and thought maybe all they had to do was get used to each other, be patient, give it time, and one day, by and by . . .

"Mel's always asking me where I came from," Ben said all at once, so that she caught her breath, "and I don't know what to say. Who do I look like?"

He was squinting at the wedding picture, standing so close that his nose was practically in it, and Molly flinched and turned away. Same old question. What could she tell him that she hadn't said before? What could she answer that would finally be enough?

"To me," she began, "you're like Grandpa Wasserman." She nudged him along the wall and pointed at the photo of Nathan's father. "He was also tall, but your nose with the high bridge, the big jaw and long face . . . those, I'd say, are from my side of the family."

He peered at the old man with the beard.

"You have his mouth," she said, "like your father before you, and also the Wasserman eyes."

He went to a picture of Nathan again and said he thought he could see it.

"Oh, those dreamy Wasserman eyes!" Molly changed course. "The first time he looked at me, I knew your father was the one."

He turned away from the photos and crossed his arms. "Tell me."

"I already told you a hundred times."

"Tell me again."

"You said you have to go, so here's the quick version." She sat in the chair that had been moved to a corner and fixed her eyes above his head.

"Naturally we were very young, your father in university and me still in high school, but from the moment we met I knew he was special. My *tateh* said he should graduate and find a good job first and that I was too young, but Nathan proposed to me anyway, which I remember thinking was brave and romantic . . . though we didn't actually marry for another two years, when he'd already started with the widgets and gadgets."

"Did he get down on one knee?"

Molly's eyes rolled up. "Nothing with the knees—we were already lying in the dandelions in Prospect Park after a picnic. There were egg salad sandwiches, a Thermos of iced tea and something good I made for dessert, I can't remember what now, and he was leaning over me, pushed up on an elbow, touching me softly where the sun warmed my face. He said the sun was shining for me and I was a flower turned to the light and my green eyes reminded him of things grassy and fresh—and wasn't that a lovely thing to say to a young girl? I passed him a crust of bread and we ate it from opposite ends until the piece was all gone and finally our lips met . . . and then we kissed a long time until I ran out of air and had to stop to inhale."

She closed her eyes and licked her lips, recalling a time when her mouth was like a plump tomato. "Then he asked me to marry him and I looked up at the trees and the sky was robin's egg blue and I didn't answer right away, I was thinking about being someone's wife and having children, the shopping and cooking and a lifetime of laundry like my mother used to kvetch about . . . but also my wedding dress, lacy and fitted, and a honeymoon on a cruise ship. Still, I had to wonder if I loved him enough to want to spend the rest of my life with him because I'd never had another beau to compare him with— but then he kissed me once more and it felt so good I said yes . . . and then he asked me again and I said yes a second time, and he went on asking me because he liked the sound of it. I pulled him up against me and his heart was banging so hard I worried it would fall out and I said over and over, 'I'll marry you, I will, I will.'"

Was that how it went—or was she saying what she remembered from a schmaltzy book? Well, it hardly mattered. Molly breathed deeply, her lungs expanding with the hope and sweetness of her youth, then opened her eyes again and saw Ben staring at her bluntly, his jaw loose.

"That's a wonderful story," he said after a long while. "Dad said all the right things."

"He had a poet's soul, like you."

She let him sit with that a while, pleased by how their talk went, and then she instructed him to carry the toybox to the basement while she made tea. He said not to bother, he had to get up early and was leaving after he took it down, but Molly insisted.

"What's a meal without tea?"

Back in the kitchen, she put the kettle on to boil and cut up some honey cake Ida had brought over when she heard Ben was coming tonight because she wanted the world to know she was a *baleboste* who liked cooking and baking and not some lazy housewife who gossiped on the phone for hours and sat in front of the TV getting fat. And yet Ida outweighed Molly by half a ton.

"He'll love this," she had said, and Molly reminded her that Ben was always watching his weight and didn't usually eat sweets.

In fact he shook his head when he came up from the basement and saw slices of Ida's cake next to the teacups, and secretly it delighted her to think of telling her neighbour he wouldn't even try it because it looked so fattening, butter and honey practically oozing all over his plate. But when he drank his tea in one gulp and said he had to go, the pleasure ran out of her.

"What, no dessert? You only just got here and already you're flying out the door."

He looked at his watch. "It's getting late."

"You hardly said a word to me, I don't even know how you're doing."

"Everything's fine, Ma. We'll talk more the next time."

"And when is this next time? When will I see you again?"

She was just about to hug him and say how much he meant to her and not let go till he promised to phone regularly and come back soon, when the doorbell rang several times. The shrillness of it made her freeze where she stood with her arms open, outstretched—as if the evil one himself were screaming to be let in.

"Who's that?" Ben asked.

"What? How should I know?"

Loud knocking on the door—bang, bang, bang! Whoever was out there wouldn't give up.

"You're not expecting anyone?"

"Who should I be expecting?"

More ringing and banging, then the doorknob started rattling.

"Don't answer."

"He'll break the door."

"Just ignore it," Ben said. "You shouldn't let a stranger in, especially after dark."

"A burglar wouldn't knock first. Better we should see who it is than stand here worrying."

Molly stuck her chest out, walked from the kitchen to the hallway with Ben at her heels and yanked open the front door. An elderly gent in a shirt and tie, with flattened sprigs of white hair, stared at her through narrowed eyes.

"Molly Wasserman?"

She opened her mouth and tried to speak, but all that came out was a small "Oh."

"Look at you!" he cried out.

Ben elbowed his mother aside. "Okay, buddy, what do you want?"

"I'm here about the room," he said, throwing back his shoulders. For an old man he was quite tall.

"What room?" Ben said.

Molly stroked Ben's hand. "This is Ida's cousin Saul. It's all right, I know him. He came from Europe last week and needs his own place but can't afford an apartment, so I said I had some extra space and wouldn't mind the company. I wasn't expecting him to show up this soon."

"You're taking in a stranger and haven't told me and Mel? You can't have someone move in without talking to us first."

"I offered to rent a room. He hasn't even seen it yet."

"Will you show it to me?" Saul asked, pushing his face up to Ben's and peering at him meaningfully.

"I'll do it," Molly said. She walked to the foot of the stairs and pointed to the second floor. "Go up and turn right, it's down the hall, facing the yard. A big room, painted blue with white around the window."

Fifty years was a long time. She saw how much he'd aged as he started slowly up the steps, no longer filling his pants, which flapped against the back of his legs. His shoulder blades poked out and pale scalp showed through where there used to be thick hair. And how did Molly look to him? She hoped his eyesight wasn't so good anymore.

"So that's why you got rid of the toybox," Ben said, coming up behind her.

"I told you, no one uses it."

"I don't want him in my bed."

"Do you even remember the last time you slept there?"

"I don't get it. You don't need the money."

"It's not about money, Ben. This is a good deed we're doing, a mitzvah . . . and I thought it would be nice having someone around for tea and conversation."

"You have a family and friends for that."

"How often do I see them? It's not the same as somebody living under your own roof. It's lonely here by myself. A house isn't meant for one."

"What about a small apartment? Something easy to handle."

"I don't want to leave my home. And Saul could help me manage, he could change washers, shovel snow, things like that, so I wouldn't have to bother Mel."

He lowered his chin and squinted at her. "How do you know him anyway?"

"Through Ida," she replied a little too loudly, and then, thank goodness, before he could ask another embarrassing question, Saul came back downstairs and interrupted them.

"I like it," he told her. "Just what I had in mind. But I'm sure you need to think about it, talk to your family. Call me when you decide."

Ben started to say something, but Molly put a finger to his lips and scolded, "Not now. I think you should go now. Say good-night to my old friend, Mr. Saul Rosenberg, and the rest we'll talk about later."

"You want me to leave you alone with him?"

"I know this man a long time, since before you were born."

Ben backed away from them, his eyes blinking nervously, and paused again in the hallway. "You're sure you don't want me to stay?"

"You have to get up early."

"Your safety—"

"I'm perfectly safe."

She blew a kiss and waved him out, and Ben left abruptly, the door booming shut behind him disapprovingly.

Her heart was chattering in her ears when she turned around to face Saul. "Well," she said, "look at *you*."

"Everybody's old now. Even your son has grey hairs."

"He's always worrying, that's why."

"I worry too," said Saul. "I worry that you hate me."

"I did once." Molly raised her fingers to one of her hot cheeks. "But after all these years, I'm not so angry anymore."

He bent forward as if to bow, so slowly and stiffly that she thought she heard his joints creak, and then he touched her other cheek with the back of his trembling hand. "You'll always look good to me."

"Come into the kitchen," she said. "There's honey cake and hot tea."

CHAPTER 6

Renata heard her eight o'clock enter the waiting room a few minutes early and glanced at the notes on her desk. Joe Marquez was a nursing assistant in a community hospital who'd lately begun to panic when he saw bloody sheets or patients' wounds. Fear and sleeplessness were causing him to stay home and miss work more and more, endangering his job and recent marriage.

Today they were going to spend two intense hours using the lancing device on the table in front of her, an exposure session likely to bring him close to fainting. She'd been staring at the pen-like plastic tool for the last twenty minutes to prepare herself for what was to come. She'd have to use the lancet to prick her own fingertips, draw her own blood, before it was his turn—and she herself had qualms about the sight of blood.

At eight she opened her office door and calmly invited him in.

Joe was a burly man of thirty-one who arrived in a crisply ironed shirt. He sat down across from her, the glass table between them, and pushed back his chair a few feet. He was slightly hunched and kept his eyes fixed on his shoes as he rubbed his palms over his knees. She imagined round, shiny patches forming on his dark pants.

Face pale, he glanced from his hands to the table. "That's the lancing device we spoke about last time," she said. "For drawing blood."

"My blood?"

"Yours too."

"How much?"

"A single drop. My finger, then yours. You said you weren't able to look at your own blood either—when you nicked yourself with a splinter recently, wasn't it?—and want to work on that too. So that's what we planned for today, to look at this device, then use it on me, use it on you. That's next on your list of things you'd like to accomplish, and I know you can do it."

He drew in his breath and gripped his knees.

"How are you feeling right now?"

"My anxiety level's going up."

"How would you rate it?"

"Fifty, sixty percent."

"Think you can take another look?"

He narrowed his eyes at the table, grimaced and turned aside.

"Where are you at now?"

"Eighty and rising."

"Let's stop here so you can do your relaxation techniques. Breathe in, hold your breath, breathe out and hold it. Let your jaw and eyes relax. Do a mental body scan, releasing any tension . . . When your fear level comes down, see if you can look again. It's important for you to do this, so please keep trying."

Twenty minutes later, when he was feeling better and could view the gadget steadily, she asked him to move closer. Inch by inch he slid his chair up to the table, until his knees reached the glass. Finally she picked up the loaded implement, the lancet needle aimed at him, and his breath quickened.

She gave him another minute before she continued. "I'm going to prick my finger now to get some blood and want you to watch. Are you ready for that?"

"Guess so."

She put the cap on the end of the device and pressed it hard against the tip of her ring finger. An image of a dribble of blood across her wedding band arose out of nowhere and she blinked it back.

When she pressed the release button there was a startling click, but she didn't react. Stroking her finger slowly, she watched as a drop of blood formed on the tip.

"If you prick us, do we not bleed?" Ben once read out loud from Shakespeare. The rush of feeling in his voice had stirred them both, and their lovemaking that night was tender and powerful. How long ago was that? Not so long that she wasn't still waiting for another hit of closeness.

She blotted the puncture, and when she put the bloodied ball of cotton on the table, other words replaced Ben's. *I'm bleeding*, her mother cried, and Stella said about the crash, *There was blood everywhere*. Momentarily woozy, Renata breathed deeply until the sensation passed.

Joe's eyes were squeezed shut.

"Can you look at the cotton ball?"

His eyelids fluttered open and closed as she asked again.

"What's your level now?" she said.

"A hundred and fifty!"

"As high as that? Off the chart?"

"Well, maybe ninety."

He was breathless, fidgety, close to crying. Renata's upper body swayed in sympathy. She asked him to tell her when he felt less anxious and ready to continue, and eventually he did.

"Would you like me to do that again? Pierce my pinky, then another two fingers? Will you watch me and look at my fingertips as long as you can?"

He clenched his stomach with his hands and nodded.

After she was done pricking three more fingers and had lined up cotton balls on the table in full view, it took more than half an hour for his fear level to drop.

Finally she asked if he was ready to go to the next step, and held out the tool. "Do you think you might like to try using it on yourself now?"

"Maybe you could do it for me one time?"

"Certainly."

She changed the needle, grasped the tool and walked around the table. His hands were fisted on his knees. She bent over, close enough to feel the heat of his red face, opened his left hand and pushed the device against his index finger.

"Okay, here we go."

He looked away and whimpered when Renata pressed the button.

"There's a tiny drop of blood on your finger, when you're ready to look, same as what happens when a sliver gets under your skin."

He peeked at it, looked down, screwed up his face and immediately began hyperventilating.

Healer or torturer? Renata wondered about herself. Sometimes it was hard to tell.

She put the gadget on the table, wiped his oozing finger with cotton. "Slow your breathing down," she instructed in a gentle voice. "That's it. You're doing fine."

She arranged his dirty cotton ball next to the ones she'd used on herself, red stains face up, and quickly returned to her chair.

He frowned at the table, then his head dropped forward and he sagged in his seat. "My anxiety's shooting up again. I can't— I want to leave now."

"You can go if you like, but I think it's best to ride this out. Take your time," she encouraged him. "Let the tension ease before you make a decision."

"I'm sweating now. Feeling sick."

"You know what to do," she said. "Use the method we practised to keep yourself from fainting." Renata directed him to tense his muscles and hold the contraction; then she watched and waited. When he seemed more relaxed she said, "How are you now?"

"Better."

"Not light-headed or nauseous?"

"Not bad."

"Would you like to rest before we move on?"

"I'm okay."

"Are you ready to hold the instrument?"

He hesitated before he spoke. "It scares me," he murmured.

"What about it scares you? What are you imagining?"

"The needle going into my skin . . . and then I'll bleed till I'm dizzy."

"Dizzy like when you're anxious?"

"More than that—real bad. Dizzy till I pass out."

"Then what?" Renata asked.

"I fall down, unconscious."

"Would that be so terrible? You've fainted before and come around quickly. Isn't it worth risking a little discomfort to get over your fear of blood?"

"I'd be so embarrassed . . . down on the floor like that."

"Do you see me helping you?"

"It's too late for that, because I've lost so much blood."

"And what happens next?" she said. "What do you think is the worst that could happen?"

"I die," he answered simply.

"Look at your finger," Renata said. "If you do that you'll see that it's no longer bleeding." She held up her left hand.

"Mine have stopped bleeding too. Maybe you can check out the cotton over there as well—five tiny spots of blood, that's all there is. Your prediction didn't come true. Nothing very bad happened to either one of us, did it."

Her client winced and shuddered.

"How real is your belief? How accurate were your thoughts about dying?"

His lips formed a half-smile.

"So maybe the next time you imagine bleeding to death you can tell yourself you're only having an anxious thought, that losing a drop of blood isn't going to kill you. How does that sound?"

"Good."

"What's your fear rating now?"

"Fifty or so."

"Would you like to go on—"

He began rubbing his knees again.

"—and use the device on yourself?"

Shaking his head and complaining of a headache, he stood up shakily, knees pressed together.

"You have to expect a few ups and downs," Renata said, "and not get discouraged. I know this is hard, but remember why you're doing it. Remember the payoff, your job and your marriage. You got through a lot today and made excellent progress."

He waved his hands in front of his face as he moved away.

"Don't forget to watch those surgery videos and make notes in your journal."

"I'll do that," said Joe Marquez, and backed out the office door.

Renata slid down into her big ergonomic chair and sucked the bruised fingers of her left hand.

The room was blinking on and off with sunlight squeezing through the slats of the partly closed blind. She rolled her chair in reverse toward the window, and heat pressed into her back like a warm palm. Like Ben's hand on her shoulder this morning on his way out.

———

Something new: When Stella walked in at ten she put a cushion on the floor, close to Renata's desk, and sat on it cross-legged. Her hands were on her knees and her shoulders rounded; her hair was tucked on one side behind an exposed ear that seemed to be waiting for the doctor to speak.

Slightly hidden by the desk, Renata was swinging her leg and had to remind herself to keep still.

"I see you've chosen a new position."

"Lucy says it's grounding."

"Lucy, your sister?"

"She took a break from the ashram and moved in at Christmas. She wants to stay till after the baby's born and help out."

"Is that what you want too?"

"She's not in the way or anything. Mostly she keeps to herself." Stella massaged one knee.

"Are you comfortable sitting like that?"

"I like looking up at you."

Renata uncrossed her legs and pulled her skirt over her knees. "Does this have anything to do with our last session?"

"My leg won't flatten."

Stella pummelled her right thigh while Renata kept waiting, even though it was clear that her client didn't want to talk. To witness your therapist collapse on the street and cry was at best bewildering and probably something you'd try to forget.

Highly unprofessional, Ben would've said if she'd found the courage to tell him.

Stella leaned forward and peered at her. "You look tired."

Renata said nothing about her previous session or that she hadn't slept well and had to use eye drops and makeup this morning to make herself presentable. She blamed Ben for that part, because he was preoccupied and didn't want to make love, leaving, her tense the whole night, their backs turned against each other like strangers on a park bench. All his talk about babies! Did he think the Stork brought them?

Stella looked past her. "Aren't we supposed to increase my exposure today and take a streetcar?"

"That's the next step on your hierarchy list . . . but first we need to talk."

"About what?"

"Last time. How it affected you to see me like that."

Stella watched her wordlessly with a gaze that dimmed and brightened like the beam of a faulty flashlight. The sun's rays from the office window heightened the colour in her cheeks.

"Maybe I frightened you?"

She twitched but was silent as Renata sat patiently, pushing her lower back into the chair to ease a spasm. It was unsettling looking down at Stella corkscrewed on the floor like that, her big head and shortened body: like an uneasy child at her feet. Between her ears Renata heard the echo of a schoolteacher scolding her to sit up—knees together, back straight!—and resisted the impulse to say as much to her client.

She rolled her chair back until her head was close to the window and sunlight touched her scalp. A peaceful, promising morning, she had noticed on the way in. A January thaw day. Christmas lights still tied to porches and awnings had twinkled as she walked by. Melting snow pooled on the streets, and every puddle reminded her that spring wasn't far off.

"I want to ride the streetcar. I think I can do that."

"Before we do anything else"—Renata sat forward—"I think we should finish our talk."

Stella unpretzelled her legs and leaned back on her hands, squinting at the window.

"What happened wasn't your fault," Renata tried again. "It wasn't because of anything you said or did."

"I know that."

"Maybe there's something you've been thinking about since then and might want to say now?"

She shook her head, half closed her eyes and began to breathe, her lips counting ins and outs.

Renata eyed her watch: there was still enough time to ride a streetcar and salvage the session. "Well, all right . . ." She was nearly out of her seat when Stella began to speak.

"It was hard to hear you crying, but then it felt okay because you were the same as me—you know, easily broken?—like a sister or best friend. I didn't think I should touch you so I waited till you got up, and after we said goodbye I kept thinking about it, and the more I did the better it got."

Renata fell back in her chair and heat rose in her face. The same? They were not. She was not a college dropout but a clinical psychologist. Not single and pregnant, with a mother who drank herself to death, an AWOL father and no one to rely on other than a sister on leave from an ashram. Although her friends were colleagues or couples she saw with Ben, people she knew only superficially, her husband was alive and well and dependable.

Her dad was also someone she could turn to in a crisis, though she hardly ever saw him now that he was remarried and living in California with his second family. But he always sent birthday cards and phoned her at Christmas.

Her dad wasn't actually here . . . and there were tensions in her marriage, *but still*, Renata thought. Still.

Stella slowly got up. She stretched her arms, rolled her shoulders, circled her knees, and then finally crossed the room and went out to find her coat.

Renata got her leather jacket from the closet, pulled it on and checked an inner pocket for her cell phone. Just in case. If Stella had contractions again they might be genuine, though the last thing she wanted was to deal with a miscarriage.

Stella was adjusting the pompom on her tuque when Renata entered and walked through the waiting room. The young woman followed her out, waited for her to lock up and then shuffled along close behind, like a duckling.

As they reached the landing on the way down to the lobby, a man coming upstairs brushed Stella's arm and she froze. She didn't like casual contact with strangers—though when she lived with Grant, she had once told Renata, she wanted to touch him all the time.

With Ben too there never seemed to be enough touching, and now and then Renata would bump into him at home on purpose. One time he jumped back as if he didn't know her, and his empty, distracted expression had brought her to tears.

She spoke to Stella soothingly and got her moving again. They were lucky enough to not meet anyone else on the stairs.

Out on the street at last, Stella was breathing hard. The streetcar stop was a block away and she moved along carefully, staying close to buildings, her head tipped and her right ear and shoulder practically meeting. Her boots became water-stained as she moved through puddles and snow, and her breathing fractured into small hiccup-like gasps.

Renata had never had such a difficult case. It wasn't hard to treat someone afraid of blood or spiders, to prick an apprehensive man's finger in the office or accompany a woman to the top of the CN Tower and coax her to look down. But Stella confounded her. What did she need that Renata wasn't giving her?

Helping her required more than changing anxious thinking and encouraging exposure to streetcars and trains—but she didn't know what.

Eventually they reached the stop. Cars and buses sped by, spraying fans of mud and slush. Stella pulled her tuque over her ears and backed away from the curb.

From somewhere a drop of water fell onto Renata's head and snaked down the side of her face. Everything was melting. The sun appeared, disappeared, and people wandered in and out of shadows and bright light, growing dim, then sharp. Stella sidled up to her, grazing her arm, and Renata flinched at the touch, her shoulders rising as she stepped discreetly to one side.

A streetcar arrived that was unsuitably crowded, so they let it go by. Stella stood as still as a pole. Several minutes later, when an emptier car pulled up, Renata got behind her and urged her forward onto the road. The doors opened with a smack and Stella sprang back, landing hard on Renata's toe.

"Nothing's going to happen to you," Renata said despite the pain. "Grab the rail and lift yourself up. I'm here if you need me."

"Let's go," the driver barked at the hesitant woman with a foot on the ground and one in the door.

Renata nudged her in, but she paused again on the top step.

"Come on, move it," the driver said.

Renata dropped a couple of tokens into the fare box, took Stella's elbow and steered her to the back of the car. Almost at the rear, she stopped by a double seat and motioned for her to slide in. Stella glanced around to size up the other passengers, some of whom were watching them, then moved to the window and sat down. Looking neither right nor left, she stared at her knees as Renata eased into place beside her.

The streetcar was rolling again, clattering on its tracks. Stella was still for several minutes; then her cheeks darkened and she fisted her hands.

"What's wrong?"

She inched across the seat until they were touching and put a hand over her breast, the other one on Renata's arm. "It's like the train," she whispered. "My heart's going crazy."

Too close, Renata thought, removing the hand from her arm. Inappropriate. "You're thinking about the accident?"

"No, I'm seeing Grant's face—remembering when we first met. I thought it was enough that he was handsome and successful and never stopped to think about the kind of person he was inside, like if he cared for me and could make me feel special, which it turns out he couldn't do. I mean, I loved him a lot, but there were times I didn't like him . . . and now he's dead and I'm going to have his baby."

Renata spoke softly. "Do you understand that your feelings had nothing to do with his death? You couldn't have saved him."

Stella pulled a tissue from her pocket and tore it up. She rolled the pieces, dropped them and flattened them with the toe of her boot. "I'm scared all the time," she said.

"What's scaring you right now?"

"This is, the streetcar. I think it's going to jump the tracks and people are going to get hurt like people got hurt before, and you . . . something will happen to you."

"Something bad?"

Stella shrugged. Then she turned around in her seat and curled into the window, thudding her head against the glass.

Renata's arm shot out and hung briefly between them. She felt a twisting of her heart as she touched Stella's shoulder and said, "That won't happen."

Abruptly Stella sat up, so that Renata's hand was caught between the seat and the woman's back.

"Bad things happen. They happen all the time and we don't see them coming. My mom was just having a drink, Grant was going to Montreal—and all of a sudden, poof, they're gone! People you know, people you don't . . . Why don't they worry crossing the street, talking to strangers, driving their cars? Maybe there's a terrorist sitting behind us who's going to blow us all to bits, or a truck's out of control and is heading straight for us! Why do people pretend things are safe and normal when they're not? Is it only me who sees the danger, the dead bodies, the pieces?"

Renata drew her hand back and dropped it, tingling, on her lap. Pale and inert, it looked like a severed hand. She saw the pieces too, but couldn't possibly say that. What could she say instead to give Stella courage: that life is always changing and mostly unpredictable and people secretly understand but choose not to dwell on it in order to get by? That loss, pain and suffering are part of the mix—and we know that, we do, though it doesn't make it easier. Our loved ones disappoint us, and we disappoint ourselves . . . but still we trip onward, struggling for meaning and hope.

"Everyone struggles, not just you" is what she finally said.

"Even you?"

She didn't reply.

Stella wriggled back in her seat, hugged her knees, closed her eyes. The bell dinged and the streetcar lurched and clanged as it sped up, slowed, stopped and started, but she sat unmoving. This too was something new and unfamiliar, her client's stillness. Renata wasn't sure what it meant.

Stella opened her eyes again. "I'm thinking about the baby now, thinking something Lucy taught me, sort of like a mantra I can say to keep her safe." She crossed her hands on her middle. "We could say it together, 'May you be safe and protected,' but first—" She grabbed Renata's hand and flattened it over her belly. "Now we can start."

Renata stared at the young woman's abdomen and seemed to see into it: blood, water and bits of flesh. *Be safe*, she aimed her thoughts at the fetus. *Live*, she insisted. But then her own stomach rolled over and she felt sick. Other people on the streetcar seemed to be swaying, and the scream of ringing cell phones and clamour of conversation pushed into her ears.

"I'm not feeling well," she said, but when she tried to get up, a sudden motion of the car threw her back into her seat.

Stella moved her face close and peered at her. "You look green."

"Motion sickness. I have to get off."

Stella pulled the overhead cord and Renata stood up. When the streetcar stopped, they left by the rear doors. Back on the sidewalk Stella smiled, her face freckled with sunlight. "Better?" she asked.

"So-so."

"Does this happen to you a lot?"

"Not a lot. Sometimes."

"We didn't get far," Stella said, but Renata only grimaced back, afraid that if she opened her mouth she would gag.

She looked around for a taxi but didn't see one. Stella was already walking, so she fell into step beside her.

They followed the streetcar tracks back the way they'd come, carefully navigating the snow-sloppy sidewalks. Renata's head was clearer and her stomach gradually settling, but now she was shy with embarrassment: once again she'd shown weakness and ruined a session with Stella.

Before long, Stella said, "This is where I turn off," indicating a side road. "Guess I'll see you next week?"

"Monday," Renata agreed, but neither moved to separate.

Her next appointment was hours away, Renata reasoned, and walking outdoors with her was part of Stella's treatment—so why not go along now and squeeze something beneficial from the session? Surely even Ben would approve her objective.

"Let me walk you to your door. The fresh air will do me good."

Stella blinked but didn't speak. They went on for another block and then turned a corner. Outside her building, they stopped and faced each other.

"Want to come up?" Stella asked.

"I don't make house calls."

"You think it's unprofessional?"

"I don't think it's a good idea."

"But since you're here anyway . . . you could meet my sister."

"Maybe another time, as part of your treatment."

Her chin fell as if her neck could no longer support her head. "You wouldn't have to come in but just say hello to her." Stella spoke to her stained boots. "I know you can't be my friend . . ."

"Are you asking me to be your friend?"

She lifted her head. "Do you think about me sometimes, after you leave the office, I mean? After you cash my cheque?"

"You'd like to know I care about you."

Stella looked as fragile as a bone-china figurine. The air between them seemed to freeze and quietly splinter.

"I do care"—thinking of her earlier session with Joe Marquez—"about all my clients." Renata paused, choosing her words. "I have a unique—a particular relationship with each one."

"Me too?"

"Especially."

The word resounded in her ears till they hurt: it was the wrong thing to say. The absolutely wrong thing. She hadn't meant to say that . . . even though it was true enough.

She mentally struggled to backtrack, but Stella was already grinning into her fingers, the corners of her mouth curved up like apostrophes. She had attractive dimples in her cheeks, Renata noticed for the first time.

The young woman looked away, caught in a daydream no one could possibly guess. Perhaps she was imagining Renata with a camera, snapping cheery photos while she fed her new-born, pushed a stroller in the park or lit a pink candle on a bunny-shaped cake for her baby's first birthday.

Renata heard the shutter clicking. Saw the family album.

"I meant to say, 'You too.' I have a particular relationship with you too."

Stella shifted her gaze so she was eye to eye with Renata, and kept smiling, her mouth wide, her skin lit with its own light. She lowered her hands and rubbed her belly, as though she were communicating with the creature in her womb, silently describing the surprising world outside. As if she knew its happiness, could feel the kicking arms and legs and hear the tiny clapping hands. As if, like Stella, the baby couldn't wait to spend time with her new friend.

CHAPTER 7

B en had been expecting someone slight and retiring, but Iris Rae was a large woman, taller than her husband, who was outside in the waiting room, and probably outweighed him by twenty pounds. Like Goldilocks, she tried out three different chairs, then dragged one to the far end of the table that stood between Ben and his patients.

"There," she said, settling in. Behind her glasses, her eyes swung from wall to wall as she sized up his office. "You know what this place needs?"

Art on the walls, some personal items on his desk and a fresh coat of paint in a soothing colour. Wasn't that the answer? Renata's office was done up in earth tones with silly names like "fawn" and "burnt sienna," but Ben had no objection to institutional beige, and his taste in decorations was a private matter unrelated to his job.

He ignored the question and asked Iris to tell him about herself.

"I'm a weaver," she volunteered. "Tapestries mostly, which I sell, show, give away or hang in my home. Did Arthur mention that our son is an artist too? He works in acrylic . . ."

Ben reached for his coffee mug on the table and took a sip. With her zaftig body and outspoken manner, she reminded him of Molly . . . which made him think of Molly's friend who'd come looking for a room, breathing his geriatric breath into Ben's face. Friend or not, he was Ida's cousin, Ida's headache, not his mother's problem. She never should've let him in.

"But that's enough about me." Iris smoothed her skirt over her knees and locked eyes with him. "Why am I here?"

"I asked you in today," he said, "to find out what you think about your husband's offer to give away his kidney . . ."

Her face puckered in seriousness.

"To your neighbour, Mrs. Stanley. What was your reaction when he explained what he wanted to do?"

"I wasn't surprised," she said. "We talked about it long before he got in touch with the hospital. It wasn't like he sprang it on me."

"He told me he spoke to the family."

"And no one went against him either. Well, our younger daughter Claire did at the start. She didn't like the idea of him laid up and hurting, but Arthur assured her it was an easy operation and she was fine with it after that."

"And you? What were your thoughts?"

"I was upset about the risks he'd be taking. Checking into a hospital is never an easy thing."

"And how do you feel now?"

"I'm worried sick, but he's sure he made the right choice and I have to respect that. I told him I'm frightened but won't stand in his way on this. I said it's okay if he wants to give Carol a kidney—and meant it too. God knows she needs one."

Ben scratched on his pad, *Wife worried but approves*. The others would be as encouraged as he was to hear that. An agreeable spouse was a good sign and could only help him sell Arthur's game plan to the team.

When he looked up, she was squinting at him over her glasses. "This surgeon"—she faltered—"the one doing the transplant. I want to know your opinion—the truth—is he any good?"

"Top-notch."

"So nothing's going to go wrong?"

What should he answer—*unlikely*? Highly unlikely? Still, it's always possible. Things do go wrong sometimes despite our best intentions and hope for happy endings, *as in all of life, Mrs. Rae.*

"I know you spoke to the nurses about the risks," he said slowly, "but do you completely understand what's involved here?"

"His chances are pretty good. Everyone expects him to come through this just fine."

"Yes, very good . . . from a medical standpoint."

She pushed up her glasses. "What other standpoint is there?"

He picked up his mug again and balanced it on his knee. "Sometimes there are other, less obvious reasons for donating an organ besides the unselfish ones, and we have to look at those too."

"What sort of reasons?"

"It's just that we all have certain motivations we're only dimly aware of."

"I don't know what this is about."

"About Mrs. Stanley. I'm asking you how well she and your husband know each other."

"Carol's lived in the neighbourhood a long time." She tipped back until her chair was balanced on two legs. "They're old friends, neighbours."

An old friend, his mother had said. Saul-something. Did Nathan know the man too? Had he worked in his father's shop? Had Ben ever met him before? There was something familiar but also disagreeable about Molly's old friend.

"Old friends," he persisted. His left eyelid started twitching and wouldn't stop. "How deep, would you say, is their friendship?"

Her chair dropped forward and she pressed her palms into the table. She stared at his quivering lid as though he were a bug-eyed insect on a glass slide. If only she would move back, he might be able to think of how to rephrase his question and move the interview forward.

"How deep?" She laughed so hard that Ben worried some-one would open his office door to ask what the joke was.

"What's so funny?" he said.

Iris slapped a hand on her breast and finally quieted down. She drew a tissue from the box between them and dabbed her eyes. "You're seriously asking me if they're getting it on?"

Ben pulled the corner of his eye, stretching the lid still, and drank more coffee. His question was reasonable and not to be taken lightly; something that had to be raised whenever the transplant couple were unrelated. Self-serving underlying motives had to be exposed. It was not impossible that Iris's philanthropic spouse was lonely or lustful and itching to slip into Mrs. Stanley's bed.

"I'm serious," he told her. "I didn't mean to amuse you."

"I'm sorry if I embarrassed you. I know it's your job to ask these things. It's just—the idea!"

How deep? flared in his brain, regarding Molly's friend, and he had the urge to bang down his mug. Instead, he stared at a year-old stain on the carpet, the result of being asked to speak to a moribund patient with little chance of surviving a long operation in order to tell him he wouldn't be getting new lungs. The man had covered his face in his hands and blubbered freely, while Ben, restraining an impulse to hug him and cry too, raised his arm suddenly and knocked over his coffee, spilling it on his notes, his pants and the new office broadloom.

Gently now, he set his mug on the table and sat back. "It may seem ridiculous, but we have to talk about this. I hope you understand."

"But it's silly," said Iris.

"I'm more than happy to arrive at that conclusion, but for the sake of argument, let's push this further. Is it possible your husband expects Mrs. Stanley to be so grateful that she'd feel indebted to him?"

She shook her head. "You don't know him. He'd never expect Carol or anybody else to be obliged to him for a gift.

And you don't know about us, how much we love each other. Tell me, Dr. Wasserman, are you married?"

"Well, yes."

"What's your wife's name?"

He stalled. "I'd rather not say."

"At least tell me how long you've been together."

"Nine years."

He ran his tongue over his teeth, hoping she wasn't going to ask next if they were happy. Somewhere in between, he figured. They still cared about each other and considered themselves a couple, though the marriage had gone from hot to tepid over nearly a decade—which was only to be expected. He could live with that, but Renata was romantic and easily disappointed. At times, he imagined, she regretted having married him or wished he were different: less gloomy and irritable; more attentive, more enthusiastic and so on. He wasn't wired for cheeriness but tried, when he thought of it, to be less of one thing and more of the other. Still, he wasn't likely to change much at fifty-three. If she were older she'd understand that you don't soften up as you age, you solidify. Everything shrinks and hardens.

If Iris asks, he won't respond.

"Arthur and I just had our thirty-fourth anniversary. You get to know someone pretty well after all those years."

He found that a hopeful remark. Twenty-five years from now, Renata might be more tolerant of his failings.

"I can't speak to his fantasies, of course," she went on, "but I know he'd never actually do anything dishonourable. Arthur wouldn't shame me."

"I see," he said neutrally, writing another note with as steady a hand as possible: *A. and wife concur, no underlying motives vis-à-vis the neighbour.* It was starting to look like Arthur was the real thing.

"There's something else I'm concerned about"—tapping his pen—"the accident your husband was involved in."

She sat up. "I was waiting for that."

"It often happens, Mrs. Rae, that the driver of a vehicle involved in an incident in which people were harmed or killed feels responsible afterward and wants to do something to make up for the damage. Do you think this might be relevant in your husband's case, especially considering his early retirement? How do you think he's dealt with this?"

"He did all he could to avoid the collision."

"Yes, I'm aware of that, but I'd like to hear about his feelings, as far as you know them."

"Naturally he was shaken up. He felt awful."

"In your opinion, is that why he retired?"

"I've been telling him for years to take his pension early. He has so many interests, like reading and gardening, and I knew he'd enjoy having more time to pursue them. Right after the accident seemed like a good time for him to stop working once and for all."

"And do you think he's happy now . . . or do you think he still feels bad about what happened?"

"People died, people were hurt—that's something you don't forget. Something he'll always feel terrible about. But it doesn't mean he'd give away an organ to even the score."

Ben unscrewed his pen and, as Iris watched, screwed it back together and let it fall into his lap. "From time to time," he said slowly, "we all have emotions we don't want to share with others." The pain of feeling inadequate. The pain of disappointing your spouse. "I'm wondering if your husband keeps feelings to himself sometimes."

Iris wiped her glasses on her sleeve, put them back on and gazed at him bluntly. "Of course I don't know absolutely everything about him, but after all our years together I can say with confidence that Arthur doesn't carry the emotional baggage that would make him help Carol only to help himself. My husband is a generous man. You have to understand that."

In fact, he was almost sure of it. Eighty-, ninety-percent sure. Almost convinced now that Arthur was what he seemed to be—a man of high principle, a bona fide altruist—and his pulse ticked in his throat at the thought.

He jotted on his pad, *Wife does not attribute husband's decision to guilt*, writing in such a messy and excited scrawl he doubted he'd ever make sense of it later.

He waited another beat, then asked, "If you had to pick an adjective, just one word to describe your husband's nature—a quality that sets him apart from everyone else—what would that word be?"

Iris didn't hesitate. "*Goodness*. That's what he's about. He came here to do this thing because he's completely good."

He pressed down hard on the page and wrote in a large script, *Good good good good*.

She was grinning when he looked up. Knew what he was thinking. She knew he'd been won over at last.

His face was warm and probably red, but he managed to say evenly, "Let's ask Arthur to join us now and the three of us can have a chat." He got up, opened the door and went to the waiting room.

When Arthur saw Ben, he flattened his shirt collar, smoothed his hair and stepped around him and into the office. Once inside, he sat down next to his wife. They joined hands without so much as glancing at each other, as though their bodies understood the rituals of comfort.

Ben had to look away. His intimacy with Renata was another thing entirely: grasping, intermittent. He wondered if they'd ever manage a more tranquil closeness.

Arthur spoke up: "Was it helpful talking to Iris?"

"Very helpful," he said. "I was glad to hear, in her own words, that she supports your decision."

"Well then, have you made up your mind?"

"He has," said Iris, her face bright as a campfire.

"If you want to go ahead with this," Ben said, "it's fine with me. I'm going to argue on your behalf when the team meets at the end of the month."

Arthur squeezed his wife's hand. "That's good news. I'm relieved to hear you say that."

"Please keep in mind, though, that I'm only one doctor, one member of the team. If the others disagree with me . . ."

"I understand. But at least we've come this far. Thank you, Dr. Wasserman."

Arthur dropped his wife's hand to zip up his cardigan, closing it only partway because he caught the end of his tie—the same diagonally striped tie he'd worn to every session—and left the zipper stuck in place. To look at him, Ben thought, you'd take him for a grocery clerk and wouldn't give him the time of day. Until you listened to him speak and felt the force he seemed to emit.

He watched as Arthur reached down to tighten a sneaker, his hair falling forward, and a quick video played in his head: Renata jogging on a beach, her ponytail flapping like the sun-bleached flag of a tropical country, while Ben chased after. Years ago he'd written a sonnet about her hair—*that twists itself around my wrist*—but now his favourite subjects were fear and empti-ness. It seemed that Arthur's notion of giving part of yourself away was a better path to meaning and purpose than poetry.

"So you'll be hearing from us shortly after the team makes its decision," Ben wrapped up.

Arthur spread his hands on his knees. "Guess that's it for now," he said, slowly getting to his feet, and Iris stood up as well, her skirt making a surf-like shushing as she moved to the door.

But we haven't finished talking! Ben stood up and rushed forward as if he were going to tackle him. "Just one moment—"

So much he wanted to ask. Arthur seemed to know all kinds of things Ben didn't. That was it: Arthur *knew*.

They were watching him, waiting. He crossed his arms and stepped back, his heart shaking in its cage. "Just—thanks for coming in. That's all, really . . . unless there's something else on your mind."

"I think we've covered everything."

Arthur stuck out his hand and Ben shook it vigorously. He expected something electrical, a tingling or pulsation, to pass from the man to himself, but felt nothing other than the clamminess of his own palm.

"If you need to see me later on for any reason, I'm here."

"Thanks again," said Arthur. Then he turned and walked out.

CHAPTER 8

Sitting on a subway car next to Stella Wolnik, Renata was pleased with herself. She'd managed to get her client on a streetcar to the station, from the station onto a crowded train and halfway across the city, and now heading back again, without any setbacks—though people stared at them constantly: the flushed, expectant woman with her eyes shut and head thrown back, breathing rapidly as if she were in labour, and the person watching over her. A caregiver, they might have thought or, because she seemed reserved, a distant relation.

Stella fluttered her eyes open and asked, "How am I doing?"

"How do you think you're doing?"

"Pretty good."

"Very good." Even Ben would have to admit her client was improving.

"How many more stops?"

"Two after this one. We'll be there in no time."

The doors shushed open at the approaching station and a few passengers got on. A young man with leaking earphones sat beside Stella and spread his feet wide apart, so that his leg touched hers. She shifted in her seat, buttoned her thick sweater to her waist and leaned against Renata; then she shuddered, got up and hugged a pole in the aisle, her bulging belly slung to one side like a knapsack. A girl offered her a seat, but Stella only shook her head and looked elsewhere.

Renata sighed inwardly, reminding herself not to expect the exercise to run smoothly; in therapy there were often setbacks. Then she stood up as well, hanging on to an overhead bar, her shoulder near Stella's chin as the subway moved onward. Some of Stella's panic seemed to hop across the space between them, landing under her jacket like fleas she couldn't shake loose. She itched all over and wished the train would go faster, skip the coming station. She wished the session were done and she was back in her office, safe and alone, or with a different client.

The women swayed in tandem as the car rocked through a tunnel. Behind the darkened windows lights flickered and streaked by, reminding Renata of the auras she experienced before getting a migraine. Her forehead ached at the thought, but she told herself it wouldn't happen: this wasn't the right time of month.

Unless it was a tension headache . . . She often got those when she was edgy and fatigued, which was most of the time now. She wondered if life would be easier in a small town: pancake breakfasts and music on the village green, long walks in the countryside. But where would she find clients? And Ben would have to start a private practice, which he wouldn't like. So after a while they'd return to the city, where the pattern of stress and exhaustion would start again.

Was there no way out of this?

At the next station a band of noisy schoolchildren shoved on, jammed together as the doors closed behind them, and surrounded the pregnant woman. They nudged her and grabbed onto the pole as if she weren't there; as if they didn't notice her slipping down.

Renata lurched forward, took hold of Stella's waist and told the children to stand back. She helped her to the nearest door, elbowing aside any passengers in their way.

She held onto her till they got off at the following stop as planned and dropped to a bench in the middle of the platform. Stella slumped forward, her hair parting at the back to show a pale seam of skin and an exposed neck. She looked like someone asleep, until she inhaled noisily, gargling and coughing as though she'd been pulled from a lake.

"All you all right?"

"Cold." She tugged at her sweater.

Renata took off her own jacket and spread it over Stella's back. "What happened back there?"

She cleared her throat. "I panicked."

"And now?"

"I want to go home."

"Are you able to walk?"

In answer she stood up and started down the platform. Renata followed closely and together they rode an escalator up to street level, pushed through a turnstile and stepped into daylight. Renata hailed a taxi and they got in.

Stella gave the driver her address and slid back in the seat. Huddled into Renata's jacket, she was quiet during the ride. When the cab reached her apartment block and stopped at Stella's building, Renata told the driver to wait, opened the car door and got out. With one hand still on the door, she helped Stella out to the sidewalk.

"Aren't you going to see me up?"

"The doorman can do that. I have to get back to the office." Though actually this was her last appointment of the day.

"He won't leave his desk and I can't ride the elevator."

"Take the stairs. You'll be fine."

"I'm not fine."

Renata nodded at her jacket—"I'm going to need that"— and Stella let it fall to the ground. She picked it up and put it on, still warm with Stella's heat, and said, "See you Monday."

"I'll pay you, if that's what it takes."

"Money's not the issue."

"Then why won't you help me?"

Because if I went up it wouldn't stop there. "We talked about this before. I don't think it's appropriate."

"I know you're not supposed to but I can't do it by myself. Not after the subway."

The cabbie honked and Renata told him to wait another minute. Then she turned to Stella. "If I do this—help you—we have to be clear about something, I'm not coming in. I'll only see you to your door."

She rocked on her heels as if she'd been slapped. "I get it," Stella said.

The cabbie stuck his head out—"You coming or what?"— and Renata paid him and let him go.

She followed Stella inside, past a doorman and mailboxes and through a lobby with mirrored walls insistently repeating the bright reflection of two women. Renata turned away so as not to see her crow's feet and worry-lined forehead and un-buttoned her jacket, which felt tight even though she'd weighed herself yesterday and nothing had changed. She ought to be more like her unseeing client, who shuffled through the mir-rored room without once looking up.

The stairway was just beyond a bank of elevators. Stella pulled open a door and began to climb, Renata at her heels, then paused at the first landing to sit down and catch her breath.

The passageway was narrow and dim. The walls were blocks of concrete, the stairs hard underfoot. Renata heard the distant hum of a ventilation system and an unknown clink-clink that made her feel like she was trapped in a submarine. It was enough to give anyone claustrophobia.

Stella rose slowly and started up another flight, wobbling a little as she went. Renata stayed close behind, ready to catch her if need be, but if her client actually fell she doubted she'd be strong enough to hold her weight or even slow her momen-tum. Then they'd tumble down to land bloody and broken at the foot of the stairs: she and Stella and the unborn baby. And wouldn't that be her fault? She grabbed the banister, light-headed, and held on with both hands until she felt steadier.

Stella had already disappeared somewhere ahead by the time Renata could move again. She hurried to catch up, and when she got to the next landing heard Stella call out, "Over here!"

She entered the hallway and saw her by an open door. "There's something I want you to see," she said.

"I thought you understood—"

"Something I've been meaning to show you for a long time. It has to do with my treatment."

"Whatever it is, you can bring it to the office."

"It's too big for that."

"Then we'll have to forget it."

"It's important," Stella said. "Really important."

What was the right thing to do? This was one of those times Renata would've liked to consult with Ben.

If she wants to share something private, shouldn't I encourage her?

Not if it means blurring the lines.

You know I don't make social calls, but this is an exceptional case.

Too risky. Walk away.

For all his education and experience, however, Ben wasn't always right. In the end it was a judgment call, and who's to say her husband's opinion was better than hers? Typically, she relied more on intuition than he did and believed her relationship with a client was a fluid thing. Her first consideration was Stella's recovery, and her gut feeling now was to follow the woman's lead. Despite the risks, she decided, there was something to be gained.

By now Stella was somewhere out of sight in the apartment, but Renata stayed in the doorway. From where she stood she saw a room furnished with a long couch, expensive-looking chairs and an Oriental rug. It was not what she had expected.

Stella reappeared holding a teacup and saucer and settled onto the sofa. She slapped the cushion beside her, inviting Renata to sit. "I know you want to leave, but you can't see the thing I have to show you from over there."

"Why don't you bring it to me."

"It's too heavy to take down."

"What is it?"

"A picture of Grant."

Now that was something worth seeing.

Curious, she stepped into the living room far enough to close the door and look around. To the left she saw a small bedroom papered with clowns wearing boldly patterned costumes. Already there was a crib in it, with a mobile of coloured letters clamped to the headboard. If it had been up to her, Renata would've chosen a woodsy scene or seascape and a mobile of planets. But it wasn't, was it.

"Do you like the apartment?" Stella said. "We got it for a good price. One thing Grant knows is real estate. 'Knew,' I mean."

Renata ignored that and asked to see the picture, but suddenly Stella jerked, spilling something in her lap. "Oh, the baby just kicked!" She waved her over—"Come feel"—but Renata wouldn't budge. Nothing good would come of this visit, she now knew.

"The picture?" she asked again.

Stella pointed. "Over there."

Swinging around, Renata saw a life-size, meticulously

painted portrait of a man. He had a head of wavy hair and good-looking features, except for his thin mouth.

"It's a painting, not a picture."

"He wouldn't sit for a portrait. It was done from a photo taken in Rome on the Spanish Steps. I liked that city a lot," Stella said. "Ever been there?"

She nodded, thinking back to her time as an intern: it was the city she saw with Ben soon after they met in the hospital cafeteria and talked about *La Dolce Vita*. The conversation excited them. He was half in love with Anita Ekberg, and she said she'd never forget the scene at the Trevi Fountain. So really it was Fellini's fault she slept with a man she barely knew and why, months later, they chose Rome for their honeymoon.

Two fairy-tale weeks. Despite rain and jet lag and a noisy hotel that discouraged REM sleep, they hiked from sight to sight with anticipation and energy, as if they were marching into a happy future together. Sometimes they recharged with cappuccinos and pizza, and once, after watching youngsters necking outrageously in front of the Pantheon, they taxied back to their hotel and made love all afternoon.

Where did that excitement go—the gratitude they once felt at having found each other? Were the ghosts of that young couple hiding under the bed? If she said magic words, would they slip into these older selves and abracadabra they'd be crazy in love again?

Surely that was still possible, even if only now and then! A few months ago, for instance, he dropped perogies on his lap and laughed till his nose ran, and when he tossed them on the table she started laughing too. In the song of their laughter was a clear note of hope that had made her remember Rome.

"He doesn't like you," Stella said.

Renata started. "Who doesn't?"

"Grant doesn't," she explained. "He doesn't like most people."

"Not even your doctor?"

"Not even Lucy, who's so, like, spiritual and never has a bad word to say about anyone. She says everyone wants to be good and wants to do the right thing."

"Is that what you think too?"

"Grant was mean to me sometimes. I don't think he ever loved me as much as I loved him. I put his meanness in the picture when I painted his lips."

"You painted that?"

She motioned toward other things hanging on the walls. "They're all mine, I did them all. Pen and ink, watercolour, graphite and charcoal."

Renata stepped forward to examine the pictures, which were mostly of furniture. Mainly Stella had drawn or painted the sofa, table, chairs and lamps of this very room. "You never mentioned this before."

"Drawing helps me see things better, in a different way, even things I know well because I see them all the time. Like what you're looking at," she said as Renata stopped before a sketch of an armchair. "It's not just a chair anymore, it's sort of special now. You can see it moving."

Renata stared at the painting but saw only pencil marks, light and dark areas and various colours. A good likeness but nothing more.

"Lucy says that things are made of ever-changing molecules, even if they seem fixed, and if you look in the proper way—I mean, with real attention—something changes in you too."

Nothing changed in her except that her legs felt heavy. But she imagined herself pulled unstoppably forward, sinking deeply into the chair in the picture—held there.

"I was like a piece of furniture Grant saw all the time but never really looked at. Lucy says he never learned to see my specialness and I shouldn't hold it against him."

Renata turned her back to the drawing, thinking of her own husband's hit-and-miss attention; her intermittent sorrow. But marriage wasn't everything. There was work, there was music . . . and loneliness happens whether you live with some-one else or not.

"But do you?" she asked Stella. "Hold it against him?"

"My sister lives with gentle people in an ashram. She doesn't know how hard it was to be with him sometimes."

Stella lowered her chin. "I'll tell you a story . . . some-thing that happened one time when we were up north. After canoeing all day we set up camp on a river and I dove in for a swim, but the current was so strong I got pulled downstream, and when I cried out for help Grant just stood there. He didn't dive in after me or throw me a paddle or even follow along the shore—he just watched me sinking. Then I was yanked around a bend and couldn't see him anymore, and finally the river got shallow and I walked out. I was so weak and banged up it took me forever to get back, and when I did, there he was, just like I left him, staring at the water. He hadn't gone after me and he didn't come running when he saw me approaching. I don't think he'd moved an inch the whole time.

"And then I had a strange thought, that my life was happening elsewhere—my real life, I mean—in a parallel universe or somewhere down the river, and I hadn't been drowning, I'd been swimming hard to get there. My life wasn't with him at all."

"Maybe he was frozen with fear and couldn't help."

Would Ben have tried to rescue her—or, like Grant, been too afraid to jump in? Fear hardens you, closes the mind and stiffens the body, and sometimes you can't move despite your good intentions.

"That's what Lucy said too. But the more I thought about it, the more I thought he never meant to help me. He let me be swept away and then was glad I was gone."

Renata's hand rose to her lips. Would Ben ever think that? Surely he would've meant to save her even if he couldn't. "If you didn't think he loved you enough to try and help you, why did you stay with him?"

"After I nearly drowned and had this idea that my life was happening somewhere else, I wanted to live alone. I almost left him . . . but, like, freaked and left school and stopped caring about being happy. And then there was the accident, you know, and Grant left me."

Stella hugged her abdomen and said to the fetus, "You don't have a daddy now, but I'll love you twice as hard."

All at once Renata's vision unfocused and she saw a long river and a lone swimmer drawn downstream by the current. *Where is my real life?* she wondered, almost tearful. Was there a better place she needed to get to? A cold, wet, solitary journey she had to make?

Her thoughts stuttered and stopped as her mind froze over. Quickly she excused herself and backtracked to the door. But before she could turn the knob, the door opened on its own.

A short woman with cropped hair, carrying a grocery bag, walked in and leaned against the door, closing it firmly. Noticing Renata, she put out her free hand and said hello. This must be Lucy, Renata supposed as they shook hands.

Rounder and younger than Stella by a few years, she didn't resemble her at all: she was shorter but sturdier, with a wide nose, large smile and clear, unblinking eyes that gazed at her keenly till Renata pulled back her hand and introduced herself as Stella's therapist, Dr. Moon.

"My sister told me all about you."

"Half-sister," Stella said.

"Different dads," Lucy explained, "and neither one stayed in touch."

Renata had half-siblings too, in California: same dad but different moms. A year after her mother's death, her father married a young woman who bore three healthy babies; then the family moved away. She knew how to reach him but hardly remembered now what he looked like, how he spoke or the feel of his hand on her head when he smoothed her hair. Whenever she thought of him she felt hollow inside, as if she'd been scooped out—so tried not to think of him.

"I was just leaving." She stepped in front of Lucy and reached for the doorknob, but as she did so her shoulder knocked the grocery bag from Lucy's arm and it hit the floor with a loud grunt. Cans of beans, a bag of rice, tofu, carrots and unidentifiable greens circled Renata's feet. Apologizing, she stooped to help her put the groceries back in the bag.

When everything was picked up and they faced each other in a squat, Lucy grabbed Renata's hand for the second time. They got to their feet at the same moment, Lucy still gripping her hand, though Renata twisted her fingers and wrist, trying to break free.

"Excuse me, I have to go. I'm late for another appointment."

And still the woman held tight, staring at the centre of Renata's forehead as if she could see inside.

"Sit with us," Lucy said. "We're going to do a breathing exercise."

"I can't stay." With a tug, she finally freed her hand.

"It goes like this," the woman said. She closed her eyes and drew back her shoulders, expanding her chest. "Breathing in, feel your breath. Breathing out, empty your mind."

Renata heard a creak and turned: Stella was shifting on the couch, attempting to fold her legs and follow the exercise, her belly rising and falling. Soon she became motionless and all sounds stopped. In an instant the room had become stupe-fyingly still.

Something scratched at the back of her throat, threaten-ing to make her cough, and Renata's mind rattled with thoughts of escaping. Lucy was against the door again with her eyes shut and would have to be nudged aside.

Renata inhaled the silence. Her lungs were tight, her ribs hurt, and who would think that something as natural as breath-ing could be so hard to do at times? Her back was feeling sore too, her neck a stone pillar. She spent entirely too much of her life sitting in chairs and should get out of the office more, though mostly there was no reason—

Reason for what?

There was no reason to not stand here, listening to Lucy breathe.

Lucy's soft exhalation faded away, like the final note of a symphony, and then she breathed in and the cycle began again. Renata's shoulders loosened as she listened to the quiet music of Lucy's breath.

But no, she couldn't possibly stay! What was she thinking? If Ben heard about this—

Reaching around Lucy, she grabbed the doorknob, turned it and pulled hard with both hands, as though the apartment door were bolted from outside. It opened only narrowly, bumping against Lucy, who fluttered her eyes and jerked. But that was enough room for Renata to squeeze through and hur-riedly slip away.

CHAPTER 9

"You look good in candlelight."

"I look old," said Molly.

"To me you're still a beauty with green-apple eyes."

She felt her cheeks heat up and fanned herself with the menu. "You were always a talker."

A squat, floating candle in a bowl of water on the table burned orange between them. Saul reached out and took her hand, squeezing it with fingers as rough and thin as twigs, and the warmth and pressure excited her, made a memory grow inside: his lips moving over her; his wet eyes and grateful hands.

"You haven't lost your grip, Saul." She was making a joke, but he didn't seem to get it.

His hand slid away from hers. "I lost everything," he said, all at once serious.

Her hand on the tablecloth, no longer held, was like a small creature now, a pink rat or hamster. She covered it with her other hand and waited for him to continue. If he meant her in particular, if she was one of his lost things, she wished he would say so. A lot of time had passed, during which she'd hardly thought of him, but still it would be nice to hear that he'd been crazy in love with her once and never should've run away.

"My children," he said. "Two girls. My wife told stories that turned them against me . . . and now I'm an old man with no one to comfort me."

What did she care about that! She crossed her arms and straightened her back. "*Nu*? Weren't the stories true?"

"No, not all of them."

Good with the talk but always unreliable, never had enough money, couldn't get a decent job—and on top of that a skirt-chaser! His poor wife had plenty to tell.

"Your wife was right to say what she said. You treated her disgracefully and couldn't be trusted."

"What about what you did?"

"Nathan never knew a thing!"

"You're so sure?"

"Completely."

"Why should I doubt you?" His eyes sparked in the gloom. "But people like to gossip. I told my wife not to listen to every *bobe-mayse* she heard, but one thing she got right—and that was the story of you."

"Who told her?"

Saul shrugged. "Not me."

Her arms fell and her shoulders sank. What if Ida talked to Nathan—just the sort of thing she'd do—and whispered in his ear the wicked things she suspected? Whether he believed her or not, it would've caused him pain and doubt he would've carried silently throughout their marriage. Her Nathan, who didn't complain. Who lost his head and shouted when the boys disobeyed him, threw things and even put his fist through a wall once, but never raised his voice to her. Who had a talent for wires and circuits—for making little doodads others used for bigger things—but didn't know the complicated workings of Molly's heart. What if he died tormented, raging, thinking she'd betrayed him? How could she live with that?

Her mouth felt dirty and she reached for her dinner napkin, only to find it had slipped to the floor. She bent over to pick it up, her face under the table, and a fat tear wet her cheek.

Nathan, if you heard something and even for an instant believed that it might be true . . . Nathan, forgive me. I never thought you'd find out and never would've left you, not for him or anyone.

She wiped her eyes on the napkin and, sitting up again, smoothed it across her lap. Saul was watching closely, his brow creased with secrets. She squirmed under his gaze and played with her empty wineglass.

"What, there's something on my dress?"

"It's just—" He shook his head. "I was thinking about us." He closed his eyes a moment, as if to see the film of their brief affair played again.

Was he thinking about the hurt he'd caused—how much she must have suffered—and how his own heart cried out for her through the years? That he was sorry he up and left without a word, without a note—not even a phone call? What kind of person gives up happiness just like that?

He was staring again. She saw reflected images of bygone days in his eyes and felt the old emotions he'd been too shy to speak about, the open-hearted tenderness they'd felt for each other. Then nothing mattered half as much as what shimmered in Saul's eyes. Not his wrinkles, thinness and baldness; not his reasons. Everything important was there, still there, in those brown-flecked irises that once made her melt inside like a Popsicle, and all she had to do was look and think hard of how it was when things were good between them—not only in bed but when they stole away for a walk too, a meal or a movie, which didn't happen often because what they liked best was time in each other's arms. She hoped he remembered it exactly as she did, that they would always share this set of bittersweet memories.

"I want to tell you something," he said, spreading apart his fingers to show how they trembled, and she had to force herself to breathe in before she fainted. "Because I know you can't see me blushing in this light."

She leaned forward, ready for his passionate confession. Had waited so long to hear it.

"Molly, the truth is . . . I'm not like I once was."

What? He wasn't making sense. "No one's like they used to be," she said to encourage him.

"I'm an old man now. I don't expect much anymore."

"You're what—seventy-five? I'm almost the same age and I expect everything."

"You had a better life. You're not so discouraged."

"Don't talk like that!" she cried, smacking a palm on the table. "Your life isn't over."

"Too much has gone wrong." He lowered his eyes, shook his head.

"There's nothing wrong with your heart, is there? Nothing wrong with your eyes and mouth or your hands either. Isn't it enough that you can see, touch, kiss, remember? Isn't it enough to love?" She drew in her breath sharply, shamed by her heated words; the way she was leading him on, still wanting more from him.

"Molly, I'm not like you. But maybe if I lived with you, maybe with you I could find peace in my old age."

She felt a small contraction in her pelvic region, like a cramp. Was it reckless to believe him? Did he mean what he just said—or was he simply flattering her, looking for a deal on the rent? With him you never knew for sure, you knew nothing beyond the moment, and then only what you guessed by listening between his words. Did she have the courage to love again?

She sank into her chair, and neither had anything more to say.

The waiter brought a bottle of wine and filled their glasses. Saul emptied his at once, but Molly only sipped the wine because it gave her headaches. Like Saul, who gave her a headache too.

In a while the waiter came back with their salads, and they turned their attention to those. Molly ate some of hers, then watched as Saul removed disks of onion and cucumber and pushed them to the side of his plate.

"What are you doing?"

"This way I get a taste but don't upset my stomach."

He used to eat anything and nothing ever bothered him—hot dogs with sauerkraut, pickles from the barrel, knishes and french fries. Who was this new man, this older version of Saul, who was fussy about his food?

"You like the salad?" he asked in return. "You're just picking at it."

"What's not to like?" she said. "Salad is salad. Some lettuce and tomato, a little oil and vinegar." She fluttered her lashes at him, sorry that she hadn't bothered to put on mascara. "But if you want to know the truth, I could make it better myself. When I cook for someone, he doesn't have to worry about what's going to give him gas."

"I'm sure you're a wonderful cook. Your husband was a lucky man."

"Whatever I did made him happy."

"You were happy too?"

"Nathan was a good man."

"That's not what I asked you."

"He loved me, he loved the boys. He wasn't perfect—who is?—but he was smart, a good provider. We never wanted for anything. What's not to be happy about?"

"Then you're lucky too, Molly. Everything you wanted you got."

She winced at what he said because it wasn't altogether true and both of them knew that—but Saul had no business asking personal questions. "Well sure, I can't complain, I got more than I deserved."

"But maybe . . . not everything?"

"*Everything* is a big word." She glanced at his eyes that were too close together, and their colour seemed to deepen as her belly tightened with a small ache of yearning.

"There was a time I wanted you," she said brashly, shocking herself, "and that—that I didn't get."

"You had me for a little while."

"Enough to make me want more." She looked off to one side and found herself speaking again before she could think better of it. "Where did you go, Saul?"

"Where did I go?" He pushed away his salad. "I went home to my family, left again for North America, back and forth all the time from one place to another, wherever I could get a little work under the table. I was a rolling stone."

"You left me for nothing?"

"I was young and mixed up, with this much to offer"—he formed a zero with two fingers—"and I wasn't running from you but from everyone, from myself."

Briefly she batted her eyes to stop any ill-timed tears from escaping.

"With me you never would've had the things you had with Nathan—money, family, peace of mind. With me it would've been complicated, nothing but trouble."

"Didn't you want those things too?"

"I couldn't live that kind of life back then. I was restless."

"But kept going back to your family in Europe. So you lied when we met and you said the marriage was over."

"I never stayed for long."

"You weren't free."

"Neither were you."

"I didn't lie about it! You knew from the start I was married to Nathan."

The waiter appeared to remove their salad plates. He poured more wine for Saul, who drank nearly half a glass before he continued. "I wanted a divorce, but my wife said I'd never see my daughters again and they meant the world to me." He took another swallow of wine. "I went home to be with them, but when they were almost grown they didn't want to see me anymore, because of this and that—whatever their mother told them. So I lost my children anyway. Now here I am the way I began, alone and longing."

Longing. She knew about that. Knew it painfully in her heart, even though she was seventy-three and you'd think all that would stop by now. But even if by some chance she lived to be a hundred, Molly would never lose the ache and fear of loneliness, that hunger for someone to share her life with. It just went on and on, like what she'd read about the slow expansion of the universe. One time she even dreamt the moon was circling her bed and she reached out and hugged it.

Many nights she woke dreamless and felt lonely through and through. She felt a hole under her ribs and something vital leaking out. Or else an itch in her arms like a caterpillar on her skin, and she scratched herself until she bled. And then she would be furious at Nathan for dying—and when she even thought of him, at Saul too.

Shivering, she rubbed her arms, pimply with goosebumps. She should've brought a sweater along or worn something warmer than a thin blouse and loose skirt because of how the temperature was never right in restaurants, no matter what the season—too cool in summer with the air conditioning turned up and in winter never hot enough. They didn't care if you froze to death so long as you paid the bill while your fingers could still move.

"There's something else I might've lost," he said. "Something important."

That would be her, of course! She stopped fidgeting, held her breath, waited for his declaration. *Now that you're in my life again, nothing else matters.* She folded her hands on the table, in case he wanted to touch them while he whispered his endearments.

She exhaled slowly and lowered her eyes. "What do you think you lost?"

"A son," he said.

"What—a *what?*" She tilted her head as though she hadn't heard properly.

He tapped his knife against his plate, seemingly calling for everyone's attention—for people in the restaurant to stop eating and look at him—and she peered at him, unblinking. Floaters like shooting stars streaked across her eyes and she shook her head to clear her sight. Two men at the next table paused with their forks up and stared in his direction as if they too had been blinded by his announcement.

"A son," Saul repeated.

Molly's throat closed so that it hurt her to swallow. Her voice became gravelly. "You have—what?—two daughters? And maybe a dozen grandkids you don't even know about.

Maybe you should make up with the family you got instead of dreaming about another one."

He ran a hand over his scalp, flattening his wispy hair. "They hate me now, what can I do? People turn against me, even my own flesh and blood."

Her ears weren't working right. What was he saying? What did he mean? The room started pivoting like she was on a Tilt-a-Whirl, and she clutched the arms of her chair to keep from falling off.

"Take Ben, for instance." He waved his hand dismissively. "Doesn't want me in your house, can't stand the sight of me."

"He's got a poet's temperament," she tried to explain her son, "and easily gets upset. Plus you caught him by surprise, he didn't know I wanted to rent the room he slept in for thirty years."

Saul raised an eyebrow. "Thirty years he lived with you?"

"Well sure, on and off. His education took time. Mel went away to school but Ben stayed at home."

"And that would make him how old?"

Her stomach was bubbling now with onions and cucumbers, and acid shot into her mouth. "Why do you want to know?" she asked too loudly, although she knew the answer. Knew it and didn't know. How was it possible to know and not know a thing at the same time?

He glanced at her and then away without responding.

The waiter brought their main dishes, poached salmon for each of them, with rice and mixed vegetables. Even in the old days they both liked fish and salads and would often order the same meals. It wasn't just in the bedroom that their tastes had been similar. Nice-looking food, she thought—but his talk had killed her appetite.

Hunched over, Saul was shovelling salmon into his mouth like a starving refugee. When he paused to look up he said, "What, you're not eating?"

"All of a sudden I'm not hungry."

"The salmon is delicious."

Molly glared down at her plate. "For what you pay in a restaurant for a slice of salmon the size of an ear, I could buy a whole fish."

Saul patted his mouth with his napkin and sat back. He counted on his fingers for a minute before he spoke. "Fifty-three, I'm figuring. His birthday, I think, was last month."

She opened her mouth as if to reply, then lifted her fork and filled it with rice instead. Grains stuck to her lower lip, fell on the table and into her lap, but she ignored them. She chewed with her face screwed up.

"Just like that you're hungry again? I can't keep up with you," he said.

She gulped water to wash down the rice, which felt like pebbles in her throat, then brushed her lips with her fingers. "Nathan raised him," she declared, "so that makes him Nathan's son. Get the picture?"

"I'm not here to make trouble."

Her voice cracked when she said, "Why *are* you here?"

If only Ben hadn't been home when Saul came to see the room! Or if she'd closed the door in his face and told him to come back another time, the next day. Or if she hadn't offered to rent to him in the first place. *Gotenyu!* What on earth had she been thinking? Why didn't she figure that if Saul moved in with her, sooner or later he'd meet Ben and start asking questions? She was no more sensible now than when she was a young wife recklessly sneaking out of the house and into the bed of a troublemaker.

"It wasn't till I met him and saw how tall he is—and Nathan such a small man, no bigger than you—that I thought, how can that·be?"

"Genes are unpredictable, you never know exactly how your kids are going to turn out. Mel's a big boy too, only a few inches shorter than his brother."

She used her fork to rearrange carrot, squash and turnip pieces on her plate, pushing them into categories of yellow, orange and red, like the colours of the candle. Like the colours of her face gone from warm to boiling.

"That's how you explain his size?"

"Nathan's father was tall, only men were shorter in those days because of bad nutrition. Ben is like his *zeyde*."

"And what about the rest of him, his eyes and jaw, the long face?"

"From my side of the family." She felt Saul watching her as she played with her vegetables, not daring to look up. Trying to calm her pattering heart and blink away the telltale wetness in her eyes.

"This is what you said to him—he looks like his *zeyde* and people from your side?"

"Family's important to Ben—he needs to know where he comes from. If looking like his ancestors helps him figure out who he is, that's what I'll tell him."

He forked a vegetable into his mouth, chewed slowly and swallowed. The knob of his Adam's apple, prominent in his thin neck, rose and fell a long way.

"Is he married?"

"Nine years."

"Children?"

"They're trying, but his wife can't get pregnant and nobody knows why."

His hand shook as he raised a last forkful of fish to his mouth. After a while he said, "Children are a blessing. I hope things work out and someday he'll have a son to name after his father."

To name after *Nathan*. What right did Saul have to break into their lives again wanting only God-knows-what? Molly's face hardened as she slapped down her cutlery. The people at the next table turned to stare, but she didn't care who was looking, she couldn't sit on her anger one second longer.

"It's your own fault," she hissed, "if there's nobody in your life. You weren't faithful to anyone, not me, not your wife— and who knows how many more you left crying in the dark! You abandoned your daughters and even now don't have the courage to make it right, then decided to live with me because you needed a cheap room and thought maybe you could start another family with a boy you never saw before. Shame on you, Saul Rosenberg, shame on your behaviour!"

Gesturing wildly, she knocked over her barely touched glass of red wine. The men dining next to them jumped a little in their seats and watched open-mouthed as a dark stream spilled forward, staining the tablecloth, and dripped slowly, menacingly, onto the floor.

"Close your mouths," she snapped at them, "it's not blood."

The waiter popped up again and Molly assured him that everything was all right, nobody even got splashed, all he had to do was wipe a small puddle off the floor. Tight-lipped, he hurried off with their dirty dishes, came back and cleaned up, spread a new tablecloth and refilled their glasses.

Saul ignored the disturbance. With his head thrown back he was squinting at the ceiling, as though watching a slide show of his good-for-nothing life.

"You're a no-goodnik who got what he deserves!" Molly summed up.

He levelled his head and peered at her. "I don't deny any-thing," he said after a pause, "but what you said, the way you put it . . . that's not the whole story."

"Not even a letter you sent me! Not even a phone call!"

"I'm sorry for hurting you. I don't deserve your kindness."

"You're a *mamzer*, a bastard, that's what you are!"

"So why did you give me a room?"

"Because I'm not in my right mind." She cupped her hot cheeks in her hands. "Because . . . I don't know why, I don't have an answer. Maybe I felt sorry for you."

"Maybe you were lonely too."

"My boys are grown, my husband's dead—maybe I was. Maybe I am."

"And maybe somewhere deep down you still have feelings for me, as I have feelings for you. That needs to be said too. We look at each other now and can't help remembering the special thing we once had."

Like steam, the heat from her face seemed to blow out the top of her head and Molly was speechless. The looking, that was it—the way he looked deeply into her eyes and past them. The way he gave his full attention, then and now, made something widen in her chest, and suddenly there was room in her for all his faults and goodness, for joy and suffering. What was this big space, this quietness, she wondered—and then she knew. Forgiveness.

"I'm not going to say or do anything to embarrass you or cause problems," Saul said. "I only want for us to be friends."

He reached over and rubbed her arm lightly, elbow to wrist, and her burning skin cooled a little. In fact, she started shivering.

"You're my last hope, Molly. Don't say it's too late."

She lifted her glass and drank some wine, even though she'd probably regret it in the morning when she woke with a headache, because she didn't want him to see her eyes welling up. Because she didn't want him to know her heart was swollen with kindness. Didn't want him to stop trying to sweeten her opinion of him. Not yet, not yet . . . because all that looking and touching felt so good, she didn't want it ever to stop.

"Let's go home," Molly said. "I don't care for restaurants."

CHAPTER 10

Mel was never on time. Ben was on his second beer when his kid brother walked in, clip-clopped across the floor in his suede boots and sat down on the next stool. He unzipped his jacket, glanced up and sniffed at the ongoing renovations.

"The Bald Eagle should be condemned."

"I like seeing the insides." Ben swept his arm over the counter to take in the loose wires, bare bulbs and still-exposed ductwork. "It's like they're making a postmodern statement or something."

Mel skewed his mouth, then ordered a drink from the doughy-faced bartender. "This place gives me the willies. I don't know why we come here."

"Because no one else does and we can talk in private."

"What have we got to say that God forbid someone should hear?"

Ben quickly emptied his glass. "We need to talk about Mama."

"Maybe we should check for hidden mikes under the bar stools."

"It's nothing to joke about. I don't like her situation."

"What situation?"

"I don't like that Saul guy sleeping in my bed."

"You sound like one of the Three Bears." Mel raised a finger and drank some of his rum-and-Coke. "Maybe what you don't like is someone sleeping with Mama Bear."

Ben coughed beer across the counter. "At their age? Impossible! He must be after her money. The man's got a pension the size of his putz and wants to steal her savings."

"No one's stealing anything. Whatever Mama gives away she gives because she wants to."

Ben had the bartender bring him another draft and stared at it briefly. He used to have beer only on hot summer evenings and never more than two at a time, but lately the weather had nothing to do with his drinking and it took three or four to ease his nervousness.

He had a long swig before he found the nerve to speak again. "I think you should know I phoned Ida Abramowitz to ask about her cousin."

"You stuck your nose in Mama's business?"

"A son has a right to protect his mother's interests."

"She can look after herself, she doesn't need help from you."

"You want to hear what I found out?"

Mel shrugged. "I'm listening. But I know it can't be good if you heard it from Ida. I never liked that yenta. When I was learning to ride a bike she told the whole world I was too old for training wheels, her boys hadn't used them since they were in diapers."

"Get over it," Ben said. "Even if you don't like her much, Ida knows things."

"Awright, so what'd she say? Cousin Saul kicked her cat? He took too many showers and ran up her gas bill?"

"He has a wife and two daughters in eastern Europe. And none of them talks to him because he's such a deadbeat, he jumped from job to job selling crap like garden hoses nobody wanted and hardly made enough money to keep them in shoes, then went to North America but did no better here."

"Since when is poverty a crime?"

"On top of which, Ida says he ran around with other women on two continents and didn't bother to hide it."

"At least we know they weren't after his money." Mel smirked.

"Ida says he was handsome once, but I saw a geezer who looks like a goalpost."

Mel checked his watch. "This is very interesting, but I have better things to do than listen to gossip. Instead of wasting time with you I could be shmoozing with well-heeled grannies dying to look young."

"We have to find out more about him. Mama could be living with a shark, for all we know."

"Go tell your wife about it. Maybe she can calm you down."

"Not likely," Ben said. "Renata likes to disagree with me on principle."

"Yeah, well so do I. Because you're a shmuck who gets excited over nothing."

"And you're passive-aggressive. You sidestep anything the least bit difficult."

"Stop already!" His voice was sharp. "Mama's not in danger of losing her savings or anything else, and she's not going to thank you for messing around in her affairs."

"We're talking about a vagrant bulldozing into her life!"

"Dr. Wasserman, heal thyself. I think you've got an Oedipal thing you haven't worked out yet."

Ben exhaled a geyser of air. "Do I tell you how to fix a nose or lift a tush? Stick to what you know and leave psychiatry to me, okay?"

The men turned away from each other, bent over their glasses like a pair of strangers and swallowed what was left of their drinks. Mel scowled at the counter, while Ben tried to quiet his mind with a visualization—the sort of trick Renata knew more about than he did. He saw them curled together in a hammock at the cottage they'd rented two summers ago: the way sunlight slid down the branches of maple trees and chipmunks stopped to peer at them; the smell of the muddy lake and how she fell asleep in his arms; the poem he wrote for her later on—"Love in August"—which he never actually showed her because if she complained about his choice of a word or the placement of a comma it would have spoiled the memory.

She often disagreed with him about petty things like errant punctuation . . . or insisting that his mother was a better judge of Saul Rosenberg's character than he was.

The visualization wasn't working: Ben was still pissed off.

His brother rubbed his hands together and stood up. "Gotta go."

"What? You just got here." Ben grabbed him by the sleeve. He wasn't ready to head home and didn't want to drink alone. "You can't just storm out. Let me buy another round."

"I'm already late." He looked at his watch. "Chloe's got a piano lesson and David's off to hockey. Every night I have to drive them somewhere, never a moment's peace."

"Be happy you have them. Without kids you drift and your life becomes meaningless."

"Don't start," Mel said, zipping up his jacket with a vehement tug. Starting for the door, he swung around for a last look. "Now I'm going to drift off to spend the rest of my meaningful night sitting in a coffee shop, the bleachers or in my car. I have a feeling your evening's going to turn out better than mine." And with that he walked off.

Ben's shoulders sank as he watched Mel's back and listened to the retreat of his boots. It was like he'd been left behind, chained to the bar stool: helpless to free himself, waiting to be released.

He ordered another draft, then sat hunched over his glass, feeling sorry for himself. His wife rarely took his side, and even his kid brother didn't look up to him. Mel had children and more money than he did, but Ben was the poet and thinker in the family—the doctor of psychiatry!—even if no one respected his opinion. It's true that Molly wouldn't like him meddling in her affairs, but she'd never question his motives. What's wrong with wanting the people you love to be happy and safe?

When he heard someone enter the lounge, Ben didn't look up. He sipped beer and studied the glass, in case it was his brother returning to apologize. He wouldn't make it easy for him. Wouldn't jump up, all smiles, and slap him on the back. He'd let Mel stand behind him, twitching and breathing hard, until he finally grumbled in the husky voice of regret.

But the person who walked in didn't come over to him. He spoke to the barkeep at the far end of the counter, waited for her to give him a drink and carried it to a table at the back of the room. Ben watched the customer from the corner of his eye—a skinny guy in a hat and coat—and then reluctantly went back to his solitary drinking, wishing it had been Mel.

He imagined a companion piece to his "Love in August" poem in which he'd describe himself a year and a half later, sitting alone in a godforsaken bar on a cheerless March evening, nursing his fourth beer. A poem about an aging man whose life, like most lives, hadn't quite turned out the way he'd expected.

He had wanted a large family, two girls and two boys, which wasn't going to happen, and wanted to write great poems or a cutting-edge medical book, which wasn't likely either. He'd trained to be a doctor who bettered people's mental health, yet found himself, on bad days, looking patients in the eye and telling them they couldn't have the organs they needed. *I'm sorry to say this, but there aren't enough to go round.*

It was always in his mind, that fist-in-your-face awareness of what his assessments meant.

In theory it was a team decision. In truth it was sometimes Ben alone who made the call, and he might be the one to deliver the news as well. It didn't happen often, but each time he had to say no was as bad as the first, when he turned down a patient who'd been a heavy drinker because he knew—Ben knew—the man wouldn't stay dry and would ruin a new liver too. After a few sessions, he'd given him the verdict as tactfully as possible and told him to return after a longer period of abstinence so Ben could reassess him . . . but the guy went home and OD'd on Elavil. As soon as he found out, Ben ran to a bar and drank himself stupid. Later that same night, he pitched and groaned in bed till Renata shook him awake.

He shouldn't get a liver, he yelled, *when others more deserving are standing in line too!*

His wife tried to comfort him with well-meant bunk about "doing your job to the best of your ability"—what Dr. Mengele thought, no doubt, as he pointed Jews left or right.

You live. You die.

And yet, come morning, he had shrugged off despair like a dirty nightshirt, gone back to the office, started again.

Now he squeezed his head in his hands to try to flatten his thoughts, then gave up and sucked down the rest of his beer. Abruptly he got to his feet and hurried to the washroom.

Returning, he motioned to the barkeep and settled his bill. If there wasn't much traffic he'd be home by eight.

On his way out he caught sight of the man who had walked in instead of Mel. He'd taken off his hat and coat and was sitting at a table, sipping a drink and reading. Something made Ben pause, something familiar about the guy—his neatly combed and parted hair, his cable-stitch cardigan—but another characteristic too, harder to pin down: a cat-like stillness, as though he were warming himself on a sunny fence.

Who else but Arthur?

Ben watched from the shadows, reluctant to approach but curious to know what book he was reading, and finally made his way to the table.

Arthur looked up at once. "Well, I never—"

"I didn't expect to see you either in a place like this."

Arthur smiled his broad smile and laughed his soft, nasal laugh. He gestured toward an empty seat and said, "Come join me. We'll pretend we're strangers."

Ben reached for the chair and stopped. It wasn't appropriate to fraternize with a patient. But this was nothing more than an accidental meeting, and all he had in mind was a chat. He signalled the barkeep to bring him another draft.

Pulling out the chair, he reasoned that theirs had never been a doctor–patient relationship in a technical sense since he hadn't actually been the man's psychotherapist but simply assessed him as a possible donor. What's more, he'd already made his decision known, had given the go-ahead to everyone involved in the case. And while there was a chance he'd be the treating psychiatrist if Arthur became anxious or depressed after surgery, he didn't think that would happen. Ten to one he'd do fine and not need further care.

His motives were above board. He just wanted to have a conversation with an interesting guy. For godssake, it wasn't like he wanted to be his best friend!

The beer arrived and he sat down.

Arthur marked the page he was reading and closed his book. "I come here sometimes when I'm staying in town," he said. "It's quieter than my daughter's place."

He lifted his drink, and Ben wondered what it was. Scotch, to judge by its colour and the size of the glass: not what he'd expected to see. Ben had never liked whisky himself, neither the flavour nor the high alcohol content—a shame because it gave the drinker an air of sophistication, a quality that didn't come easily to him with his common taste in food and booze.

"Am I intruding?"

"Not at all. I used to be on a tight schedule when I was a working man, but in my retirement it seems that time just keeps getting larger. It's like blowing up a balloon and finding out there's more space inside than you ever thought."

Ben's life was carved into sixty- or ninety-minute patient assessments, one session after the next, and hour-long staff meetings. Coffee and sandwiches were gulped down in between. Monday to Friday he went to bed around eleven, was lucky to be asleep by midnight, woke at six-thirty. On weekends he often felt restless and muddled and let Renata plan those days, which filled up quickly with shopping and other chores, movies, newspapers, workouts, meals out and maybe, if they still had the energy, a roll in the hay. There didn't seem to be enough hours to get it all in.

How had his life gotten so cluttered and shallow? If only there were more time to read and write poetry; at least to while away some hours thinking about it. Early Sunday morning on the days Renata slept in or after supper those nights he wasn't totally beat or when he couldn't fall asleep and snuck into his study were the only minutes possible for investigating his inner world. Desperate, he sometimes even locked himself in the bathroom and soaked in the tub with a book or ducked underwater till ideas and images floated up . . . but inevitably she knocked on the door and asked him to hurry up, they had to be somewhere soon, and all his thoughts would drain away.

A few rushed, irregular hours: never enough!

He reached out and turned Arthur's book around on the table. The title was unfamiliar, the author someone he didn't know, the cover mysterious: orange squiggles, pale animals, stars and a bare tree. "Who's the poet?" Ben asked.

"Roo Borson. She lives in Toronto."

"You never said you liked poetry."

"It never came up before. The topic was always kidneys."

"I like it too, but because of my schedule I don't read as much as I should." He sipped beer to wet his throat. "I even manage to write a few lines every now and then. It's a long-standing hobby."

"Good for you," said Arthur. "Tried that myself, but it didn't come to much. I think I'm better at reading."

"Read something now," said Ben. "Read something out loud. Whatever you were looking at. Whatever impressed you."

"This one, then." He opened the book to his marked spot and explained that the speaker was standing on a bridge that overlooked a river. "That's all you need to know." Then he began to read in a surprisingly dramatic voice.

"'On the last night of the year / the swans set sail at evening. / Then among the boats and fireworks / we can see the black water, / the city in the river. / That's where all our life is, / beyond the grief and failure, / the wake among the reeds.'

"That's just the first stanza. Powerful, isn't it?" Arthur's eyes were lit up. "It makes me feel hopeful."

"It says our life is in the reeds. What's hopeful about that?"

"Or that it's beyond them, beyond grief and failure. Our true lives are somewhere else. At least that's how I see it. But listen, I'll read more.

"In the next part the narrator, still looking at the river, sees a whole world there. I don't know what kind of world— remembered, imagined or another reality—but here's how she describes it:

"'Down there / down there / what is that place now / but a hill studded with lights / and a pine tree that doesn't move with the wind? / Wherever there is summer, / wherever the crickets sing to it, / that place is. / But longing is a wind that blows through you, / and like the pine that is nowhere / you do not move.'"

He closed the book and gazed at an unpainted wall. "It leaves me astonished. As still as that mysterious tree."

Ben pinched his forehead, trying to squeeze clarity from the skin between his fingers. Longing hurts, he was thinking. It digs up your insides. It's something we automatically want to run away from.

"I don't understand why the speaker just stands there."

"Well, I can't be sure of this—I don't know the poet's mind and can only say what it means to me—but maybe if she hurried off the feeling wouldn't 'blow through,' if you see what I'm getting at. She couldn't fully experience it before letting it move on unless she was standing as still as that tree in the wind."

"I think it would be smarter to step aside when you see it coming."

"Maybe it doesn't frighten her, so there's no reason to move. Or how about this: she's stunned by the force of her emotion and can't move. Or maybe she's dreaming of something else and longing takes her by surprise."

"I wonder what the poet meant."

"What do you imagine?"

"She can't move? But I'm guessing. What's your opinion?"

Arthur shrugged. "All of them, one or two, none of the above. I don't have an answer. What matters most to me is that the poem is intriguing, and for that I am grateful."

Ben picked up the book and rubbed it between his hands, as if there were a genie inside he could set free. His first wish? To slow time. His second, for serenity: to let more of the unsettling things of life blow through. The third? That was easy. What he always came back to. A tangible thing, even more alive than poetry, that he and his wife would co-create. He put the book down again.

"I long for a lot." This was followed by a shy inhalation when he realized he'd spoken aloud. He polished off his fourth—or was it his fifth?—beer. "Like travelling," he said, veering off. "I'd like to experience different places, go home and write about them. Write an amazing poem."

Which wasn't exactly a lie, if not what he wanted most. If he were granted a fourth wish, it might very well be that . . . although, in light of past vacations, travel was more appealing as a concept.

"I've thought the same thing. Go somewhere distant and new, get away from everyday life, become another person—a great poet, someone like that. Maybe cross paths in the air with the very people I meant to see, on their way to visit me! Wouldn't that be something," Arthur laughed, "waving from my plane as they waved back from theirs."

Ben smiled crookedly. He never became someone new when travelling; was never moved to write about his experience afterward. All that unpleasantness of waiting in big airports, talking to hurried strangers, finding clean hotels and affordable places to eat, driving on narrow roads jammed with buses and Vespas or dealing with salespeople who spoke in baffling tongues while he tried to explain that his wife had blisters on her feet and a terrible migraine and was threatening to fly home, so he needed to buy aspirin and Dr. Scholl's foot pads. At the end of a day in a foreign place he stank from nervous sweat.

"But now I think something else," Arthur concluded, "that if you want to write, find a quiet place and do it . . . or pick up a good book and throw yourself into that. The rest is distraction."

Ben stared at him openly. It was like he was chatting with a man he'd never met before: a random encounter in an out-of-the-way bar with a nondescript guy you could easily over-look, who nevertheless proved to be fascinating company. "Arthur, you surprise me. I never would've guessed we had poetry in common, that we'd be talking like this."

"What did you think when you sat down—the subject would be kidneys and living donor transplants?"

"I thought we might start there."

"I'd rather talk poetry and save the rest for your office. Wouldn't you, Doctor?"

Ben nodded, light-headed, and gripped his mug to brace himself. Empty again. An empty glass. That last beer was get-ting to him, but he dared to order another. Scowling as usual, the bartender carried it over and set it down.

Doctor or poet? The question came forward in his mind unexpectedly, demanding an answer he didn't have. Right now he felt like no one at all.

Once he'd planned on being both, like William Carlos Williams. As an intern he could handle double shifts on little sleep and still manage to jot down lines of poetry daily. He didn't mind skipped meals or the slop served in the hospital caf, and wrote about his girlfriends and the pleasures of the body. But now, even with twice as much sleep, he woke muddy-headed and tired, relying on coffee to keep him going. More times than not his body was a source of pain—aches in his shoulders and knees, gas and indigestion—and he wrote almost nothing.

"Read to me," he finally said. "Read again about the river."

Arthur opened the book and began, speaking more slowly this time than he had before, glancing at Ben and pausing at the end of a line to let him absorb the words.

Ben grew still and let his head hang forward. The poet's words swirled in his brain. Then one by one, phrases of his own pushed up and opened like flowers. *A bellyful of bubbles. An earful of crickets. A tear in the river below.*

Arthur closed the book and stared at the cover through half-shut eyes. When Ben looked up and saw him, a word blossomed in his mind. *Lovely.* Just that. The poem was. Arthur was. The bartender. Ben himself. In that peculiar instant, everything in the bar was exactly as it should be, beautiful and perfectly formed. Everything was so right—the dirty table, bad lighting, even the ductwork—that his eyes became runny and hot.

He swiped at them before Arthur could notice his silly tears. Sentimental, boozy thinking, that's all it was, he thought. He'd change his mind tomorrow when he got to the office hungover and saw once more that everything was, in fact, wrong.

Life *wasn't* lovely. He only had to think of people desperate for organs if he needed proof. Not just the few he refused, but also the ones he approved who died regardless—died in anguish—waiting for a liver or lung. Or the lucky ones who finally got an organ but whose bodies rejected it. Or those who lived through surgery and tolerated the transplant only to hate the results—their circumscribed, drug-reliant, medically managed lives. Sometimes even now he'd wake up at night shouting, *Live, live*! until Renata reached out and stroked him calm again.

He had a last swig of beer and woozily pushed himself up. His feet felt wet in his shoes, and he pulled up a pant leg to see if he was bleeding. But that didn't seem to be it.

Arthur said, "Are you all right?"

Of course he wasn't all right! Anyone could see that he was sinking in black water, up to his shins in it. Up to his knees now! Trapped among snaky weeds and life-sucking leeches: a boggy life, a life in the reeds. His days marked by small failures, separateness and sorrow. A small, sad, stuck life. Didn't Arthur *know* that?

How much did Arthur know? Intoxicating question. Ben himself knew nothing. Nothing at all! He bent his fingers into fists and wobbled with the effort of not falling over.

If Arthur knew about happiness, he ought to share the secret with Ben—especially considering how well Ben had argued his case and sold him to the team. The man owed him one!

But what if he didn't know what made him happy? What if Ben had misjudged him and Arthur was a lightweight, his thoughts the depth of a wading pool, and Ben was merely wasting time?

When he stumbled into the back of a chair, Arthur suggested he sit down and have a cup of coffee.

"My wife's waiting," Ben said. "Have to go."

"You're not driving, are you?"

Ben waved him silent, then lurched out the door and into the murky night.

The cold air stung his face and made him more alert, but his feet, sliding in his shoes, wouldn't follow his commands. He staggered around the parking lot, trying to kick car tires because he'd lost feeling in his toes and wanted it back. No longer sure which vehicle was his since they all looked alike in the dark. Wasn't it stupid, he thought, that someone should want one car over another because of its colour and shape? Weren't they just big toys? Shiny distractions to make us forget mortality? That's it, distractions! Cars should be identical, equally priced and non-polluting, distinguished from one another solely by their licence plates.

He heard Arthur calling him back from the doorway, but Ben didn't turn around. Wanting to get away fast and still not finding his car, he charged out of the parking lot and reeled around a corner. This street or that street, it didn't much matter since there was nowhere he wanted to be. He focused on the slap-slap of his feet on the pavement and was airily free for the moment of thought and design.

Finally he stopped before the marquee of a cinema and looked up. The letters were small and ran together as though they'd been sloppily painted, but he didn't keep up with movies and wouldn't have recognized the names even if he could read them. He went inside, bought a ticket for something about to start, found his way to the right room and banged his knee on the edge of a seat and his elbow on a drink holder as he plunked down in the back row. A man and woman to his left turned their heads and glared at him, like he was a pervert who'd come here to jack off . . . and wouldn't it be funny if he'd walked into a porn flick!

But after the show began he saw it was an art film. A big-eyed, pretty blonde who reminded him of Renata with her pearly skin and long hair was hiding out in a backwater town called Dogville, working in houses and shops for the townsfolk—except there weren't actual buildings in the picture but grid lines and props. He wondered if he'd gone into a theatre by mistake and was watching actors on a stage, but forgot about it once he got caught up in the story.

His eyelids felt papery as he looked at the movie and time passed. More and more anxious now, he watched the sweet blonde get raped, chained and collared and taunted by the townies. A young woman tortured by churchgoers gone amok! Why was this happening?

He wanted to leave but didn't, and as he gaped at the screen his sympathy did an about-face and all at once he was mad at the girl, inflamed by her passivity. A person of dubious virtue—not unlike Arthur! Weren't they the same, those two, a pair of stunned innocents who left it to others to shield them from ugliness? All they did was smile dumbly and leave you twisting in the wind, so why was it surprising that people might abuse them?

And yet when the villagers were killed at the end of the film, he was so glad that he popped up in his seat and shouted, "Awh-right!"—and the couple sitting in his row hissed at him to be quiet.

"Sodomites!" he barked at them on his way out.

He managed to find his way back to the parking lot. After searching up and down he even spotted his Volvo, the one with the plate that read CEAS 211—which he took to mean that his life would end at 2 a.m., 11 minutes, though he didn't know on what day. If he waited another two hours before flopping into his car and weaving onto the highway, it just might happen tonight.

But he didn't stay longer, and was lucky enough to arrive home without having an accident. Later he would hardly remember the drive, his clearest memory being that he dropped his keys when he got there and couldn't be bothered to look for them in the muddy yard.

His temples were beating as he rapped on the front door. He was already getting a hangover, which didn't seem fair since he'd hardly had a chance yet to enjoy being drunk.

Renata finally opened the door and stood before him in the nightgown he liked best—the one of such fine cotton her nipples showed through—and he said, "You're so beautiful."

"Where are your keys?" she asked.

He nodded over his shoulder. "Somewhere out there."

"There's an extra one hanging in the garage. You put it there yourself."

"Can't remember where. Did I say how gorgeous you are?"

"Under the window and behind the box of junk you promised to get rid of but never did."

"Come on, Renata, let me in." He opened his arms to her. "The neighbours are watching."

"I don't care."

He shoved past her into the hall, shutting the door behind them. "What're you upset about?"

"You got me out of bed . . . but I wasn't sleeping anyway."

"Why not?"

"I was worried sick!"

"Let me tuck you back in. I can help you fall asleep." He eyed the erection distorting the front of his pants. "Look what you did to me."

She didn't seem interested. "Where were you all night?"

"Having a drink with Mel. I told you this morning."

"You said you'd be home early."

"Tomorrow's an easy day, I don't have to be in till ten." He crossed the hall, sat on the stairs and patted a step. "Come sit with me." His plan was to back up discreetly, one tread at a time, pulling her with him till they reached the upper landing and tripped into the bedroom. To ditch his clothes and curl up with Renata under cool sheets.

"You were not drinking with Mel. At least not the whole time."

"What are you talking about?"

"Libby said he was home by seven, he had to drive the kids somewhere. What were you doing the rest of the night?"

"I can't believe you called Libby. Checking up on me like that." His head was really hurting now. Before they hit the bedroom he'd back into the small bathroom just off the landing and wash down some ASA. "I thought you trusted me."

Renata was rubbing her arms, gazing at her bare feet. She

had utterly wonderful feet, soft, pink and slender, with straight toes in perfectly descending order, big to small. He hadn't sucked her toes in a while but planned on doing that tonight.

His penis bumped the zipper of his fly, trying to get out. "Are you going to sit with me or not?" He waved her over.

She hugged herself and shook her head. Not a good sign.

"You don't often stay out late, and Mel never does. I couldn't imagine who or what was keeping you," she sniffled, "and then I started thinking something terrible had happened, a heart attack or car crash."

"Why didn't you think that I stayed on to drink alone or shoot the breeze with the regulars? Or maybe I was writing poems—why not imagine that? Why think the worst?"

"You could've phoned to say you'd be late."

Not going well. His erection deflated and he pushed himself up a step. "Since when am I not allowed to stay out a few extra hours without reporting in?"

"It's easy enough to let me know."

Strategically he should've stood up and walked over to her, wrapped her in his arms and apologized for his thoughtlessness; but his head was throbbing now, his stomach rolling. Suddenly it was more important to score Gravol and ASA than take his wife to bed, so he stretched out his cramped legs and climbed another two stairs.

"I left after Mel did, but it was still early so I went to a movie. The film was just about to start and I got a ticket and rushed in and never thought to call you."

"What was the name of it?"

She was trying to sound casual, but he heard wariness in her voice. "You know how I am, how I never remember what they're called. Something with *dog* in it."

"What was the plot?"

"It was actually pretty interesting. That blonde actor—Nicole Kidney?—holes up in a small town where everyone treats her horribly, confirming my opinion of the fundamental degeneracy of humankind." He backed up another step, as though nothing more could possibly be said after that.

"A movie takes two hours. What did you do then?"

"This one was very long, more like three hours."

"There's still another hour you haven't accounted for."

"I can't believe I'm hearing this! What are you accusing me of?"

"I'm trying to make sense of what you're saying."

"Maybe I went back to the bar. Maybe I stopped at a coffee shop and thought about the movie. What's going on here? You want me to log my time?"

"Wherever you went, whatever you did, you weren't thinking about me. You weren't being considerate."

At this point he could have, should have told Renata about meeting Arthur. *I ran into someone I spoke to in the office about donating his kidney. Of all people to meet in a bar!* He could've eased her mind by speaking the truth—but didn't.

Like after the first time he interviewed Arthur and later decided not to talk about it with his wife, he wouldn't share this encounter either. He didn't want her input—her questions and opinions about having a drink with a would-be donor; her arguments and censure that were sure to upset him and ruin the experience.

You never should've sat down with someone you'd assessed. What a risky thing to do! Even riskier, wouldn't you say, than taking a pregnant phobic outdoors on a snowy day?

Wouldn't it be just like her to cling to old grievances and wreck his fun with a cutting remark!

And Ben thought this too: that Arthur was as special and fragile as a unicorn who, like that poor exploited girl in the movie, needed protection. Goodness was a delicate plant that had to be watered and helped to bloom. The fact that he hadn't yet figured out the code of Arthur's generosity didn't mean it wasn't real. He only had to be patient.

By keeping his secret, he was not only steering clear of his wife's self-righteous anger but also safeguarding Arthur Rae and everything he stood for.

Ben bumped himself up the final stairs to the landing, ducked into the bathroom and shook Aspirin into his palm. As he filled a glass with water, Renata swished past in her ghostly, diaphanous gown, on her way to their bedroom without saying another word. Both of them understood that he would spend the night on the couch, which seemed like a suitable arrangement at the moment. He didn't want her lying stiff and snivelling beside him, soaking the mattress with her difficult emotions.

He was free at last to fall into a drunken, mind-erasing sleep.

CHAPTER 11

Stella asked for the aisle seat, and Renata said that was fine, she understood that sitting by the window might be hard for her. Kids sometimes throw rocks at the glass, Stella went on, or else watching the scenery could make her feel sick and she wouldn't want to cause a fuss struggling over Renata's knees to get to the bathroom.

"It's only a short ride," Renata explained when they'd settled into their seats, "but if all goes well we can take another trip soon and go as far as Kingston—"

"Unless I have my baby first," Stella interrupted, "and then we'd have to put it off. I wouldn't want to travel right away with an infant."

"You're due the end of June, which gives us some time."

"We don't know—you *never* know, my mother used to say, because her daughters were preemies. She actually said it the last time I saw her . . . so long ago that I don't remember much else, only that she smelled sort of smoky and greasy, like chicken nuggets or fish and chips."

"She'd stopped looking after herself?"

"She kept herself clean when Dad lived with us, and then with Lucy's father, but neither of them stuck around . . . and in the end we just became a messy family of females. When Lucy got pregnant at sixteen, Mom laughed and told us for the zillionth time how lucky she was that her girls came out easy—*I wasn't due for another month,* she said, *but you never know.* Lucy said she ought to drink and smoke as much as Mom did to keep the baby tiny, and Mom smacked my sister's cheek. Soon after, she came home not pregnant anymore and ran off with a drug dealer, and then there was just me for Mom to rely on, only me to shop and cook and wipe up the vomit. She couldn't even sing by then, her voice totally ruined, so I tried singing instead, but my voice was no great shakes and it wasn't the same thing at all as having your mother sing to you."

The train started moving, and Renata was glad it was leaving on schedule. Circling her watch around her wrist, she thought that the day would be long and exhausting and hoped there'd be no delays.

As the train left the station, Stella dropped her chin to stare at her knees, and her hair fell forward. She tucked it behind her ears but strands came loose, and she kept flipping them back and around, which discomposed Renata, who began to play with her own hair.

Finally she lowered her hands to her lap when she saw Stella peeking at her, studying her green shirt, grey jacket and matching skirt. Slyly Stella moved a hand close to Renata's thigh, as if to touch the fabric, but then drew it back again.

"I like what you're wearing," she said, "and your perfume."

The intimacy of her remark—words that would've been welcome from Ben but not from a client—made Renata wish she had thought twice this morning before routinely applying scent.

"Does your husband like you to wear perfume?"

"Why do you ask?"

"I was thinking about your marriage just now, that's all, imagining the two of you sitting down to dinner with good food and wine and both of you dressed up, you smelling of perfume, talking about your work."

"We don't discuss our clients." Renata crossed her legs and jutted her knees at the window. The train picked up speed as it pulled away from Toronto, and she felt a slight rumbling in her chest and gut.

"Sometimes, you know, I had nice meals with Grant too, especially after I dropped out of school and he was trying to cheer me up. He'd bring home takeout from upscale restaurants and even expensive wine. Once he brought me daffodils, also a cushion for my chair and hand-painted napkin rings carved to look like elephants. Those were my favourites and I still use them all the time. Whenever I reach for a napkin I remember that he thought about me, even if only now and then."

"Those are good memories."

"But still I didn't trust him, he was too unpredictable. One day he brought gifts, the next he didn't notice me. I never thought he'd stay and was shocked when he finally invited me to meet his folks. I figured he would move out—if I didn't move first—and live alone in a house with his iPod, computer and flat-screen TV, and when he was gone I'd become new and happier, like Lucy did in the ashram.

"So now he's truly gone but I'm carrying his baby and my head's still full of him, I keep having nightmares."

"You *can* become happier," Renata insisted, "but you have to be patient."

Stella turned her back to the aisle and faced her fully. "I never asked you this before"—massaging her abdomen—"and you never mentioned it, but I was just wondering if you and your husband have kids."

Renata straightened her legs and concentrated on controlling her voice. "No, we don't," she said, then quickly changed the subject. "I see you're rubbing your stomach. Are you comfortable? Would you like to stand?"

"We're doing great, aren't we?" She grinned at her belly, and Renata had that queasy sense she often got with Stella that another boundary had been breached.

Half an hour later the train stopped in Oshawa, then started moving swiftly again, rolling through a landscape of tracks, gravel, power lines and the brown hills of early spring already turning green in spots. Renata stared out the window, lulled by the repeated scene. But in a while the train seemed to be going even faster—too fast, Renata thought—reeling and stuttering, the wheels chitter-chattering, and she swayed against the armrests as Stella did the same. Every time she bumped the chair the young woman caught her breath, and soon she complained that the baby was punching her insides and things were sloshing around in there, making her anxious.

Renata reached into her tote and passed Stella a fashion magazine to distract her, though possibly giving her photos of skinny blondes in tight clothes she couldn't wear wasn't such a good idea. Still, it opened neatly on the shelf of her belly and seemed to hold her attention, and eventually she grew quiet. Renata pulled out something for herself to look at, *The Journal of Cognitive Psychotherapy*, and read a few paragraphs, but found it hard to concentrate. Passengers in front and behind and across the aisle were yammering at one another, talking into their cells, or else tinny music was escaping their earphones, and even Stella distracted her, humming for no discernible reason as she riffled through her magazine—that "Frosty the Snowman" song, although it was April and they hadn't seen snow in weeks.

She put away the journal as Stella's song grew louder. Was she trying to comfort herself? Thinking about Grant's death?

The magazine slid to the floor as Stella leaned forward all at once and cupped her belly.

"Are you in pain?" Renata asked, but Stella shook her head.

"There's a horrible movie playing in my brain," she said, "pictures popping up that I don't want to watch, but the way the car's rocking me I can't help but look out the window and see the view—rivers, trees, sky, fences, houses and dark fields—all of it smeared and watery, rushing past. All things making me remember what I want to forget."

When the train passed a crossing, clanging and hooting, she swung up her elbows and slapped her hands over her ears. Her eyes squeezed shut.

"I don't want to look but it keeps showing in my mind—the trip to Montreal and Grant sitting next to me, his red ears, angry mouth, and me stumbling over him to get to the bathroom . . . and then the room collapsing like a stepped-on sandcastle. I'm seeing myself banged up, trapped in the bathroom again, my ears exploding with the screams of people in their seats . . . and when I get back to the car I see them all broken or torn into bloody bits, Grant broken most of all, like Frosty without a head.

"It's happening again, like I'm having a nightmare wide awake"—her breathing quick and shallow. "I see his shiny-wet hair, his dead eyes and grey mouth, the gash below his chin and his neck dark and leaking—"

Renata told her to breathe—*breathe!*—but Stella said she couldn't breathe, her lungs hurt when she inhaled, her lungs weren't working. She opened her eyes and whimpered that everything was blurry now, she thought she was dying.

"You're not dying," Renata said, "you only *think* that. Tell me what's happening. Talk to me."

Stella coughed hard before she said through her teeth, "It's like my throat's full of blood, and if I open my mouth wide my clothes, the seat and carpet and the back of the chair in front of me and even *you* will be stained red forever."

"That's not going to happen."

"I feel like I'm sinking, like I'm going under, sucked down . . . pulled into a sea of blood filling my ears, filling my mouth, plugging my nostrils and the hole between my legs, and I'm tumbling like I'm sleeping, like I'm deaf, dumb, blind, numb.

"There's tightness in my lungs now and heaviness every-where, but mostly just this slow fade, just this tiny voice saying, *Let go and die already, that's all you have to do.*"

"You can't die," Renata said. "You have to stay, you have to *live*. I want you to think about breathing in, breathing out, and count the breaths, one, two, inhale, exhale."

Stella peered at her a long time before she spoke again. "You're like a mermaid, wavy and green, with a bubbly under-water voice only fish can hear, and you smell like a lake and water lilies in bloom."

"Stella, are you listening? Do you understand what I'm saying? Look at your fingers right now and start counting out loud—five, six, seven, eight . . ."

"The baby," Stella groaned suddenly, bending over her abdomen. "She's jabbing me with her elbows and knees."

"She wants your attention. She wants you to remember there's a new life inside you, a child you have to take care of now and forever. You have to think of her too."

Stella ran her tongue over her lips, then began to speak. "One, two, three, four . . ."

Renata joined in and they counted together in one voice, but didn't stop at eight or ten. The numbers kept increasing, like they were counting stones on a beach or fish in a barrel, till someone a row ahead swung around to shush them because he was trying to work. Stella angled her body left, dropped an ear to her shoulder and pressed as far back as she could to get away from the stranger, but Renata only smiled at him and promised they'd be quieter, and the man turned around and went back to his computer. Renata resumed counting, but very softly now, with a finger to her lips and her face close to Stella's until she started whispering too.

"Keep going," Renata encouraged her. "We're almost there. We're coming into our station." Impulsively she caught Stella's hand and squeezed it.

Outside the window, just ahead, were a blue sign with oversize yellow VIA letters and a red maple leaf, and a square brick depot with a Canadian flag on top. People pressed together on the platform were small at first but zoomed in larger and larger as the train slowed.

"We'll get off here," Renata said, "and take the next train back."

As she rose, Stella swayed, fell back in her seat and had to try again. Renata asked if she needed help, but Stella said she could manage.

Carefully she got up as the train wheezed to a stop, her belly like a hibernating bear unwilling to move, and heaved herself into the aisle. Renata scrambled after her. When people brushed against her while grabbing bags or lining up, Stella jerked her head, raised her hands and listed to one side. Standing close behind, Renata reminded her to visualize a summer's day, a sandy beach, and to focus on her breathing.

When the line began to move, they followed other passengers down the steps, off the car and onto the platform, where a crush of people were waiting. They stood aside until the platform started to empty, Stella's back to the train that finally slid away into the afternoon.

As soon as the crowd thinned, Renata took Stella's elbow and steered her into the overheated, overly bright depot. A pair of ticket agents looked calm behind their counters as they chatted with travellers and tapped at their computers, never glancing up when the two women passed, and Renata was reassured that things would proceed routinely.

Stella took a seat in a corner, locked her purse between her knees and stared at an overhead screen reporting the arrival and departure of trains. Renata watched the screen as well from an adjoining chair. A westbound train wasn't due for another hour.

Stella said she was trying to see a beach on the screen and herself running barefoot and inhaling clean air. But the baby wouldn't stay still, and every time she turned over, Stella was startled back to the station and schedules and dozens of strangers, and her mind filled with trains again.

"What happened back there?" Renata asked gently.

"It was just like I told you—the bathroom and passenger car and everybody screaming."

"You were remembering that. It wasn't actually happening."

"And Grant too, mostly Grant. Then—"

"Then what?"

"Then everything was hurting."

"In your body?"

"In here." She pressed her fingers over her heart.

"Can you say more about it?"

"Only that I had to get off . . . and don't want to be in the depot either. The baby probably thinks so too because she keeps butting her head, trying to escape."

"You're not"—Renata held her breath—"having contractions?"

Stella shook her head. "But she's kicking so hard, you know, it's like she's in a big hurry to get out and away."

Renata peered at the schedule on the screen as if she could change it and said, "It won't be too long," and Stella misunderstood, thinking she meant the baby—not too long till she was born. She hoped the baby would get here sooner than expected, she said, because she was worn out from carrying that extra weight, from peeing every half hour and not sleeping well.

"Mostly when I can't sleep I go to the living room"—Stella spoke in a hushed voice—"and stare at Grant's portrait. It never looks the same twice, like somehow he's taken over the picture from the inside and changes the colours to suit his mood. Sometimes his eyes are the way I painted them, medium brown with green flecks that remind me of budding trees, but other times they're shiny black, and though I can't interpret his look—sad, angry or nothing at all—it always makes me think I've done something wrong."

"Why don't you take it down?"

"Lucy told me the same thing—take it down and hide it— but I said I can't do that. She worries that after she goes back to the ashram no one will be around to stop me from staring at him, and I won't be able to put all that behind me and move on.

"But it's not just the portrait. I see him other places too, even when I don't want to, even here at the depot. Like right now on the overhead screen there's no schedule, no beach, it's just Grant up there with his wide forehead, straight nose and sticking-out cheekbones . . . and I remember licking his face, the taste of his aftershave, my tongue on his stubble and the soft places under his chin, but best of all his mouth on mine, sucking away my consciousness." She paused to look at Renata. "He's not finished with me yet, and I'm not finished with him." Then she turned to the screen again, where the schedules had blinked off, leaving only a blue square.

"Now his face is breaking up, it's like there's poor reception"—her voice rising steadily—"and his hair's falling out in strings, his skin's peeling off and his perfect nose and cheekbones are cracking into pieces. Now there's nothing left but a *skull*."

A freight train clamoured by and the room began to vibrate with thunderous noise, and Stella covered her ears with her hands and said to the blank screen, "Go away. Leave me alone!" Several people glanced her way even though they probably couldn't hear her over the blast of the train, but if she noticed their attention Stella didn't seem to care. "It wasn't my fault!" she yelled, then slumped against Renata and asked why it happened.

"There are lots of things we don't know," Renata said. "It just did."

After the train passed, the room became quiet enough for the swish of turning newspaper pages to be audible. The overhead screen showed words and numbers once again as Renata touched Stella's wrist and whispered, "It's okay."

"But sometimes I *wanted* him dead. Is that okay too?"

"We all have thoughts like that now and then about the people we love."

"I wanted him dead that day."

Renata said she understood that those were troubling thoughts, but Stella didn't answer. Instead, to her astonishment, the woman pulled her into her arms, as close as she could manage with that big belly up front, and wouldn't let go—even when Renata tried to break free.

Her back was stiff in Stella's hold, but all at once it softened and then, without thinking, Renata shivered, reached out and cupped the back of Stella's head. She rubbed her hair in circles and kept repeating in her ear that Stella had nothing to do with the crash, he didn't die because of her, regardless of her feelings, and everything was fine now, everything was all right . . .

Stella pushed her face into Renata's neck and began to weep, her tears wetting Renata's shirt.

"Why are you crying?" she asked.

And Stella said because it was the best moment of her life.

CHAPTER 12

S he said no."

"Excuse me?"

"Mrs. Stanley doesn't want to go ahead with the transplant."

Arthur looked at him blankly. "Did something bad happen to her? Diabetes? Cancer?"

"Mrs. Stanley changed her mind."

"No! I can't believe it."

Ben watched him silently. He seemed, at the moment, as fragile as a baby chick. His eyes were beads, his nose sharp, his hair greyer and wispier, less tidy somehow than when they had first met.

Lately he'd been noticing hair. Most balding guys he knew were older than he was, but a frightening number looked to be his own age. It was hard enough dealing with the slowdowns and burnout and shrinking possibilities that came with the middle years, but having to face these alterations without a protective coat of hair was unthinkable.

Arthur moved slowly as he unzipped his cardigan, opened the collar of his shirt, rubbed the back of his reedy neck. Then he asked the expected, why?

Ben softened his voice and said, "I'm not at liberty . . ."

"I'm sure it's not because of me—because it's my kidney—so there must be medical reasons. If she's not ill with something new, it has to be the surgery. Did she get scared when it looked like it would actually happen?"

He could answer simply that, according to her doctors, an unforeseen clinical problem had indeed cropped up—*They spoke about an unanticipated complication. I can't be more specific than that*—which is generally what he said in cases like this to appease the would-be donor. But he offered Arthur something more.

"All I can say is that she's thought about it again and decided to remain on dialysis at this time and not go through with the transplant."

What he couldn't say: that her psychiatrist and nephrologist believed she was tired of the whole affair—of surgical and pharmaceutical "miracles," as she called them, and the chronic problems a new organ owner would face—and made up her mind to continue on dialysis without further stepped-up medical intervention. Neither depressed nor delusional, they decided. Competent to make such an unexpected choice, she'd frustrated and confounded her doctors and nurses alike. Here was a patient who rejected not just an organ, but their concentrated efforts to improve and extend her life!

Arthur squinted at the doctor. "Why doesn't she want to live?"

"We can't discuss her verdict. I don't have permission to tell you more—and all of us, including you, should respect her privacy."

"I'll talk to her myself, then. I think I can persuade her she has everything to live for."

"I can't keep you from speaking to her, but I urge you to bear in mind that Mrs. Stanley thought this through and made a decision not to proceed and nobody, not even you, can make her take your kidney." Though he believed that if anyone could talk her into it, Arthur could.

"Somebody has to try."

"Many people have. It's a complex process to arrive at these decisions, and the team has worked hard to persuade her that a transplant is her best alternative. She knows what her refusal means, knows that she can reconsider at a later time . . . but for now she's chosen dialysis. The staff have done as much as they can. No one has the right to force her to change her mind."

"I have the right to try."

"About this matter of rights . . . I hope you understand that you don't have the right to be a donor, Arthur, just to be considered one. The patient, however, has the right to make an independent choice and to say no."

Arthur smacked his thigh. "But I know I can save her!"

Ben drew back reflexively. Rarely did a possible donor react this way when he realized he'd been refused. Sadness and relief, yes; confusion, disappointment. But not this doggedness.

"I know it's hard," he tried again, "when things come to a halt like this, and also I appreciate how much you want to help her. But even though you may not agree with Mrs. Stanley's choice, it must be respected. I'm asking you not to pursue this privately. You'll only exhaust her and won't change the outcome."

"That's your opinion. I want to speak to someone else."

"The team agreed that I should be the one to inform you of Mrs. Stanley's wishes. You can meet with the transplant co-ordinator, if you like, but I promise you she won't say any more than I have."

Arthur stiffened in his seat. "The team did this, didn't they. She won't go ahead with it because they scared her out of her wits."

Ben said nothing.

"Always in a hurry. Impossible to understand with all their medical jargon. It takes courage to put your life in the hands of doctors and I don't think Carol's brave enough, she doesn't like taking risks. The way I see it, she decided it was easier to say no to surgery, more tests and drugs, and to go on the way she was—and no one talked her out of it. No one cared enough to sit with her for ten minutes, speak plainly, hold her hand and get to the bottom of this!"

Blame the doctors, Ben thought, because they denied you the chance to be a hero. Because you'll carry shame and guilt throughout Carol's shrinking life.

Arthur shoved his chair back, jumped up and circled it, his neck pink above his collar. "That's what you're not saying. That's why she said no!"

When Arthur finally stopped pacing, Ben spoke carefully. "I see this has upset you. I wonder if her change of heart is making you uncomfortable for more personal reasons."

"What are you getting at?"

He gestured toward Arthur's seat and waited for him to sit. Ben watched as he sat down, crossed his arms and legs and swept back his hair. He took note of Arthur's swinging foot and his eyebrows flattened to a single line, like the slot of a mailbox, and the cork that bobbed in his neck as he swallowed repeatedly. The man's irritation was reassuring somehow: his ordinary anger.

"It's often bewildering when someone behaves unexpectedly," Ben said, "as Mrs. Stanley did by turning down your kidney. Especially after so much time and preparation."

Arthur unfolded his legs and fixed his eyes on Ben.

"I know you think her refusal makes the medical system look bad, but what I'm getting at is how her decision affects you. How does it make you feel about yourself?" he prompted.

Arthur lowered his gaze, considering the question. "It's frustrating, naturally." He looked up. "Not good."

"It makes you feel less good?"

"I was sure she wanted this. She hated the dialysis, complained about it to everyone. I guess I feel a bit useless now."

Ben's shoulders shot up. Had he missed something earlier? Was Arthur at risk of hurting himself?

"Everyone wants to feel good, but I'm wondering, in your case, how pressing the need is. Just how important is it that you feel useful?"

"I think a lot about helping out, if that's what you mean."

"Do you think about it often?"

"Not all the time, no."

"Are you tempted at this point to offer your kidney or any other organ to someone else who needs one—someone who needs your help?" Would damaging yourself make you feel better in some way?

"Not my kidney, not my liver, not any part of me," Arthur said deliberately. "I wanted to help Carol, but she doesn't want my help anymore. I'm never going through this again."

"But when you've thought this over in the quiet of your home, is it possible you'd change your mind?"

"This whole thing—" He shook his head. "I've had enough."

Ben leaned over to make a note in Arthur's file—*Doesn't want to repeat this*—and gently closed the folder. He was satisfied he'd done his job but also felt let down: Arthur wasn't quite as unusual as he had thought. Dejected, disappointed, he was like any number of people Ben had interviewed. In all too familiar ways, like Ben himself.

When he looked up, the lower half of Arthur's face was moving, as if he were sucking candies. Then he spread his hands over his face: he was crying. The sounds he made were like the grunts of somebody being punched.

Ben felt the urge to put a hand on his shoulder or offer a Kleenex, but just sat quietly and waited for him to stop. Cry for her and everyone else on the waiting list, he was thinking. Cry for the team, for you and me. We all deserve a few tears.

Arthur drew a handkerchief from his pocket and blew his nose. When he was composed again he asked, "Are we done here?"

There were no other questions. It was time for Ben's closing remarks. He steepled his hands, then pushed his fingers up under his chin and spoke in a practised voice.

"Your generous gift—your compassionate offer—is still an impressive one. Mrs. Stanley's final decision was a blow but doesn't diminish the value of your proposal."

Despite the Honest Abe delivery, Arthur seemed unconvinced. He hunched forward and said, "But tell me, Dr. Wasserman, what good is a gift that wasn't accepted? For all my trouble, what was gained?"

What indeed? Exactly. Nothing was solved, no one saved. Not much to show for everybody's efforts. A waste of resources, if you looked at it like that. A useless expenditure of energy on the team's part, Arthur's, and his own—but none of this could be disclosed.

Ben stared back mutely, wanting nothing more than to sink into his chair and sleep. Instead, he forced himself alert by focusing on Arthur's tie. It was shockingly loud and its geometric pattern clashed with his striped shirt. He switched his gaze to Arthur's glaringly white tennis shoes, which only made his eyes hurt.

At last he spoke up. "This has been a difficult experience for you, and I want you to know that I'm still here to help you.

If anything comes up that you'd like us to talk about, say, in a week or two, feel free to call me." He stood up. "I'm sorry things didn't work out the way you wanted."

Arthur rose and zipped his sweater. "I'm sorry too . . . but thank you for all you've done. I know you did as much as you could. When I said those things about Carol and her doctors, I wasn't including you."

Ben was surprised at how glad he was to hear that. His heart rose in his breast as he reached over the table to shake Arthur Rae's hand.

But then he wouldn't let go. He held Arthur's fingers, pressing the bird-like bones as he peered at him, and the man silently met his look. Ben's chest seemed to swell with a breath blown into him, and he felt a kind of spreading-out—a stretching of his senses—so that he was aware of every vein and joint of Arthur's hand. Every line and pore of his skin. Every surface in the office. Every room in the hospital, and spaces beyond it.

The moment ended abruptly.

Ben shoved his hands into his pockets and drew back. While Arthur pulled on his coat, he busied himself at the table. He turned to file notes in a drawer, and when he heard the man leave he sat on the edge of his desk, his hands and feet tingling. His thoughts floated away, away, as out of reach as helium balloons set free, until his mind was empty.

Minutes passed, though Ben wasn't sure how many. Eventually he got his jacket and went out, locking the door behind him. He passed other offices, walked through the waiting room and along a wide corridor, then turned left. He took an elevator down to the lobby, where he moved through a set of revolving doors. Turning onto the street that bordered the hospital, he sideswiped a man who was leaning against the building, drinking a coffee.

"Sorry, didn't see you," he said to a splash on the sidewalk. Glancing up, Ben was startled to recognize Arthur Rae. He gawked at him as though he'd bumped into a stranger.

"Are you all right?"

"No damage." Arthur brushed a spot on his coat.

He forced a smile—"That's good"—and waved as he turned to go, but when he started walking again Arthur was at his side. He stopped, shuffling in place, and struggled with what to do next. They'd already said goodbye and shaken hands in his office. *Well then*, he could say, and scoot across the street . . .

While he weighed his possibilities, Arthur studied him up close, eyes pinched as if he were seeing something painful in Ben's face. Then he said, "I'm not going straight to my daughter's but out for a drink first. Maybe you'd like to join me?"

"No!" His voice was almost shrill. Hunching his shoulders, Ben stared at his feet and the gum-stained sidewalk. "It's just— not a good idea."

"I don't often get a chance to talk about poetry. That's why I asked. I didn't mean to alarm you."

Ben remembered the poem Arthur had read to him at the Eagle and longing, like a chilly wind, blew right through him.

An innocent drink, a quick chat. Why was that a big deal?

Idiot! You lonely fool. Don't even think it!

He thought of them standing on a bridge, peering into a river, and knew that if he jumped off Arthur would try to save him. And if he didn't jump he could stay there with this man, drawing strength from his nearness, unsure of what was going to happen next, but unafraid. He heard again, *you do not move*, and imagined them like that: shoulder to shoulder, perfectly still.

Yes, lonely and foolish.

"One drink," Ben said, and added for good measure, "You know that if we do this I won't be able to see you again in my office—professionally speaking—though of course if you wanted to meet with someone else I could easily arrange it."

"I thought we were finished with all that."

"Just so you understand."

Arthur suggested they go to The Bald Eagle again, which only seemed right.

They agreed to take Ben's car and headed toward the hospital lot, arms swinging, in step. Anyone seeing them would take them for a couple of friends and not give it another thought. He didn't have enough friends, he thought as they walked along. Only Mel, who didn't count because they were related, and two or three overloaded doctors he worked with and saw socially now and then.

Just the same, he glanced over his shoulder a few times to make sure no one from the hospital was watching. He didn't see anyone he recognized on the street. And not a single person he knew, aside from his brother, ever drank at the Eagle.

A low-risk situation, Ben reassured himself. Strictly between the two of them.

And really, when you considered it calmly, now that their professional relationship was over, why shouldn't they have a drink? Why shouldn't two men with an interest in poetry and metaphysical ideas sit in a bar and talk? Too much of Ben's life was literal and matter-of-fact. The heart, he thought, was more than a pump beating in someone's chest!

When they got to the parking lot, Ben unlocked his car and dropped into the driver's seat, Arthur beside him. With a final peek in the rear-view mirror, he swerved out of the lot and drove in stop-and-go bursts in rush-hour traffic. Finally he pulled into a spot behind the Eagle, and they got out and went inside.

To his relief the place was as empty as always, and they chose the same corner table where they'd sat last time. Ben ordered drinks at the bar, and if the silent bartender remembered him she didn't let on.

Back at the table, he couldn't think of how to get the conversation going and played awkwardly with his beer. Arthur was quiet too, which surprised him. Didn't he want to talk poetics? Wasn't that why they were here? Ben slid down in his seat, knees jutting out like those of a schoolboy waiting for the three o'clock bell.

Minutes later, he made a start. "I guess you'll be staying at your daughter's again."

"I leave for Cobourg tomorrow."

"Do you like living there?"

"We love our house and gardens."

Arthur swirled Scotch in his glass and Ben drank some beer, counting the seconds as he wondered what to say next. It was like they were on a date or something—meaningless chatter and uncomfortable silences. Like the first time he'd spotted Renata in the hospital caf and stared at her cleavage till her supervisor, Gord White, introduced his intern . . . and then he asked about her job and other dumb questions and nodded like a woodpecker at her replies. When Gord finally left them alone, he couldn't think of anything but *Seen any good movies lately?*

Luckily she'd just seen a Fellini retrospective and the conversation took off. Fellini, God bless him, saved the day.

So now he asked about movies, but Arthur only shook his head. "Don't go out much," he said.

What more could Ben say to someone who was neither a friend nor his patient? He knocked back his beer and narrowed his eyes at Arthur, willing him to say something smart and arresting, but the man only smiled back, one eyebrow raised, and Ben was sorry not to have shaken free of him when he had the chance.

The bartender opened a window close to their table and dusty air pushed in, warm and heavy, stirring the hair on Ben's wrists. He wanted to be in his car, driving home with the windows down.

"April already," Arthur said. "I'll be in my garden soon."

"Is that one of your hobbies?"

"I like growing vegetables. Beans, tomatoes, that sort of thing."

Ben nodded politely, though he found the topic nearly as boring as the weather and was already planning his escape.

"But my favourite plant is garlic. *Allium sativum.*"

"To ward off vampires?"

Arthur laughed at Ben's joke. "Keeps away mosquitoes too. It's quite an amazing plant—an antibiotic and anticoagulant, among other things."

Ben became more alert. The fifties were perilous years and health matters concerned him. Already his cholesterol level and blood pressure were rising, and this winter he'd caught a flu and more colds than usual.

"I've heard that it's good for you."

"Strengthens the immune system."

"Lowers your blood pressure?"

"And cholesterol," he agreed.

"Is it hard to grow?" Ben asked. He was thinking of a square of dirt behind their townhouse where Renata once unsuccessfully tried to grow roses. No reason he couldn't add fertilizer to the soil and throw in a few cloves.

"It's pretty straightforward. You plant in November and the shoots come up in early spring. We snip the scapes in June and harvest mid-July."

"How much of it do you grow?"

"Softnecks and hardnecks in twelve rows a foot apart, twenty-five cloves to a row."

He did the math: three hundred bulbs. Too big a project for a backyard enthusiast. Ben's attention shrank again. The conversation wasn't going anywhere interesting. As soon as he found an opening, he'd mutter an excuse and leave.

But Arthur was going strong now. "You must be wondering what I do with so many bulbs."

He wasn't.

"We use some in cooking, but give away a lot too. My daughter's 'Chicken with 40 Cloves of Garlic' is delicious."

"Nice hobby," Ben said. He looked at his watch and pushed back his chair.

"It brings you close to nature and teaches you synergy. It teaches you to honour the mystery of all that grows."

Synergy was just the sort of word to give Ben pause. He moved up to the table again. Maybe they were going to have a meaningful talk after all.

"What about you?" said Arthur. "What do you do to relax?"

"Me? No time for that."

"Not even with your wife?"

"She's as busy as I am. By the end of the day we're too bushed to even cook a proper meal."

"Doesn't your poetry give you pleasure?"

"Sometimes," he allowed, "when I'm not in a hurry. When there's actually time to sit and think."

"What do you write about?"

"Oh, the usual," Ben said. "Love, hate, life, death—what everybody writes about."

"You must have a great deal of material to draw on, given your profession."

"I don't write about medical stuff. I need to get away from that, all those dying people."

Arthur peered at the unpainted walls and had a long drink, and Ben imagined he was thinking of Carol Stanley.

"Though sometimes they truly inspire me," he added.

Arthur recovered. "Have you published anything?"

"A few poems here and there. Not enough for a book."

"But someday you might—"

"My stuff isn't that good."

"Maybe you're not the best judge. Let me hear something now. You must know your work by heart."

Say something out loud? It was one thing to mail a poem to a little-read journal, another to recite before an actual listener.

He stared at the bars, blocks and circles of Arthur's tie, which appeared to be moving. What if he thought Ben was an amateur, a dilettante? What if he laughed outright, like Iris had in his office?

Stalling, he reached for Arthur's glass—"More Scotch?"— but the man said no.

"Well, I need a refill." He went to the bar and bought a draft. Not for the first time, the bartender frowned at him for no apparent reason as she passed him a full mug. Maybe even she thought he was untalented and ought to keep his poems to himself.

When he came back, Arthur was smiling expectantly, his hands folded on the table.

Ben hung his head. "I've never read any of my work out loud before."

"Not even to your wife?"

"I don't want to depress her."

"You think they're depressing?"

"Maybe not the love poems."

"Say one of those, then."

Ben's face grew warm, and he raised his mug to hide his cheeks.

"Don't be embarrassed. We're just having a drink together, talking about poetry. If you don't want to do this, we'll move on to something else."

But he did want to do this: be a poet, read aloud. Something short, he bargained with himself. Just a few lines. Three or four dozen words said to a one-man audience in a near-empty bar. Surely he could manage that!

Arthur's gaze was bright and steady, and his hands still. He looked both keen and patient at the same time.

"Just one," Ben said. "It's called 'Love in August.'" He gulped beer, dried his lips with his fingers and began.

"'The hooks are pitiless in the trunks / of maples with cringing leaves; / the cloth strains beneath its double burden and forgets to breathe. / Grass wilts, the lake recedes, but we are too enwrapped to move: / Nothing is as heavy and selfish as hammock love.'"

Arthur cleared his throat, but Ben broke in before he could speak. "I wrote that years ago. My work's much better now."

"I like it. I really do."

"You like it?" he repeated. His face and neck were burning.

"Read it to your wife. She'll be crazy about it."

"You don't know Renata. She'll find something wrong and want to correct it."

"At least you'll have tried," said Arthur.

"Tried what?"

"To reach her."

His eyes were leaking. Ben got up, excused himself and hurried down the corridor that led to the washroom; was in and out quickly.

Heading back with dried eyes, he was moved to call Renata, so he leaned against a wall and pulled his cell from his pocket. As he punched in the numbers, he was seeing her in the hammock that day at the cottage, feeling her summer-fresh body in his grateful arms.

She answered on the second ring. "Where are you?"

"Having a drink. I'll be home shortly."

"I've been waiting and waiting! I was just going to call you. The samosas I picked up are stone-cold."

"I was thinking about our time at the cottage . . . thinking about you."

"You're at The Bald Eagle, right? Why don't I join you? I can use a drink tonight."

"No!" He didn't want Renata bumping into Arthur. "No"—more softly now—"I've already had enough."

"I'll come drive you home."

"I'm not drunk, just tired."

"I think you should sit tight and wait for me to get there." She paused, then drew a loud breath. "Maybe I can finally meet whoever it is you're drinking with."

"Don't be silly. I'm on my way."

He hung up before she could form another sentence and fell back against the wall. The good feeling was gone now. She'd ruined his evening in seconds flat—and all because he was running late. Because she didn't trust him. And now his harmless secret had become problematic. He returned to the table to say he was leaving.

Arthur pointed at his mug. "Aren't you going to finish your beer?"

"I have to go home now." He took a giant step back, flinging his arm toward the door.

"I wonder if we'll meet again."

"Don't know." Ben shrugged, moving again in the direction of the exit. Stay cool, he told himself. Even at warp speed, it would take Renata fifteen or twenty minutes to get here.

"If you come to Cobourg sometime—late May, for instance, when everything is blooming—my garlic will be several inches tall and you can have a look."

"Come see your garden?"

"I'll be at my daughter's the last Friday of the month, so we could even take the train together Saturday morning."

Renata wouldn't like it and they'd wind up arguing.

But why did he have to share every part of his life with her? What was wrong with riding a train and going to the country without her, for a change, to watch things flower and grow? What was wrong with whimsy?

Arthur wrote his number on a napkin and gave it to him. "Think about it and let me know."

Ben smiled at the curious thought of travelling to Cobourg to stand in a green field of three hundred garlic plants reaching for the spring sky. He had no idea where to steer his life next, and Arthur's garden seemed as good a destination as any.

CHAPTER 13

They were sitting across from each other in the living room, feet up on the old trunk that served as a coffee table, relaxing with books and glasses of wine. A window was open and the room smelled pleasingly of a neighbour's chicken dinner. He was reading a chapbook by a little-known poet, and Renata was partway through a biography of jazz singer Sarah Vaughan.

This is what they did best, Ben paused to reflect after studying a tender poem about a pair of lovers: sit together in a room or elsewhere—the place didn't matter as much as the fact that they weren't conversing—each absorbed in private thoughts, yet conscious of the other; aware that something larger was going on between them, a comfortable connection as simple and true as love.

And that was enough, he thought. More than enough. Times like these, he considered himself a lucky man.

If only he didn't have Arthur on his mind.

Renata put her book down and picked up her wineglass. "This is nice, isn't it. Just sitting here like this."

"I was thinking the same thing."

"Remember our Cuba trip the winter before last? Drinking mojitos in our tiny hotel room, reading maps and *Lonely Planet*; cooking smells from the dining room . . ." Smiling, she looked out the window. "I'm reminded of that now."

"We had a great time there."

"Wouldn't you like to take another trip together? A place where we can rest and unwind?"

"Nothing wrong with staying home," he said, glancing around.

"This is fine too, but a change of scenery would do us good."

"I can't get a week off anytime soon."

"It doesn't have to be a week. Even just a weekend."

"Sure, we'll talk about it. But right now it's late and I'm hungry"—he crossed the room and helped her off the sofa—"so let's have supper."

Tonight it was kimchee and Korean barbecue, microwave-heated again, from the takeout Goody Grill. The wine was making him sleepy and dull, and though the ribs on his plate smelled good, Ben could hardly taste them. Renata, on the other hand, ate with gusto, using her fingers and disposable chopsticks and now, between bites, was telling him about a trip with one of her phobics.

Ben sat up, alert again, when he heard her say, "We got as far as Cobourg."

Here was the perfect chance to mention his plan to visit Arthur tomorrow—*Speaking of Cobourg*—which he still hadn't brought up. He'd have to use the right words and right tone of voice . . . but no matter how he delivered the news, she wasn't going to like it.

I hardly see you all week and then you're gone on Saturday? is what she would probably say—instead of encouraging him to be more adventurous and make new friends. Instead of understanding his need to spend the day with a man who read poetry, rather than pushing a cart in a superstore.

Sometimes, Ben, it's like you're not my husband at all.

Said with a sigh, no doubt. And he would be pained to know he'd let her down once more in some indefinite way having to do with what she called his "self-absorption." Yet again he'd feel like the well-meaning but self-absorbed, sadly inadequate partner of a young wife.

But despite his failings, he still believed Renata respected his rectitude and professional expertise. So how could he confess he'd befriended a man he had interviewed more than once—an almost patient, as it were—and watch with shrunken eyes as her face collapsed anew with shock and disappointment?

You want to spend time at the home of a patient?

He's not exactly a patient.

Then what exactly is *he?*

Disappointment, disapproval, disillusion. How much would she tolerate before giving up on him and shopping for someone who could make her happier?

He thought himself a decent guy who liked doing the right thing, especially where his wife was concerned, but in this case revealing the unabridged truth would threaten their relationship. Even so . . . he had to give her something.

Briefly he considered spinning a whopper—a bioethics conference in Niagara Falls or an urgent consultation in Timbuktu—but she could easily check that out. One call or e-mail to a colleague and the jig was up, his guile revealed, his marriage strained. And for what? he had to ask. A day with a gardener who could turn out to be as unremarkable as toothpaste?

No, for the right to do an innocent, spontaneous thing for his own fun, even if it wound up being a mistake.

Shutting his eyes, he acknowledged his stubbornness, his reckless unwillingness to come clean and face the music. Renata would probably judge him as cowardly . . . but wasn't he merely expressing the instinct for self-protection? Didn't that deserve consideration and regard too?

And so he decided that revealing *part* of the truth would be best all around. Better to be guilty of the sin of omission than an outright lie.

"You're not listening," Renata said.

He opened his eyes, took a long breath and began. "There's something on my mind . . . that I want to say," he edged forward. "I won't be home tomorrow . . ."

She stopped chewing. "Not home?"

". . . and don't expect to be back till suppertime."

Putting down her chopsticks, she swallowed what was in her mouth and picked up a napkin. Slowly she cleaned her lips and wiped her greasy fingers one by one till the silence made his gut hurt.

"Really?" she said at last. "And here I was thinking we could take a trip this weekend, maybe drive to the country and spend the night in a B & B."

"How about a nice dinner out Saturday evening?"

She sniffed at him, noncommittal.

He prodded the red-orange lump of kimchee on his plate, and when he raised it to his mouth with the chopsticks it slipped through, wetting and staining his shirt. Quickly he picked it off, jumped up to dab at the spot with cold water and sat back down, feeling her eyes on him the whole time.

"I thought it would be good to spend time together out of town, like I was saying earlier."

He watched without speaking as she lined up scattered grains of rice on the table and imagined she was seeing the two of them on a country road, striding parallel into the sunset. But her knitted brow and turned-down mouth when she looked up denied such a fantasy.

"The weather will be perfect tomorrow for a picnic."

He was feeling worse by the second now, more and more certain that no matter what he said there'd be tears and accusations.

"But I guess whatever you're doing is more important than spending the day with me."

"Don't be like that," he said.

"You might have told me sooner you had plans for the weekend. Didn't you think I'd want to know?"

He pinched the bridge of his nose. "I only decided yesterday."

"Decided what?"

"To visit someone I know who lives in Cobourg."

"*You're* going to Cobourg?"

"Tomorrow morning, by train."

"No one's going with you?"

"I'm going alone."

He wiped his forehead with his hand. His answers were making him sweat, the way one small fib led to another: an accumulation of untruths he'd soon lose track of.

But if he'd said he and Arthur were travelling together, she might have offered to drive him to the station and meet his friend—and Arthur mustn't chat with her, not now or ever. A man like that wouldn't lie. *We met in his office*, he would say. *I wanted to donate a kidney to my neighbour* . . . And Ben wouldn't ask him to. What would a man like that think if he learned that Ben had deceived his wife?

"You're spending the day there?"

He nodded. "That's right." In fact, it would be a relief to go without her and not have to worry about Renata's reaction to the Raes or what they might think of her. Nothing to distract him from the pleasure of their company.

"So how do you happen to know someone from Cobourg?"

"The guy was in town and we met at the Eagle."

"The guy?" She slit her eyes at him. "That doesn't sound like you. You're not very sociable."

"He's interested in poetry. That's the connection."

A man with a poet's soul. *A man like me*, he thought, and all at once his blood was beating hard in his temples. Ben was a poet, goddamnit! and poets had to feed their souls with singular encounters. Wasn't he entitled to his own friends and experiences? Allowed to be a free spirit, at least on his days off? If he was drawn to someone who interested or attracted him—not in a sexual way, but something subtler, more refined—wasn't that reason enough to follow his impulse?

"Does he have a name?"

"Arthur."

"A last name?"

"I forget. You know how I am about names."

"You must know his address."

"He's picking me up at the station"—widening his eyes into clear, still puddles—"so actually I don't."

"What about a phone number?"

"I wrote it down somewhere . . . but just call my cell if anything comes up."

"You don't want to give me your friend's number, do you."

He sat taller in his chair. "I don't want you embarrassing me by phoning him to verify my story."

"I wouldn't!" she huffed.

"It hurts me to hear how suspicious you get when my plans don't include you. Like the time you phoned Libby to check on me—"

"And you *weren't* out drinking with Mel."

"I don't have to account for every second I'm not with you. We agreed that I'd call you when I was running late, and the next time I was I did, just like I said I would. End of story!"

Renata fell silent, her eyes flashing, and Ben said quickly, "I want to visit a new friend, a man who loves poetry. Why is that a problem? He's way more interesting than your colleague, What's-his-name, and his boring wife we had dinner with last week."

"My friends aren't boring."

"That old windbag, Elmer Fudd—"

"Helmut Flood."

"—and his anorexic wife who spent five days in Paris and won't shut up about it. I never want to see *them* again."

"Stop it!" She pressed the heels of her hands into her eyes. "We were talking about the weekend."

He paused to reorder his thoughts. "Look, I had no idea you wanted to get away, so I made plans yesterday and don't want to change them. Why can't we go to a B & B next weekend? I'd be happy to do that."

"I don't want you to change your plans. I just want to know the truth about your friend in Cobourg."

"I'm not having an affair, if that's what you're thinking."

"I don't know what to think." Her eyes welled up and she wiped them with her fingers. "Something's wrong with your story, but I don't know what."

"Wrong? What are you saying? I'm not doing anything *wrong*. I'm not sleeping with Fudd's wife or drinking my life away, neglecting the kids we don't have—!"

"*What?*"

He shook his head clear. "No, I didn't mean that. I shouldn't have said that."

She swatted her plate off the table. Balls of rice, bubbles of grease and wormy threads of pickled cabbage flew in all directions, landing on the floor with a splat, and the plate shattered.

His ears were burning. Goddamnit! Gone too far this time and needlessly hurt her. He had to stop mentioning kids. What the hell was wrong with him?

She glanced at the muck on the floor, then trained her eyes on him. "You can go to hell, Ben."

Didn't even raise her voice, which, given the content of the message, took him aback. She seemed implacable, her mind made up as she scraped back her chair and stormed out.

He looked down at the broken plate, the shiny pieces smeared with food; at the crap all over the hardwood. Everything was a mess now. The best thing to do, he figured, was stay out of sight a few days and hope she'd get over this. For starters he'd wake up early tomorrow and try not to run into Renata on his way out.

And maybe when she calmed down he'd say he was sorry and tell her the uncut story of Arthur Rae.

———

Saturday morning Ben bought his ticket in Union Station and found that Arthur was already waiting in line at the boarding gate. He caught up to him, shook his hand and slapped down his shoulder bag. He'd brought a sweater and extra socks, the weekend paper, and a book of poems to read on the train and talk about if there was time.

Arthur, dressed in a stretched-out pullover, shirt and tie, carried a sack of groceries. A hockey bag at his feet bulged as if it were crammed full of melons and grapefruits. As the line bunched forward he explained that they'd be boarding soon, shifted his bags, and said nothing more. Nervous to be standing here with him, Ben supposed, or edgy around trains.

Ben felt tense too. Staring ahead at the dreadlocks of a pair of teens leaning into each other, he was having second thoughts. Instead of driving to the country with Renata, he was travelling with someone he hardly knew to a town he didn't care about to see sprouting garlic. He drew back his shoulders as if the guy behind him were tugging his shirt and breathing into his ear that it wasn't too late to turn back.

But then the lineup started to move. Reflexively he followed the people in front, as the people behind followed him. At least they'd be riding along Lake Ontario, he thought as he shuffled ahead. He always liked seeing the lake, the blue, hopeful spread of it on a clear day.

An escalator took them to the loading platform, where he climbed up after Arthur into the last car. They shoved their jackets and heavy gear into an overhead bin and sat down on the lake side, Ben in the window seat, as Arthur suggested, so he could have a good view. In the aisle seat, Arthur drew a book from among his groceries and spread it on his lap as the train pulled out of the station. A poetry anthology. He soon was absorbed in reading the index.

Ben let him be and looked out the window, where everything was green and blooming in the May sun. After a while of
silence, he shook open his paper, offered a section to Arthur,
who passed in favour of his book, and crammed the rest of it
into a pouch on the seat-back facing him. A headline in caps
read WHERE ARE WE GOING?—and he wondered as much
about himself. What was he doing here? What had made him
get on board, and what did he hope to learn from the man sitting next to him?

"So why am I going to Cobourg?" he said out loud, then
chuckled to show he wasn't altogether serious.

Arthur put his book face down on his knees and considered the question. "Roethke here would say we learn by going
where we have to go."

Ben closed his paper. "I know that poem, 'The Waking.'"

"I never tire of reading it."

"Is that what you live by?"

He laced his fingers behind his head. "I wanted to be a
teacher but hired on to the railroad at age twenty-two because
my dad told me to. He was a trainman, and his father before
him, so I guess you could say it was the family business."

Ben cringed to imagine a life spent selling component
parts. "I was supposed to join the family business too, but my
mother wouldn't have it, so I got to go to med school."

"A life can go in any number of ways," said Arthur. "Turns
out I learned a lot by not getting everything I thought I wanted."
He dropped his hands onto his lap and squirmed back against
his seat as if trying to get at an itch between his shoulder blades.

"I liked being an engineer . . . and try not to think about what might have been."

Something about his body language caught Ben's attention. "I get the impression that you don't like looking back."

"That's more your field than mine," said Arthur.

"Maybe we should've talked more about your childhood during one of our interviews."

"What else do you need to know?"

"I'm not sure," said Ben.

"My dad was a conductor and my mom stayed home and did the best she could with four kids, just like I told you."

"I thought there were three of you."

"My younger brother died." He twisted again in his seat, and Ben took note of this. "Mostly my dad was away, my mother run off her feet. I hardly knew my parents."

"Doesn't that bother you?"

"Both of them are long dead," he said. "I don't dwell on it."

Something cold moved in him, and Ben asked, "Did you feel ignored?" And so became a man willing to go to extreme lengths to get attention. Willing to rip an organ from his body and give it away.

"Every child wants more of his parents' time, but eventually you figure out it's not going to happen. You learn how they operate and try not to take it to heart."

"So you think they were good parents?"

"Okay for me." He paused. "Maybe not for my brother."

"The one who died?"

"Dad said he had to join the railroad like his brothers, but John wasn't strong enough—he was more like my mother—and wouldn't do it. My father didn't understand anything about him."

"What are you saying?"

"He threw himself in front of a train."

Killed by a *train*? Like the trucker and passenger who died in November because of the locomotive Arthur was driving? A corkscrew turned in Ben's gut. Queasy, he stared out the window again at a landscape of power lines and box-store shopping malls that only made him feel worse.

He should've told me right off.

"I didn't see it coming"—Arthur slumped in his seat—"and wasn't able to help him."

Couldn't help the people who died in the crash either. Couldn't help hitting the truck. What was it Arthur had said during their first interview? That he blew the whistle, rang the bell, put the brakes in emergency as soon as he saw the truck skid toward the crossing . . . *but you can't stop a train on a dime.*

Guilt compounded. Therefore, because of his overwhelming guilt, he became self-sacrificing, compelled to save the needy.

"Why didn't you say all this in my office?"

"You would've made assumptions about my wish to donate an organ that weren't true."

"How do you know they *aren't* true?"

"I know what I think and feel. My brother's death was terrible, but not enough to make me give a kidney to my neighbour."

"You didn't tell the whole story, only as much as you thought I should know." And you, Dr. Wasserman, should have asked more about his past from the get-go.

"I answered your questions honestly."

"But not as completely as you might have."

He didn't reply.

"The way I see it, you were being manipulative. What does your conscience say about that?"

"You would have found me competent and well informed in any case and allowed me to go on." Arthur crossed his arms and legs and tipped up his chin, his Adam's apple bulging in his neck like a knuckle.

Arthur's parents, brother John, the people who died in the crash and Carol Stanley: it was all a big jumble now. How much could he know in the end if the man either was unaware of hidden motives or wouldn't acknowledge them?

Abruptly he got to his feet and, bumping Arthur's knees, shoved past him into the aisle. Walking along the corridor, he stumbled as the car swayed, the weight of their conversation pressing his bowels, and finally locked himself in a washroom that stank of piss.

He should've done a better job interviewing Arthur, but at least the man's kidneys were still intact. Ben would have to settle for that.

The wringing in his gut increased as he sat down on the toilet and shut his eyes. In the dark behind his eyelids, Ben had a vision of the day he refused a career in component parts and Dad threw a dish at the wall, shouting that his first-born should follow in his footsteps. Mama waved her arms and said, *You're acting like a lunatic! He wants to be a doctor! A* doctor— *what's wrong with that?*—and though it was crucial to have her on his side, Ben had stood between them with his hands over his ears and his heart caving in.

That's how wretched he felt now.

And felt last night too, cleaning up the mess in the kitchen after Renata ran out. Picking up the cracked plate, seeing its innocent blue glaze and milk-white core, he'd remembered her as a young bride; remembered when the thought of her made him faint with lust; when she was more important to him than anything. Now, more times than not—yesterday, for instance— other things came first.

. . . whatever you're doing is more important than being with me.

How apt to be spending the day with a man who'd told him a story and withheld key facts, as Ben did with Renata. He was more upset with himself, though, than with his companion, because he thought deceiving his wife was a bigger wrong. And Arthur's intention in concealing information was to help Carol Stanley, whereas Ben was looking out for Number One.

Renata was probably awake by now, delicate in her sleepiness; puffy-eyed and tangle-haired, her nightgown hiked up. Deliberate as she punched pillows and smacked the sheet and blanket on his side of the bed smooth before stamping off to the bathroom. Glad now to have him out of the house and out of sight, he told himself.

The mystery of married life was how you got from happy to not-so-happy without even noticing.

He sat another minute, then stood up, fixed his pants and stabbed a red button with his finger to flush the bowl.

What did he know about anything?

Ben walked back to his seat. He climbed over Arthur, whose eyes were closed now, and slipped quietly into place without disturbing him. When a VIA attendant came by, pushing a rolling cart, he bought himself a coffee and returned to his paper. Horrible things were happening in Africa, the Middle East, the Caribbean, Asia—floods, drought, earthquakes, war and disease—and closer to home there were ongoing trade disputes, health-care crises and economic downturns. He read a while longer and then, sad and discouraged, put aside the paper and picked up the book he'd brought, a collection of Rumi poems he still hoped to discuss with Arthur at some point.

He read inattentively till his brainwaves flattened, and in a while, despite the caffeine in his veins, he dozed off.

Ben awoke to the static of an overhead speaker and the announcement in English and French that Cobourg was the next station. Arthur touched his shoulder and waited till he opened his eyes, then stood and moved into the aisle. Ben hitched up his shoulder bag and got in line behind him.

Iris was waiting on the platform when they got off. She was just as Ben remembered her: a tall woman, wide in the hips, with thick socks, Birkenstocks, and glasses on the end of her nose. She hugged Arthur and smoothed his hair. Turning to Ben, she pumped his hand vigorously and said she was glad to see him.

He followed them to the parking lot, where Iris unlocked their van. Arthur chose the passenger seat and Ben
sat in back as she swerved out of the lot and drove through
the downtown. She and Arthur spoke at once, interrupting
and completing each other's sentences as they pointed out
scenic delights: old homes, grassy parks, nineteenth-century
churches and the main street with buildings painted white,
yellow and green.

As they drove along a smaller road heading away from
town, Iris told him the story of an owl in their backyard and
about a neighbour's chicken farm. Arthur reminisced about a
plowing match last year, a bumper crop of strawberries and
mornings spent making jam . . . spinning a rural fantasy that
grabbed at Ben's heart. If only he and Renata led a simple life
in the country and were more in tune with nature!

"Almost there," said Iris.

Just ahead he could see Lake Ontario, glittery blue in
sunlight. Nostalgia sweetened him as he thought again of the
cottage—the one they hadn't rented this year because of other
commitments—and a pair of kayaks, cold beer, a crooked
dock, easy love. In his mind's eye he saw Renata jogging along
a rocky shore, elbows working and her shoes slapping the
wet stones as the lake breathed in and out around her narrow
ankles . . . and there he was chasing her, as if her bouncing
ponytail were the gold ring of a merry-go-round he needed to
snare to solve his life.

Arthur reached through the gap between the front seats
and shook his knee. He pointed at a small house with dark,

drawn curtains, a closed-in sun porch, tall shrubs out front and weeds growing up through the cracks in the pavement.

"That's Carol's bungalow."

Ben winced to think of her lying alone in there, but if Arthur felt uncomfortable as well he didn't show it.

"Remind me to trim her yews," he said to Iris.

Farther along the same street, they turned into a driveway and Ben saw where the Raes lived. Their two-storey home was close to what he'd pictured: white clapboards, gabled roofs, multi-paned windows and an open veranda. A graceful and serene place.

Everyone got out of the van. Iris went directly inside with the groceries, but Arthur wanted to show him around and started across the lawn, swinging his arms wide to take in everything—apple, pear and plum trees, berry bushes, flower beds. Ben hurried to keep up, his shoes making kissing sounds as they pulled away from the wet grass.

Beside the veranda was a square kitchen garden where lettuce, herbs, radishes and rhubarb were coming up. Arthur crouched, scooped up a handful of dirt and held it close to his nose. Spreading his fingers, he let the soil run through. "May is such a wonderful month," he declared. Reaching to one side, he lightly touched a rhubarb leaf. "If you look closely you can see something alive in it."

Ben saw a green leaf.

The man straightened, brushed his hands on his trousers and moved back. Pulling Ben's sleeve, he turned him in the direction of a bigger garden behind the house. "Come with me," he said, already walking away.

They stopped beside tilled ground lined with rows of garlic. That's it? Ben thought. *This is what I came for?*

Arthur moved forward among the plants, opened his arms as if to embrace them and stood in a T shape, as still as a scarecrow. He stayed like that a long time, and it wouldn't have surprised Ben to see a flock of swallows perch on his branched arms.

Several feet behind him, Ben hunched his shoulders and didn't come closer. Was he expected to stay back or move up and join in? Standing in place, he shifted his weight. Yet even from a distance he could feel Arthur's pleasure, and that's what finally drew him into the garden.

Looking more closely, he saw that some of the garlic leaves resembled blades of grass, while others were thick and leathery. At the head of each row, a wooden stake with a white tag showed above the soil.

Arthur turned and lowered his arms. "That's where I write the names of everything I plant," he said, following Ben's gaze. "I grow different species, some from Europe and Mexico with cloves the size of a man's thumb."

He moved away from Ben and spoke to the plants themselves about his day in the city and his trip home. He complimented their healthy leaves and thanked them for growing.

Ben took a step back.

Arthur picked up a trowel and wandered unhurriedly among the carefully mulched rows. Heaping straw close to the bottom of several plants, he patted it around the stalks as if tucking them into bed, then brushed the tips with his fingers.

Farther along he stooped to pluck a few weeds, mumbling and clucking his tongue at a knot of stems.

"What are you saying?" Ben asked.

"I warn them before I pull"—glancing at him sidelong—"to give them a chance to prepare."

"You think they can hear you?"

He shrugged, looking down. "In one way or another."

Ben's shoulders lifted again. Arthur was turning out to be a different person than he'd imagined. Squinting, he looked past the man and his garlic and settled his gaze on a cedar hedge—an ordinary, neatly trimmed, solid, suburban hedge.

But then, although the air was still, he felt an odd sensation, like a breath blown across his hand. Hairs rose on his fingers, and he stared at them as though they were somebody else's. What happened next confused him. He sensed, or thought he did, a slight distortion in the atmosphere in the garden.

In that instant he might've turned and run back to the station—but his shoes seemed to be stuck in dirt and he couldn't move. Peering at the plants around him, he could swear that the young stalks, like an army of new recruits, stood straighter under his gaze.

Ben started trembling.

Minutes went by, though he couldn't say precisely how long he stood there. From the corner of his eye he noticed Iris watching. By the time she called them in for lunch he couldn't think straight anymore; his head felt heavy and swollen to pumpkin-size. By the time Arthur stretched out his arms like a diver, spoke again to the garlic and turned toward the house, Ben could no longer trust his eyes. It looked as if the green spears were so many dogs' tails, wagging goodbye.

Arthur touched his shoulder and steered him away. "Working with garlic," he said while they walked, "you have to pay attention to more than their physical needs, to more than just good soil, water and sun. My plants produce exceptional bulbs because I love them and want them to flourish."

Ben's legs were rubbery as he blundered alongside.

"Here we are," said Arthur when they got to the house. He put a hand on Ben's back, nudging him forward, and Ben tripped on the doorsill, landing woodenly inside.

Glancing around, he quieted a little. The place was as snug as a nest, with twig furniture, rag rugs, and textiles in earthy tones, the familiar colours of Renata's office he didn't especially like . . . but here they seemed just right. There were tall windows everywhere and sunshine patterned the walls. A hanging tapestry—something of Iris's, no doubt—done in muted shades and a swirly pattern of spirals, momentarily threatened his balance, and he looked away.

In the kitchen, wood was stacked by the Findlay Oval cookstove, and Iris herself was reading a book in a rocker by a window. When she heard them she got up, boiled water, filled a teapot and pulled three mugs from a warmer at the top of the stove. Arthur invited him to sit at the table, and Iris served tea with a platter of carrot sticks and egg salad sandwiches. Still wearing his jacket in case he decided to bolt, Ben dug in, thinking of what his mother always said before eating, that things looked better on a full stomach.

He had a broad view of the grounds through a French door, and each rectangular pane seemed to frame a magical scene. Lilac bushes with purple blooms, bird feeders, evergreens, thickets of wildflowers: everything surreal in the fullness of its colours and glassy tranquility. He felt caught in a dream where ordinary things were unaccountably strange and all that he'd learned in his life was suddenly useless.

Soon after lunch, while Arthur was cleaning up, Iris gave Ben a tour of the house. On the second floor, in what appeared to be a guest room, she pulled an album from a shelf and asked him to sit beside her on the daybed. Together they looked through pages of photos of the Raes' three children and a pair of grandkids, snapped at various ages, Ben nodding politely as he bit back his envy. When they were finished he felt tired. Peering at him, Iris suggested that he have a nap. Without objecting, he stretched out on the bed as she put the album back in place and slipped away, closing the door.

Ben awoke a while later, unsure at first of where he was. He stumbled downstairs and into the kitchen, where Iris and Arthur and a man wearing a plaid shirt, Wellingtons and an eye patch were sitting around the table, chatting about earwigs, beetles and other insects. The stranger had his sleeves pushed up, showing freckled arms and blue-veined hands, and was absent-mindedly stroking a chestnut-coloured dog.

They stopped talking when Ben approached. "I'm sorry," he addressed the Raes. "I don't know what's wrong with me, falling asleep like that, twice in one day . . . Maybe I'm coming down with something."

"No need to apologize. A busy man like you is probably sleep-deprived," Iris said, "and should rest whenever he can."

Arthur pulled out a chair for him, and he sat next to the stranger. "This is Ben," Arthur said. "Ben, say hello to George."

Ben muttered something and the man grinned back at him. His sinister eye patch reminded him of Halloween, a night he had shrunk from as a boy, reluctant to dress up and canvass the spooky, dark streets.

When Iris turned her attention back to George and asked about his health, the man started in about his wife's arthritis and unpaid medical bills, then lastly got around to his damaged cornea. His story made Ben think of a country and western song, and he wondered if the man's dog was going to roll over and die. Then the conversation switched to rafters and two-by-fours, plywood and siding. Because of his blind eye, George was having difficulty building a tool shed.

"I can help," said Arthur, and Ben sucked in his breath: he wants to give him a cornea! But when he continued "I'm good with a hammer," Ben understood his mistake.

"I'll stop by after I drop Ben at the station."

George's dog put his head on Iris's lap and she bent over, lifting his snout, so that they were practically eyeball to eyeball. "Rusty, I haven't seen you in ages," she said to the dog. "What have you been up to?"

"Chasing rabbits out of my garden," said George. "They're after the lettuce."

"George grows amazing vegetables," Arthur told Ben. "The rabbits can't get enough." He turned back to his neighbour: "Tell him your secret."

"Just this"—George laced his fingers and held them out—"that all living things are interconnected. We're part of one energy field and have to cooperate with each other, if you see what I mean."

Ben did not.

"Plants have the same biological charges we do. Like the pull of the moon and stars, a person's feelings affect them. A good attitude helps them grow."

Arthur nodded encouragement.

"If you're quiet in a garden, you can probably pick it up. Once you feel that life force you'll know what I'm talking about."

The fruits and vegetables Ben knew lay inert in supermarket bins, feeling nothing, and didn't care if you liked them or not. The man leaned closer to him, and Ben thought he caught the whiff of beer on his breath, which would go a long way toward explaining his spiel.

He shot a glance at Arthur, who was scratching the dog's back, and decided it was time to leave. Call a cab if he had to and catch the next train back. Home early, he'd tell Renata the man turned out to be some kind of weirdo and so he left as soon as possible. Sliding to the front of his chair, he was about to rise, but George beat him to it and was already standing.

"See you later," he said to Arthur. "Got to get back to my garden."

He shook hands all around, holding Ben's an extra beat and giving him a sly wink, as if to say there was no need to take all this seriously.

Arthur saw his neighbour out and came back chuckling. He passed around a plate of cookies, but Ben waved it away, saying he had to be going.

"You're not staying for dinner?" Iris seemed taken aback.

Ben checked his watch. "I'm sorry, but I told my wife . . ."

"We understand," said Arthur, raising a finger, "but let me show you one more thing." He scooted into the living room and put on an LP. It sounded classical but Ben heard the music only faintly, from far away, and thought there must be some sort of problem with the system.

"It's not for us," Iris said, "it's for the garlic. He tied a speaker to the porch."

Arthur came back to the kitchen. "They like Bach's violin sonatas," he explained, "and Ravi Shankar on the sitar."

He motioned to Ben, who waved goodbye to Iris and followed Arthur outside for a last look at the garden.

The music swelled as they approached, sounding liquidy in his ears. Ben entered the patch and stopped. It seemed that the garlic spears, already a couple of feet high, had grown a little taller and were turned toward the speaker as if it were a second sun.

"They can bend even more, depending on the music. They do well with Haydn and Beethoven, even jazz, but rock music stunts their growth." Bach played from the speaker as Ben watched and said nothing, his tongue thick in his mouth. Beside him,

Arthur reached out and spread his fingers, and Ben turned his eyes to that, as though he might slow his thoughts by staring at Arthur's hands. And then his gaze swept up, across the garlic beds and farther, to a slice of blue water just visible through the trees.

A breeze blew through him, and he smelled the fishiness of the lake, the loaminess of moist soil—smelled the air itself, which was fresh with buds and newness—and he exhaled a long breath he seemed to have been holding since he first got to Cobourg.

He rolled back and forth on his feet in time with the music.

A few minutes later, a feeling passed through him: a wave of something resonant—electromagnetic?—or, more poetically, a flapping of wings under his skin, along his arms and legs and in his solar plexus. There was tingling and pressure and urgent scratching at the back of his mouth that made him cough. He was suddenly alert, alive, to unknown sensations.

Arthur rubbed his hands together and glanced at Ben, his eyes bright.

"I felt something," Ben said.

"Good for you," he answered.

"A kind of tickle"—stroking his arms—"that made me want to laugh."

"Go ahead," said Arthur. "Laughter's good for the garden."

So Ben drew a full breath and uttered a big guffaw that came from down deep. When it was over he did it again, making an even louder one.

"No stopping you now," said Arthur, grinning himself. Then he swung toward the house and started to walk away.

Ben didn't follow. He stayed behind and breathed in the sweetness of the garden.

Sunlight warmed his nose, and beyond the rows of garlic a tent of leaves bowed and swayed, dropping shadows to the ground. Somewhere past the long trees, beyond the lake, beyond the hills . . . somewhere in the distance, he thought, was another place, a fabulous, harmonious world unlike this one. In that parallel dimension where other lives were happening, his own life was different too. In that place everything was hopeful and easy: there was his true life.

He planted his feet in the dirt, lifted his arms overhead; became light and quiet. Leaning into Bach as he sucked up the goodness of the earth through his heels, Ben stood still.

CHAPTER 14

When he walked in Saturday evening, Renata was gone. Rarely did Ben come home to an empty house, and his heart started racing.

He searched the rooms downstairs, then the ones upstairs, and checked the bedroom closet. When he saw her clothes hanging there, no empty hangers, he relaxed a little: she'd be back soon. She was out shopping, at a movie, having dinner with a friend—one of any number of benign possibilities.

He made himself a peanut butter sandwich on whole wheat and emptied a container of milk, past its best-before date, into a teacup. The milk was off but he drank it anyway, thinking with a squeezed throat of bygone days when Molly served him fresh milk and Oreo cookies after school.

If he'd known his wife wasn't going to be here when he got back, he would've gone to Molly's for a home-cooked meal—or had dinner with the Raes and taken a later train . . . and might've hung on to the special feeling he had there a little while longer. Hoping to keep his buoyant mood as long as possible, he hadn't phoned Renata to say he was on his way. Even so, his frame of mind had already changed by the time he reached the station. The rest of his day, he understood as Arthur said goodbye, was going to be a letdown.

He fixed a cup of decaf and carried it into the living room, where he stretched out on the sofa with his feet up on the arm. Having finished the last of the milk, he had to take his coffee black and, not liking it, gulped it down. Good or bad, it was part of his nightly ritual, one of the many rites he performed to induce sleep—like wearing blue pyjamas or reading a medical journal for a half-hour before bed. Unlike Renata, he didn't fall asleep and stay asleep with the ease of a child. One night, restlessly watching her in a deep sleep, he cradled her head in his arms and she didn't wake. Not even when he blew hair away from her pale face and kissed her smooth forehead.

Too distracted to read or write, he turned on the TV and clicked through the channels before settling on the news. Nothing good was happening anywhere in the world, which he'd already gleaned from reading the paper on the train, and a few minutes later he aimed the remote at the screen and switched to another station.

He caught the tail end of a nature show about frogs that made him long, unexpectedly, for Cobourg, and after that watched an old flick with Rita Hayworth looking incredibly hot. And still Renata wasn't home.

Why hadn't she phoned *him*, left a message, even a note? He could try her now on her cell . . . but it hardly seemed right after chewing her out last night about not trusting him and checking on him when he did things without her. It wouldn't escape her that he was asking *her* to account for her time, and she wouldn't welcome his call.

He reached for the mobile and dialed the number anyway.

Renata didn't pick up, which heightened his distress, and he didn't leave a message because she'd know anyway from caller ID that he was trying to get her. He had said he'd be here at suppertime, hoping she'd agree to a make-up dinner out, and never dreamed he'd wind up spending tonight alone, worrying where she was, with nothing in the fridge but sour milk, a single egg and slices of old bread.

What if she'd gone out to buy food and been hit by a car? What if a deranged ex-patient had attacked her? Maybe she'd been mugged and was slumped in an alley, calling his name! Bad things happened all the time.

He ran upstairs, changed into old flannel pyjamas and brushed his teeth so hard he probably scratched the enamel. He even used the Waterpik—though normally, despite the sorry state of his gums, he ignored it—because its loud rattling muffled the noise in his head, and then he had to wipe the counter around the sink because he'd made everything wet. But only minutes had gone by. What else was there to do?

Ben clipped his toenails, which mostly he didn't do until they got so long they snared his socks, and then he snipped hair from his ears with a new electric gizmo he'd bought in a flush of shame because he never expected to be a geezer with wayward hairs.

Then he sat on the edge of the tub, banging his heels against the side. And still Renata wasn't there.

After that he got into bed with an out-of-date magazine and flipped through an article—"The Psychosocial Principles, Parameters, and Implications of Unrelated Living-donor Organ Transplantation"—which made his eyelids as heavy as paper-weights, and soon became drowsy.

A long time later, when he heard the soft click of a latch, he thought it was Rita Hayworth opening his bedroom door and sneaking into bed with him.

He sat up, gritty-eyed, the journal sliding off his chest, surprised that there was no one in a slinky gown beside him. Then he heard clanging and what sounded like a falling chair, so he got out of bed, checked the clock—almost three!—put on his slippers and went to greet Renata.

His worn slippers smacked the floor as he made his way downstairs in rumpled pyjamas. Entering the kitchen, he saw that her upper half, in an untucked scarlet blouse, was deep inside the fridge. A cup of tea was on the island, a stool fallen on its side. His eyes teared to see her safe, but what came out of his mouth was a growl.

"Whose bed have you been sleeping in, Goldilocks?"

She pulled out her head. "No milk. You didn't leave me a drop for tea." Then she turned to face him, hands on her hips. "But maybe you don't actually know how I take my tea. Maybe you don't know *anything!*"

"I know it's three in the morning."

"You'll have to find one of those 24/7 stores to get milk

for my tea, but that's good practice. High time you thought about somebody but yourself."

Her hair was frowzy, her eyes smudged with crescents of mascara under the lower lids, and she smelled of alcohol. A whimper sounded in his throat.

"Where have you been?" he said.

"*You* wanna know." She smirked. "You wanna know where *I've* been. That's rich."

"My wife's gone the whole night, I have a right to ask where."

She squinted at the kitchen clock, an ugly thing made to look like a blackboard with chalk numbers, the hands shaped like pointers, which Renata had bought at a yard sale despite his objections. "Only half a night," she said. "The sun hasn't risen."

The way she ran the words together was like mosquitoes buzzing—*sunhaznrizn*—and he felt stung.

She stepped around the fallen stool and hunched over the island, nodding at her teacup. "Almost cold . . . and you still haven't gone for milk."

"I'm not dressed."

"So *get* dressed." She kicked the stool for emphasis.

"Maybe you should pick that up."

She curled her lip at him. "Wanna see something?" Hiking up her skirt, she showed him a bump on the bare flesh of her left thigh.

He winced. Looked above her head. "How did that happen?"

"The stool." She pulled her skirt down.

"That's hard to believe."

"You don't have to believe me." She pushed away from the island. "I don't believe what you say either."

"What are you talking about?"

"Where *you* went today."

"You know I was in Cobourg."

"Right. With your *new friend*."

"So what part don't you believe?"

She pursed her mouth, defiant.

"I told you before, I'm not cheating. I really did spend the day in Cobourg with Arthur. As for you—"

"The stool, I told you. *Told you before.* You'll have to trust me on that one."

"All right, I will," he said, "because I have faith in you." He snorted indignantly. "Unlike you, of course, who never trusted me from the start—"

"Start of what?"

"Our marriage."

"I'm sure I did, back then." She shook her head in a wide arc. "But not so much recently."

"What's wrong with 'recently'?"

She met his look. "Everything."

"*Everything?*" He gaped at her.

"Don't you know how lonely I am?" She gave a single sob, then covered her mouth with her hand and waited a beat to regain her composure. "It's like you're not my husband—like I don't even have one. And," she said, grimacing, ". . . no baby to sweeten things." Quickly she looked down.

But he'd already seen it, in a flash of eye contact: her sorrow, discouragement—and blame . . . yes, that too. She was holding him responsible for all of the heartbreaking ways life had let her down. And even if she was only partly right . . . he was partly wrong. More wrongdoing and guilt.

As if on cue Renata said, "My heart's broken, Ben, into sharp little pieces."

They blinked at each other across the island. He didn't know what to say next. A bubble moved up his throat. If he opened his mouth just then, he feared he would start crying and never be able to stop.

Finally she wrinkled her nose at her cup of tea—"Well, if there's no milk, I'm not going to drink that"—leaned back, swung around and padded barefoot into the hall.

He followed at a distance. In the living room, he watched her collapse on the sofa and wriggle onto her side with her skirt bunched up and her legs so pale she reminded him of Snow White. He sat at the end of the couch and studied her bare toes, as skinny as matchsticks. She looked so cold and fragile that his heart pinged open, and he wanted to rub her feet in his hands. Wanted to put ice on that miserable lump on her thigh, no matter how she got it.

Everything's wrong, repeated in his head, but he shook it away. Renata was drunk and emotional. Exaggerating. Dramatizing. Didn't really mean that. Whatever was wrong could be fixed.

To warm her, he pulled a throw from the rocker and covered her legs. She startled as it brushed her skin, then kicked it away decisively, got to her feet and went upstairs.

Ben walked behind her and reached their bedroom door just as she closed it and latched it from inside. There was only a hook and eye on the door and he could've shouldered it open if he chose to, but didn't. Shut in his face like that, it made as strong a statement as if locked with a deadbolt.

He rapped lightly, calling her name, and when she didn't answer him, knocked harder, spoke loudly. "Renata? Are you all right?"

He jiggled the knob but the door held fast. When he flattened an ear against the wood, he heard her opening drawers, as well as his pounding pulse. He waited till he felt more composed before he spoke again. "Please open up, okay? I just want to talk to you."

And still no answer. He shoved against the door but there wasn't any give. She must've pushed a chair or something against it. "Look, I'm getting worried now. What's going on in there?"

The creaks and bangs grew louder. He turned his shoulder to the door and thumped it repeatedly. "Can't we discuss this? Given our training, we ought to be able to communicate openly." More or less, he didn't add.

He smacked his hand against the door until his palm was stinging. "I want to hear about your loneliness—and all that."

He heard the squeal and scrape of something moving across the floor and took a step back as the door swung open with a small puff of air. The curtains were drawn, the bedroom dim and grainy. In the doorway stood Renata, dressed in jeans and a baggy sweater, her eyelids hooded, her hair tied back except for some loose strands.

As she picked a hair from her cheek, he moved forward to kiss her, but she jerked back and put up her hand.

In her other hand was a suitcase.

"Where are you going?"

She stepped around him into the hall. "I'm leaving you."

"*Leaving* me?"

She walked to the staircase.

"You're drunk," he said. "Overwrought. This is no time to make a big decision like that."

"Not so drunk I can't hail a cab and get away from you." She started downstairs, bumping the suitcase behind her. "My life isn't here anymore," Renata called out. "My real life is somewhere else."

Ben ran to the head of the stairs and hung on to the newel as his legs gave way and he slid to his knees. "I don't understand you. Don't understand any of this. Can't we sit down and talk?"

She reached the bottom and jerked her head around to look up at him. "About what, our *marriage*?"

"Basically, nothing's wrong. Sometimes we get along and sometimes we don't. But you have this rosy—this idealized version of marriage in your head and think it's always supposed to be wonderful."

"Talk, talk, talk. You don't even know what's wrong, that's the problem."

"So tell me, I'm listening!" He swayed forward on his knees. "I love you, Renata. Don't go."

"Yeah," she said, "you probably do."

With that, she hooked a purse on her shoulder, opened the front door and stepped into what remained of the night, rolling her suitcase behind her.

He knelt at the top of the stairs for a long time, and when his legs began to ache, shuffled back to the bedroom.

Though it didn't seem possible, at some point he must've slept because, turning over, he was stunned to see the bed half empty and Renata gone. He stared at her pillow, at the furrowed sheets and blanket, at the dip in the mattress, and touched the cool, bare spots that should've been flesh-warm. His eyes clouded over as his memory returned in a rush, but Ben was too weak and pumped dry to shed tears. At last he edged out of bed, and in that motion understood how much he hurt all over.

How well did he know his wife, and how much did she know about him? he was thinking as he scuffled to the bathroom. What she didn't realize was how carelessly people knew each other in general. Married people most of all.

———

Now what? Renata thought as she stood at the curb. A headache was starting. She wasn't a good drinker—and at The Bald Eagle of all places! Nothing was more depressing than spending Saturday night in a rundown bar where the few male customers were too drunk and pathetic to even try to pick her up.

She yanked her suitcase down the street until she spotted a taxi, climbed in, and had the driver take her to the office.

With a swipe card she got into the building easily and up to the second floor. Arriving at her office door, she unlocked it, entered the unlit waiting room and banged into a table— another lump on her leg—before finding the light switch.

Inside the main room the window blind was pulled up, and from outside a yellow lamp shone a square of grainy light onto one of the office walls, enough for her to see by. She threw her purse on the sofa, put her suitcase on the desk and stood where she could see out. The leafy maple behind the glass looked eerily black against the artificially glowing street, and the muffled rush of passing cars was the loneliest sound ever.

The queasiness in her stomach was worse than the pain in her head. She urgently needed Gravol. Emptying her suit-case, she found the pills and swallowed them, and then fell onto the sofa and into a groggy sleep.

When she woke up hours later, thinking she was at home, she flopped over, expecting to slam into Ben's back, and instead rolled to the floor with a thud. Now she was fully awake, mouth dry and head crackling.

The bathroom was down the hall. She used the toilet, washed in the sink and downed a couple of Advil with luke-warm, metallic-tasting water straight from the tap. At home Ben had surely gone to the store by now to buy milk and was in the kitchen drinking coffee, possibly still mad, but just as possibly contrite, missing her badly. Either way, she hoped he was as miserable as she was.

Back in the office, she wondered where to go next. What perfect, solitary place had she been imagining, and what did she hope to find there? Clearly she needed a plan. Move into a hotel? Get an apartment? What was she supposed to decipher on her own that she couldn't get to the bottom of living with Ben?

Was her "real" life—the one more conducive to happiness—a solitary existence? A life in which, if she cried in bed while in the clutch of a nightmare, there'd be no one to embrace her? Would she be able to soothe herself . . . or pull a blanket over her head and lie motionless on her back, stuck by a blade of fear, the way she'd done when she was young and her mother paced the haunted rooms?

She would need to get a pet.

Renata shivered; hugged herself. Whatever she was suffering was best faced, cried over, thought about and examined in a familiar environment. What better place for that than her own house? Even though her husband hurt and angered her sometimes, she still felt safe there. Home was the safest place she knew.

Even though he might be—but probably wasn't—lying about his new friend.

She ought to phone at least and tell him she was all right, but that seemed more than she could do at the moment. She'd deal with it when her headache eased.

She spent most of the day on the sofa with her eyes shut and didn't get hungry till late afternoon. Waiting a while longer, she went out at five for a dinner of eggs and toast, took a walk around the block, returned to her office with a magazine from the waiting room and sat down in her swivel chair—Ben's practical birthday gift. There was no getting away from him.

She glanced at the bright cover without really seeing it and tossed the magazine face down onto a pile on her desk. What a gutless coward she was! Gone less than a day and already losing her nerve. Wanting to call home like a teenage runaway. No! she decided, abruptly pushing herself up and moving to the window, where she put her palms against the glass and blinked at the sun-struck tree.

If she ran home too soon, he'd never take her seriously. *She* wouldn't take herself seriously either. This way it would be undeniably clear that their marriage needed help; that Ben had to work harder at making her happy; that they should adopt a child once and for all or forget the whole business. This way he'd pay attention, look more carefully, see things as they are.

But if she stayed away too long, would he take her back? Her plan would come to nothing if she didn't have the option of returning home. If her only alternative was living alone with a dog or cat and a new set of problems.

And then she thought this too: that she could be happy any-where, with or without Ben, alone or not; that there were always choices. A confident, mature thought. The maple nodded approval.

Out of that instant of level-headedness, Renata decided it was better to compromise and find solutions in a long-term relationship—exactly what she usually counselled her clients.

She sat in her swivel chair again and played with the levers, adjusting the height, the tilt of the seat and back support, until she arrived at a middle-ground answer: to stay tonight and leave tomorrow, after her last appointment. Stella was arriving at ten, her first client of the day. Surely she could get through the night and pull herself together by then.

———

In the morning Stella didn't show.

She'd never missed a session before. Renata phoned her apartment at ten fifteen and again an hour later, but nobody picked up. She left a worried message asking her to call the office as soon as possible.

Her desk was covered with papers needing attention, but Renata wasn't in the mood. She'd already hidden her suitcase in the closet and didn't have another appointment till late afternoon . . . so why not take a walk? With that, she locked up, went down to the lobby and out.

The day was warm and brilliant, and she shielded her eyes as she looked at the maple stretching up to her office. Its leaves had already turned from glossy yellow-green to the darker shades of late May.

Stella's baby wasn't due till late June, she remembered. Any number of things could have made her miss her session.

She wandered the busy streets and finally walked into a café for a sandwich. Over tea, she used her cell to check the office phone, but there were no messages. Nothing on the cell either, although she'd been secretly wishing Ben to call.

As it happened, she had stopped in the neighbourhood where Stella lived. Once she left the café, it hardly took her out of her way to walk another few blocks and swing by her building.

And when she got there, it only seemed right to knock on her door and see if Stella was okay. If no one was home she'd return to the office and do some paperwork until her next client arrived.

The doorman wasn't around, so Renata went directly through the mirrored lobby to a bank of elevators and rode one to the third floor, not quite sure which apartment was Stella's. When nobody answered the first door she tried, she moved along the corridor and knocked on another one.

Lucy opened the door a crack and then, seeing who it was, opened it wider.

"Stella missed her appointment and she—d-didn't phone me," Renata stammered, "and I was in the area . . ."

"Come in." Lucy glanced behind to where her sister was rubbing her abdomen and walking a path on the rug. "Stella's in labour."

"Oh, but it's too soon!" Renata stepped around her and into the living room, going no farther than the edge of the carpet.

"Her contractions are close together. We're just getting ready to go to the hospital."

All at once Stella doubled over, groaning loudly, and Lucy ran up to her, locked an arm around her waist and told her to pant—"Like this"—exhaling small gusts of air.

Renata stared but didn't speak.

"Get her bag and sweater from the bedroom"—Lucy pointed—"and phone for a taxi. The number's on the fridge."

Puffing, Stella moved to the door, half draped on Lucy's arm. Renata made the phone call, grabbed her purse and Stella's things and ran after them, slamming the door.

She caught up to them in the hall just as an elevator stopped and opened. When they got on and the doors closed, Stella hugged her belly and seemed to be holding her breath. Lucy cupped her elbow, reminded her to breathe and repeated, "You can do it," until they reached the lobby.

The cab was already there by the time Stella scuffed out, and they helped her into the back seat. Lucy gave directions as she slid in next to her sister, and Renata sat up front holding Stella's things on her lap. Her hands were cold and she buried them in Stella's sweater. She didn't want to be on her way to Maternity with a woman in labour and planned to leave as soon as they arrived at the hospital.

When they pulled up to the main entrance, Lucy and Stella got out. Renata fished in her purse and opened her wallet to pay, but she only had twenties and the driver couldn't make change. Another cabbie got involved and it took time to sort out. When at last she turned to say goodbye, the other women had disappeared.

She pushed through revolving doors, hugging Stella's sweater and bag, but didn't see them in the hall. After a couple of wrong turns, she stopped to ask for directions and finally found her way to Maternity on the fifth floor. They weren't there either.

She followed a sign to LABOUR & DELIVERY and spoke to a nurse at the desk who said Stella was being assessed and urged her to wait in the lounge. And so, bundle in her arms, Renata entered a room with upholstered chairs and a loveseat, brightly painted kid-size tables and plastic seats, two humming snack machines, and a TV mounted on a wall, showing cartoons. Fingers of sunlight coming through the window blind seemed to be trying to snatch her away.

Erect on the edge of the loveseat, she told herself she clearly wasn't needed and could go now. Lucy was here and Stella was being well looked after. Lost in the great upheaval of contractions, she'd never miss Renata—and in any case, the last thing she wanted was to see a birth. Already her heart was beating fast and doing flip-flops.

As she got up to walk out, a nurse stopped in the doorway and said, "Dr. Moon?"

She held out the sweater and bag as if she were a courier who had to be on her way.

"You can take that in yourself. Stella's in the labour room and asked to see you."

Dragging her feet, she followed her to a room at the end of the hall where Stella, in a hospital gown, hair matted and knees raised, sat partway up in bed while Lucy fed her ice chips. The nurse spoke briefly and left.

"I brought your things"—Renata presented them—"and now I—"

"Don't go. It's happening fast." Stella cringed, fisted her hands and wailed at the top of her lungs as her belly heaved.

"I can't stay." But Renata's words were lost in the commotion.

Then, her legs suddenly loose, she stumbled back against a wall and shut her eyes. In the blackness under her lids she saw herself in bed too, feet in stirrups, with a doctor between her knees. She saw blood on her mother's gown and thought, *All dead!* as the sweater dropped, the bag dropped, her legs became liquid and she started slipping down the wall.

Immediately Lucy slid a chair under her, gave her water and asked if she should get the nurse. Barely hearing through clogged ears, Renata slowly shook her head.

Somewhere in the distance, Stella was calling for Grant, crying out his name till the sound of it popped open Renata's ears. Standing beside the bed, Lucy spoke calmly to her sister and rubbed her back.

Renata wanted to run away and tried to rise, but pushing down on her thighs she felt no sensation, her legs a pair of logs, and she dropped into her chair again. She couldn't close her eyes, wide open now and determined to see what was happening, and her tongue was uncontrollable too, making impossible sounds.

Lucy was murmuring, "Ssh now, everything's fine," to her or Stella or both of them—but everything *wasn't* fine. Didn't Lucy know that?

The nurse came and went and a doctor did the same: it was all happening full tilt. Hurried noises erupted in the corridor, and suddenly they were back to help deliver the baby. The walls shook with bellows that could've been Renata's for all she knew, and Stella was in a squat now, Lucy gripping one of her legs, and the nurse told Renata to grab hold of the other. But that was more than she could do.

She staggered out, made it to a washroom and threw up. Looking at herself in the mirror—her red-eyed, grey-skinned reflection—she almost wept. Then she went back to the lounge and fell onto the loveseat. Her mouth tasted awful, and every part of her felt sick.

She bought a ginger ale from the pop machine to settle her stomach, sipped it till she was steadier found her cell and daybook in her purse and cancelled her afternoon. Holding the phone in her shaky hand, she remembered Ben. The need to speak to him was strong, to talk herself dry about all that had happened—especially being here while her client had a baby— and she hoped he would listen and not speak. When she was done, she'd tell him she was on her way and leap out onto the street, into the softening afternoon.

Yes, she would do that.

But as she began pushing the numbers a family walked in, and she dropped her cell back in her purse. Two kids plunked down at two different tables, the dad sat on a chair, and the mom put her hand in a sack and fished for something. Moments later she passed out dinner rolls, offering one to Renata too, as if they were old friends.

Renata thanked her for the bun and put some of it in her mouth. Chewing the sweet bread made her feel better.

"Dr. Moon?"

The nurse was back, beckoning. Renata smiled at the family and followed.

She got no farther than the doorway of Stella's room. Inside, Lucy was bent low over the bed, gazing at a wrapped-up package in Stella's arms. When Stella turned to Renata, her face was as shiny and golden as taffy. Even from across the room, she felt the young mother's joy.

"Come see her," Stella said. "She's little but she's healthy."

Renata moved her legs forward and inched up closer as Stella lifted the baby. Looking down, she got a glimpse of black hair and a round face like a small rutabaga.

"Congratulations" was all she could think to say.

As the nurse approached the bed with a blood pressure cuff, Renata saw her chance and escaped into the hallway. Quickening her step, she arrived at the elevators, took one down and walked out of the hospital.

The street was busy and noisy. Dogs barked, squirrels chittered, drivers rattled by in trucks or wheeled past in sleek cars. People talking to their cells hurried along the sidewalk, and no one seemed to notice the dazed woman going by.

———

She got home after seven and went to the kitchen for something to eat. Ben was sitting on a stool, spooning cereal from a bowl. An open box was in front of him, as well as a container of milk and a bottle of juice. He might have been there all day, slowly working through breakfast, or hadn't had the energy to cook a hot supper.

He glanced at her when she came in and went back to his food.

"One of my clients had a baby, a preemie, and I was there

for the whole thing. I just got back from the hospital." She sat down beside him. "I think it was harder for me than for her, but I managed to stick it out."

He stared at his bowl and chewed, giving no indication he understood what she said or if he'd even heard her.

"I'm starving!" she sang as she got a bowl from the island, filled it with cereal, added milk. She matched his movements as she ate. In the tilt of their heads and focused expressions, in the rise and fall of their spoons, they were each other's reflection.

Perfectly in step, she thought, like newlyweds trying to become one person: the way they were when they married and she innocently believed she would find wholeness in Ben's arms. In fact, she'd been separate and lonely since childhood and might always feel that way . . . but bald truth was more than she could brave right now.

"I spent the night in my office," she told him as if he'd asked, "and missed you the entire time. Sorry I didn't call, I was so hungover, but I certainly meant to."

He made a noise somewhere between a groan and bleat, and she put down her spoon and reached for his left hand. His spoon dropped from his other hand but he didn't pull away, which she took as a good sign.

"Want to talk?"

He drew back the hand she was holding. "I wanted to talk Saturday night. I don't want to talk now."

"Please don't be angry."

"How *should* I be after you walked out and didn't say where you were going or when you'd be back—*if* you'd be back?"

"Sort of like what *you* did."

"Not in the least! I said I was going to Cobourg and told you when I'd be home—and wasn't gone two nights!"

"Just one, actually. You can't count Saturday."

"You find this amusing?"

"I find this painful." She skimmed the rim of her bowl with a finger and stopped. "I was drunk, in a tizzy, and acted impulsively. I didn't mean to hurt you."

"You abandoned me, for godssake! Of course you meant to hurt me, a *lot*, and you did."

"I'm really, really sorry"—addressing the soggy flakes in her bowl—"and honestly, I thought about you every minute I was gone and would've been here sooner if not for my client."

"So now we kiss and make up?"

"We both made mistakes, Ben."

"Your mistake was bigger."

"What did you tell me Saturday night about marriage not being wonderful all the time?"

He frowned. "Don't remember."

"I don't expect you to forgive me right away—"

"That's good, because I can't." He hunched his shoulders, pushed back the stool and rose. "I'm going to bed."

"But it's too early, not even dark. Let's sit in the living room."

"I didn't mean *both* of us. *You* can sleep on the couch tonight."

His face was drained and hangdog, an odd greyish-pink, his hair uncombed and his eyes gone flat with gloom: his head like an old, deserted house. She wanted to stroke his brow and

sing an alluring song, make whatever promises he needed to
hear. Bring him back.

"Let's forget it, Ben," she said. "Let's just try again."

"Try what?"

"To get it right."

He stomped out of the kitchen and she followed him as
far as the stairs, calling his name until he was out of sight. Then
she entered the living room, leafed through a magazine, read
some of her Sarah Vaughan biography and finally gave up and
lay down on the sofa, her bed for the night. Bunching a cushion
under her head and covering her body with the afghan, she
tossed about.

How to win him over? A nice meal, words of endearment,
hot sex—or was it better to do nothing, sit tight, give him
space and see how things played out?

Turning onto her hip, she settled into place on the hard,
narrow sofa . . . not half as comfy as the one in her office.

I'll think about it tomorrow, Renata decided.

But in the end, Scarlett O'Hara couldn't keep her man.

CHAPTER 15

Stella was sitting near the desk, holding her infant. Light from the window brightened her face as she readjusted the baby in the sling over her shoulder. She hadn't been to a session in more than a month, and Renata was pleased to see her.

"I'm glad you came to the hospital. Lucy said it was pre-ordained, you know, like you were drawn there."

"Has she gone back to the ashram?"

"Two weeks ago. I miss her but we're okay."

"Is there someone else who could help you? Did you speak to Grant's parents?"

"I promised to visit sometime and show them the baby, but that's all we talked about."

The infant started mewling. Stella fixed the sling so the baby lay horizontally, then lifted her sweater, pulled out a breast and watched her latch on and suck.

Discreetly, Renata looked aside.

The baby was slurping. "You're hungry," Stella said to her, then glanced at Renata. "Doesn't she look happy?" She lowered part of the carrier to give Renata a better view.

Renata crossed her legs and focused over her client's head. This was supposed to be a working session, not a social engagement—though everything was changed now and it might be impossible to get back on track.

"You haven't asked me her name yet," Stella said between making kissy sounds at the baby.

What *was* the child's name? And what did it mean that she didn't know, hadn't asked, and didn't want to ask now?

The infant made bubbly noises as she pulled Stella's nipple, and Stella gazed back at her with unblinking eyes. A self-sufficient unit, Renata observed: like no one else was in the room, in the world even.

What was it like, she wondered, to make a new human being, name it, nurse it—and suddenly lose it? How could a mother survive *that*?

You couldn't. Not entirely.

"I named her Katrina," Stella offered.

"That's a pretty name."

Her mother had named the girls June and both boys Kenneth. If Renata had been the first to die, the dead baby girls would've all been given *her* name. She would've been replaced by one embryo after the next, her specialness of no concern to a woman whose objective was to bear a live child.

Stella spoke with her eyes on the child. "She has a middle name too."

"What is it?"

"Lucille."

"How nice for your sister."

"And another besides that."

"A third name?" Renata's leg swung like a branch in a storm.

"Katrina Lucy Moon, I call her."

"Katrina Lucy *Moon* Wolnik? What kind of name is that?"

"It's meant to be a thank-you."

Renata uncrossed her legs and slapped at the folds of her dress—her stupidly wrinkled dress that wouldn't lie flat—then stretched her neck, squeezed her shoulders and made other movements to ease the tightness under her skin.

The woman was paying tribute, so why be upset? That was the way to see it—not that she'd been roped to Stella's baby for all time without even being asked.

"No one's ever named a child after me before," she said.

"Does that mean you don't mind?"

"Naturally I'm flattered. Nevertheless, I don't think—"

"Maybe you'd like to take her?" Stella put away her breast, rearranged the carrier, scooped out the infant and balanced her on outstretched arms.

Renata leaned away from the girl hovering between them. Take her in her arms the way she used to hold baby June—blue eyes staring and her wiggly-piggly fingers reaching for Renata's heart? Stella was asking her to hold Katrina like that?

She slid her hands under her thighs. "I don't think it's appropriate to name your daughter after your therapist."

Stella took the child back and crinkled up her nose, exposing her chipped tooth. "There's something else I came here to tell you, about us."

Renata put her hands on her lap and laced her fingers; then she pressed the knuckles into the soft spot under her chin. A conversation about "us" sounded like one that could end badly.

"I don't think I need to keep seeing you professionally. I appreciate your help and all, but everything's different with Katrina in my life now. I want to stop treatment and see how it goes."

Doesn't need to see me? Something small and hard as a marble rolled against her ribs. A client wants to leave and she didn't see it coming? How could she have been so blind?

"I want to end now—like, this will be our last time."

"I'm surprised to hear that," Renata said, recovering. "Often a young mother on her own needs support. Was this a sudden decision?"

"When Lucy left I saw that I could care for Katrina myself . . . and after that I started thinking about therapy, how all that had to change."

"All that?"

"Our relationship."

"What about our relationship?"

"I want to leave . . . but don't want to never see you again."

"You can always come back if new problems crop up."

After being on her own, Stella might decide that she still needed treatment and show up again. Or not. Clients rarely returned after their goodbye speeches. Probably she'd walk out with her child in another minute and be gone for good.

"I want to see you . . . like a friend."

"That's not possible."

Stella shrugged, straightened the baby in her sling, stood up and turned to go. "I'm taking Katrina to the park now, if you want to come." Slowly she moved from the office to the waiting room.

Friend or therapist? Renata knew the right thing to do, what Ben would advise her, the professional guidelines. But what she *wanted* to do was another matter. Her thoughts circled, leading nowhere—go, go . . . don't go—until she impetuously sprang to her feet and ran after Stella, barely remembering to lock up.

It was hot on the street, the air thick. Renata squinted at the too-bright morning. Cars shimmered in the light and everything seemed molten. The leaves of the maple in front of her building were droopy and washed out, and it worried her to look at them.

Stella eased the baby more deeply into the carrier to keep her out of the sun, then turned in the direction of the park and began to walk, not with shy, halting steps but with a strong forward stride. People moved aside for her, as though the Red Sea itself were parting to let her through, and Renata scuttled to keep up.

When they reached an intersection, Stella slid her toes over the curb, looked both ways and scooted across. She was grinning like an Olympics road-crossing medallist when they got to the other side.

She chose a meandering route instead of a direct one, and they walked side by side along quiet residential streets of burly trees and brick homes with bay windows, pitched roofs, and dormers on the upper floors.

One of them caught Renata's eye, smaller and shabbier than the houses on either side, with a narrow path to the entrance and lopsided wooden steps going up to a porch that was missing spindles. Two children chased each other around a square brown lawn, the girl shouting, "Stop!" and the boy answering, "Catch me!"

Renata didn't know the house, didn't know the children, but a memory grew behind her eyes. She saw herself sitting on the lawn of her childhood home, her sister between her knees . . . when all at once the baby stood and took her first steps. And the sight of Junie wobbling into the world made her heart trill, made her think the child was walking just for her.

Dead for no reason. Kenneth first, then June.

Abruptly she turned and hurried on.

A while later they entered the park. There weren't many people around at this time of day, so they walked alone in the shade of evergreens and maples, then back into the hot sun as they climbed a grassy hill that led to a playground. The noise of excited children rose as they approached, and as if she were answering them, Katrina burbled in her pouch and tried to lift her head.

Stella was the first to speak. "There's something I want to ask you," she said, "about the baby."

"Infant development isn't my specialty."

"Nothing like that." She waited a beat. "It's something more personal."

Something embarrassing, to judge by the sudden darkening of Stella's cheeks. Instead of slowing, Renata sped up. Her dress moved between her legs with the swish of windshield wipers, and as she walked she plucked the fabric away from her damp thighs.

Stella caught up to her. "I want to know if you'll be Katrina's godmother."

Renata halted mid-stride, sweaty and speechless. The next moment she pitched forward and veered away from the playground toward a distant clutch of trees, where it looked to be cooler and darker.

Stella was at her heels. "You don't have to do much, it's more symbolic," she explained. "The idea is to be, like, a spiritual guide and teach her religion."

"I have no religion."

"Were you baptized?"

"Yes . . . but I don't pray and have no beliefs. I'm not a practising anything."

"I don't care about that. All you have to do is come to the baptism, stand at the font with Katrina in your arms and promise to see that she's brought up in the Church. Then the priest pours some water on her head, says a prayer and it's over."

"I'd be holding her the whole time?"

"She's not a fussy baby."

Renata stopped walking. "I don't have the necessary faith, I assure you. Can't you ask someone else, Lucy or Grant's parents?"

"I'm supposed to ask a friend."

"I'm not your friend, I'm your therapist . . . and wouldn't feel comfortable at your daughter's christening."

"You're not my therapist anymore."

"Ex-therapist. Same issue. I know it's an honour, but for many reasons . . ."

"You don't have to decide now." Stella moved close, thrusting the girl under Renata's nose. "Will you think about it first before you give me an answer?"

Katrina joggled herself in her sling, extending her neck, and followed every motion of Renata's head with blue, beaming eyes. Her forehead was large and creased, her mouth a gummy crescent. When she reached over the side of the pouch, the wagging of her chubby fingers was hypnotic.

Renata stared at the baby's eyes, which seemed to reflect her own and drill down into her. Watching the child's open face, something occurred to her: how alike they were in their fragility and need for love.

Lovely baby girl, she thought.

All at once her forehead prickled inexplicably, as though Katrina were sending her a message. *Lovely* flashed again in lit-up letters on the dark screen of Renata's brain.

And then there was another mysterious transmission, something beyond words, and her whole face felt kissed.

Renata was close to tears. "I'll think about it and let you know," she said to Stella softly.

Flushed, she turned away from them, murmured that she had to go and started back to the office.

CHAPTER 16

How's it working out with my cousin?" Ida said.

They were standing nose to nose on the patchy square of shared lawn in front of their houses that hadn't been weeded in so long you couldn't find the grass among the violets and dandelions.

"He pays the rent, doesn't make noise, keeps his room clean." Molly shrugged. "What more do I need?"

"You're a person who gets what she needs. I have to admire that."

She didn't actually need Saul. She wasn't so old that she couldn't take care of herself, and her boys could help out with the house, if it came to that. After all these years she was used to filling her days with shopping, cooking and TV, and God knows Saul didn't contribute much money-wise.

Molly's front door had swung partly open and was letting in bugs, so she hurried to close it. Ida followed her up the step, waiting for a reply.

"What are you saying?" Molly said.

"I'm not saying anything . . . except I was thinking, since you used to know each other well, it must be nice living together under one roof."

It was nice, in fact, and she liked that he was here. He made her feel good inside, made her feel things she hadn't felt in a long time. But she wasn't so stupid as to say that to Ida.

"Mostly I knew him through you" is what she answered. "Anyway, he's no trouble."

"He used to be lots of trouble."

"That was then, this is now."

"Maybe you're right." Ida smiled. "He walks like a robot that needs a new battery. On the other hand, you never know. Old habits die hard, and he's not in his grave yet."

Molly pushed open the door she had just closed. "I have to start cooking, the family's coming here at six."

"He used to be handsome and now he's like a skeleton, but that's what time does to you. Look at me, how everything hangs." She held out a bare arm and made the under part swing. "Still, it's easier for the men, there's always women who want them, who can't stand being alone." Ida peered at Molly. "Saul was a ladies' man, am I right or am I wrong? Could talk them out of their bloomers without hardly trying—depending on the lady, of course. Some are always easier than others."

"What would you know about it? What do you know about anything!"

Molly rushed inside the house and slammed the door behind her. Such a stupid yenta! She was so angry and out of breath she was dizzy.

She sat down on a bench in the hall and let her lungs fill. Sure he was a talker and she'd thrown off her clothes for him, but all that was long ago. Everything was different now that they were just friends. And sure he still flattered her—but why not enjoy it? There wasn't much to like about getting old and drying up, so why not be happy that a man still found her pretty, even if only for her green eyes, pink cheeks and other bits and pieces? Everything he said about her freshness and liveliness made her feel flirty again, like when they first met, and where was the harm in that?

She liked having him around. In the morning she liked that there were two cups instead of one, two napkins, two spoons and two bowls on the table. In the evening she looked forward to chatting with him over supper, because he listened well, and to when he took her hand and wished her a good night's sleep before retiring. To think that such a small gesture, such a few simple words, could make her heart swell and hum! Anyway it was summertime, so why shouldn't she feel as wobbly on her feet as a lamb?

Not that she was over the moon. Only the young can love so intensely, and she was more level-headed in her old age. What she had was quieter. A quiet feeling.

Fond of him, that was it. Molly was fond of Saul, and Saul was fond of Molly. Not what you'd carve on a tree, but more likely to give them both a little comfort.

Calm again, she got up, went to the kitchen and found him at the table squeezing lemon into a teacup.

"Want me to make you a sandwich?" he asked.

"I'm not hungry." She sat again.

"Who were you talking to?"

"Your cousin, the witch."

"What's she got to say for herself?"

"Very cagey, that one. Never lets you pin her down. But what she was getting at is that I'm not a nice person."

"This has to do with me? Because of our history?"

"She wants me to be ashamed, especially now you're living here."

"And are you?"

"Certainly not!"

He grinned, showing puffy gums. It would be a mitzvah to pay for his periodontal work if she could find the money.

"What's so funny?" Molly asked.

"Two ladies fighting and gossiping over an *alter kocker* like me is more than I ever dreamed of."

"Enough already. I have to cook."

Molly pushed herself up, pulled a turkey from the fridge, stuffed it with something from a box and tied up the drumsticks. Then she made a big racket looking for a roasting pan buried in the crowded drawer under the oven.

"Finish your tea and go. I don't like someone in the room when I'm working, it breaks my concentration."

"You want me to help you?"

"There's nothing to do once the turkey's in the oven."

"I'll sit here quietly, then."

She screwed up her eyes at him. "Since when do you sit at my heels like a puppy? What's the matter with you today?"

"You have to ask what's wrong?"

Molly spread her hands on her hips. "You're not nervous, are you?"

"Why should I be nervous? Your son who wants me to move out and your other one I never met are coming for dinner with their wives you don't care for and *kinde* who ignore the velvet rope, jump on the sofa and give you palpitations. What's there to worry about?"

"I took down the rope for good."

"So that makes everything right?"

"Everything will be wonderful. Mel's going to love you, he's got a heart the size of his head, and Libby . . . well, she's not so bad. Rope or no rope, I'm pretty sure she'll keep the children out of the living room, she learned her lesson last time. Renata you shouldn't worry about, a very intelligent if undernourished shiksa who anyway is always polite, I have to give her points for that. She never says anything rude."

"And Ben? What about him?"

Molly crossed the room and plopped the turkey into the roasting pan she'd put out on top of the stove. "Ben's Ben. What can I say?" She flicked her fingers at the air. "Don't ask me to speak for Ben, I never know what he's thinking."

"How much does he know about me?"

"Only that we're old friends."

"You didn't say anything more?"

"That's what I told him!"

She wheeled around with such force she knocked the roaster off the stove and sent it clanging to the floor. The turkey, landing near the pan with a trail of stuffing beside it, looked too much like a naked, desecrated corpse.

"See what you made me do?"

They stared at the dead bird, neither one of them showing any willingness to pick it up and put it back together. Molly shoved the roaster with the toe of her shoe. "They're coming in three hours and there won't be anything to eat."

Saul hung his head and sighed, which wasn't very useful, she thought. Why didn't he clean up the mess? Why not take her in his arms and hold her till she calmed down enough to get the turkey fixed and back in the oven?

"Molly," he said out of the blue, "I'm going to ask you something very important, and you have to answer yes or no."

"Can't it wait till later?"

"Is he my son or isn't he?"

"Ben?"

"Who else?"

"I don't know!" She gave the turkey such a kick it skittered halfway across the floor. "Why do we have to talk about this now? What do you want from me?"

"All I want from you is the truth."

"I just said *I don't know*. How can I be sure, when I was sleeping with both of you?"

He raised his head, his jaw loose. "What? You slept with Nathan too?"

"Nathan was my husband! You think I should've told him to sleep in the basement?"

"I thought . . . never mind what I thought." He ran a hand over his scalp. "In my opinion, Ben has a right to know I could be his biological father. And nowadays, with DNA, it's not hard to check."

"You want him to do a test to see if the man he loved was really his father or if some total stranger is? You'd let him maybe find out his mama was a whore and his papa a cuckold—and this you'd do for *his* sake?"

"We owe him the truth."

"You think he'll want to do this test and risk learning such a truth? You think the truth is always so wonderful it must be known and no one should refuse it, no one should remain in the dark? And what if, God forbid, he goes ahead and finds out he actually is your son. Do you think he's going to love you all of a sudden because of a test? You think he'll ever love you at all? This much I promise you, not in a million years!"

"That's not for you to say."

What was going on here? He told her he hadn't come back in her life to make trouble, yet now he was talking biology and DNA.

"The father is the one who puts food in his son's mouth. You didn't stay long enough to even know I was pregnant."

"If I knew you were carrying my child—"

"You would've run faster!"

"I didn't go because of you. I was a *greener* who had to

find work and send money to his daughters. How could I let them starve?"

"You could've asked Nathan for a job in his factory."

He clicked his tongue tsk-tsk. "You know I couldn't do that."

The room was turning slowly. Molly put a hand to her throat and sat down again, her breathing so laboured now she thought her lungs would give out.

Reaching across the table, he pulled the fingers of her free hand into his palm. "I never stopped caring for you, I want you to know that. You were always special to me, and you still are."

Molly's ears were flaming as her fingers curled under his . . . and slowly the fire in her heart began to burn down. If she truly meant something to him, surely he wouldn't say anything to Ben that would make her unhappy.

Looking into his eyes at last, she saw that they were wet. Tears pooled in the deep pockets under his lower lids, but he didn't turn away from her. What was more beautiful, she couldn't help thinking, than a man unashamed to cry?

Surely such a man could be trusted to keep a secret.

How lucky she was, really, to have rediscovered an old love. How lucky to find a companion in her final years when her body was falling apart and, among other complaints, would probably need a new hip—though she kept postponing doctor visits because of a dream about a drunken surgeon cutting her with shaky hands, and now, thank God, there was someone else to fret about.

Saul had an unmistakable tremor in his right arm and walked clumsily sometimes, and if, God forbid, it should turn out to be something awful like Parkinson's he should know right away and start taking drugs . . . though men were all the same when it came to their health and wouldn't see a doctor even if they thought something serious might be wrong. Bury your head in the sand, she'd say, and soon they'll bury the rest of you too. Which would be unbearable.

Her hand was hot in his as she gazed at his runny eyes. He seemed so small and fragile, with his long face, loose neck and feather of hair, that instantly she forgave him his trembling arm and stiff walk and all the other ways in which he wasn't a young man anymore. But even though their bodies were shot and she spent nights worrying they wouldn't live to see the dawn, she wouldn't want to be twenty again if you paid her and have to relive those heartbreaking days of guilt.

Still, when he squeezed her hand, their fingers rubbed together in a way that brought back memories of their youth: hard muscles, full breasts and Saul growing big against her leg with excitement as his lips moved over her. She didn't think Nathan had ever *imagined* such abandon—but still she'd loved him deeply and hoped he had always believed that.

Her eyes rolled skyward. Was he looking down on them now, she wondered, seeing her hand in Saul's and knowing the truth about them? Was he sorry that he never had time for her when he was alive, that work always came first and he let her stray into the arms of another man?

Did Nathan forgive her?

Was he even capable now of forgiveness? Did she really think that consciousness, feelings and memories survived death?

What she supposed was that everything disappeared when your brain stopped working: what you did or didn't do; all that sorrow, passion and pain. Her biggest hope was that when she was ready for the grave, her memories would float away and she would finally be at peace.

But who could say what actually happens in the next world. Better to be peaceful in life. Better Saul should keep quiet and no one should get upset—her son in particular.

She drew her hand out of his. "You won't say anything tonight to embarrass me, will you?" she asked. But he only sighed in answer, and she wasn't sure what that meant.

Things would happen as they did.

Ben was a grown-up, after all. What would be so terrible if one day he found out he was full of Saul's genes? Surely he'd understand that Nathan was his father in every other respect and that's what really mattered. That *lineage* and *ancestry* were just hoity-toity words somebody made up to feel superior, and why should you care what they put on your tombstone or whose bones were lying in the next plot? Even sons and daughters forget you before long and get on with their own lives. That's just the way it is. Sadness, guilt and aggravation come to nothing in the end, so why make yourself miserable?

He wouldn't take the news well.

Ben was a worrier who didn't have enough of Molly's good sense or wisdom. He wanted a family with cut-out dolls for his mama and papa and snugly babies on his knee—which was just foolishness. Life's a twisty-turny thing and all you get, if you're lucky, is a slice of what you hoped for. If only he understood that living's hard for everyone, not just him, and you have to grab what comes your way . . . then maybe he'd be thankful for his smart and pretty wife, his job where he saves lives, his brother who admires him, and also for Molly herself, who didn't always act right but loves him one hundred percent.

Then maybe he'd relax. He wouldn't spend so much time waiting for miracles, but if they happened, be surprised.

Touching Saul's arm, she said, "Dinner will be late." Then slowly she got to her feet, put the turkey back together, laid it in the roaster and pushed it into the oven.

"Maybe you should've washed it first?"

She turned around to face him and saw that he was smiling, his arms wide open. What she wanted to say was that her floors were so clean you could eat off them and not worry, but Molly only walked into his embrace and was silent.

When he kissed her cheek, his lips felt like dried fruit. Not the way they were over fifty years ago, but what was the same anymore? The most important thing was the feelings they still had for each other, quiet or not. The rest of it, the getting old and worn out, couldn't be helped.

She blew at the tuft of hair standing on Saul's head, and it bent like grass in the wind. The thing was to be surprised.

———

For this, a special occasion, everyone sat on the plastic-covered couch and chairs in the living room, except for David and Chloe, who were watching something noisy on the TV in the basement. Molly worked in the kitchen, making a salad of tomatoes that hadn't fully ripened. She sweetened it with Russian dressing, which her boys were crazy about, so no one would notice anything wrong.

If she stopped moving and listened she could hear them in the next room, mostly Mel's big voice and Saul's like the sound you make grating raw carrots—which reminded her to boil a pot of water for the vegetables and check on the chorus line of potatoes in the oven, baking an hour now. When she opened the door and pricked them with a fork, they were already soft. Stabbing the turkey while she was at it, she saw pink juices and knew the bird wasn't done. But so what if they had to wait? No one would starve. There were bowls of nuts in the living room and chips for the children downstairs, and anyway they were too busy talking to think about food.

She heard Saul ask a question and Mel start in with "Breast reduction and enhancement, eye lifts, tummy tucks . . ." Then he introduced Ben, "a transplant psychiatrist," and one of the daughters-in-law—it had to be Renata—spoke up in a mouse voice Molly couldn't make out, but she must've said something funny because everybody laughed.

Gott in Himmel, Molly thought, such professions her boys had! Sure they were doctors, that much she'd seen to, but why not a podiatrist or better yet a cardiologist, specialties she understood? At least Ben played a part in saving sick people's lives, even if he didn't touch them, but what did Mel do besides make pots of cash? He cut up otherwise healthy people who thought they weren't pretty enough and made old women like herself try to look young by flattening their bellies or giving them facelifts—operations Molly wouldn't have in a million years because it's the beauty of the soul that matters, that's the part that shines through and makes you attractive. Saul could tell her son Mel a thing or two about that.

But suddenly it was quiet in there. From downstairs she heard the blare of the TV, but nothing from the living room. Even Libby the big-mouth, who always had something bad to say about everything, and even Renata, who knew enough to keep the conversation going nicely and not leave anyone out— especially Saul, the newcomer—had nothing more to say.

What was happening? Maybe they stopped talking because they didn't like him. Maybe they guessed he was more to her than just a boarder paying rent and didn't think he was good enough to be part of the family—like she always thought about Libby and Renata, though at least she was polite to them. Were Mel and Ben glaring at him with crossed arms and hard lips, making Saul so upset he wanted to run away, pack his bags and drop out of her life again forever?

If she heard him in the hall she would dash over, grab his sleeve and not let him past the door, then say to her children that *they* had to get out. What kind of monsters were her sons who couldn't make a man in their mama's house feel welcome!

The bam-bang of the basement TV entered her brain and pulsed in her temple. She closed her eyes and rubbed the painful spot with her fingertips, but the stillness in the next room was making her headache worse.

They should thank him and be grateful he was making her happy! She raised her boys to be considerate of others, although she couldn't speak for their wives. If no one would talk to him, the only thing to do was call everybody into the kitchen and get the evening over with.

She swallowed two aspirin from a bottle she kept on the spice rack especially for times like this and dropped carrots and Brussels sprouts into boiling water. Next she finished setting the table, put out the salad bowl, turned off the oven and opened the door. The potatoes would be soft and the turkey undercooked, but even risking salmonella was better than leaving Saul in a room full of vultures.

She hoisted the bird onto a platter and put the potatoes in a covered dish. The sprouts and carrots were nearly done—fashionably undercooked for a change—when Molly poked them with a fork, so she drained the pot over the sink and tumbled the vegetables into a bowl. "Come upstairs!" she shouted at the top of the steps to the basement, but if David and Chloe heard her they didn't respond. Let their mother deal with them, the two little hoodlums, or let them go hungry—it would teach them a lesson about respecting their elders.

She arranged the food on the table, spilling a drop of grease on her good white tablecloth, first stain of the evening, and covered the spot with a wineglass. Ben had insisted on wine, which Molly didn't usually serve, but if that's what it took to get the family to sit down together, so be it. She opened bottles of red and white and set them down at either end. Saul still liked to drink, she remembered from their dinner in that fancy-schmancy restaurant, and if not for her headache she might have had a sip herself, just to quiet her nerves.

She wiped her hands on a paper towel, tugged her skirt at the waist to make the pattern of stripes lie straight and went to the living room.

No one was moving. They looked like they'd been freeze-dried. Saul, hunched over with his hands between his knees, was on one side of the sofa, while Mel was at the other end, arms spread across the back. Ben sat in an easy chair, staring at the closed-up fireplace that didn't work, and Libby leaned against the mantel rather than squeeze between Saul and her husband. Renata had chosen the one leather chair, from Nathan's office, that Molly hated for anyone to use because it might wear out, and was smiling at Saul with her mouth curved up at the corners and stuck there. Unlike the rest of them, at least she was trying.

"Come and eat." She spoke more sharply than she had meant to. "The food's on the table."

Everybody jumped up like someone had pulled a fire alarm and followed her into the kitchen.

Libby screamed at the basement stairs, "Get up here right now!" and the children pounded up the steps, shoving each other and whining, Davey-did-this and Chloe-did-that. "I don't want to hear it," Libby said. "Wash up and sit down."

They soaped their dirty hands in the sink and dried them on a dishtowel, which Molly found disgusting, but she held her tongue because things were already bad enough. Libby made the children sit apart, on either side of her, then Mel and Renata sat down, but it wasn't clear who should be across from

Molly, Ben or Saul. Right after Nathan died, the seat at the head of the table went to her elder son, but now they paused to look at her for direction.

"Let Mr. Rosenberg sit there tonight."

"My father's seat," Ben said, more to himself than anyone.

Molly's belly hardened. Was Saul going to speak out and ruin the evening after all? Ruin the rest of her life? Was it foolish to have trusted him? Not now, she silently begged.

He wet his lips and opened his mouth, but she cut him off before he could start. "Nathan's no longer with us, God rest his soul, and it's only good manners to let Saul have his place."

Ben stumbled back, like someone had pushed in front of him in line at the store.

"Come over here." Renata patted an empty chair. "Does it really matter where you sit?"

Molly had to admire the way Renata settled the question, her no-nonsense manner that was also gentle somehow. But Ben gave her a sour look, crossed his arms and kept standing. Because he'd lost his seat to Saul, or was it something between them? At Mel's birthday party last month, she remembered, June seventeenth, he wouldn't dance with his wife and was grumpy the whole night. But with him you never knew if something was up or it was just a passing temper.

In the end, Ben sat down and stared at the tablecloth. Molly loved him dearly, but she knew it couldn't be easy being married to a moody man. You had to give Renata credit for patience. More and more, she'd begun to appreciate her daughter-in-law's character.

Saul slid onto his chair and grinned across the table like a birthday boy who'd gotten what he wished for, but Molly turned away from him. His smugness annoyed her.

She asked Mel to carve the turkey, as per usual, because he was better with a knife than anyone, and the children stopped kvetching and wiggling for a second to watch their father slice the bird.

"Who wants what?" he asked, and everybody lifted their plates for white or dark meat.

Libby spooned vegetables from the bowl onto her children's plates, while Renata gave out baked potatoes, Ben poured wine, and Molly pretended for one happy instant that the three generations of her family at the table were respectful, agreeable and fond of each other.

Glancing around, she saw that everyone, including Saul, was busy eating quietly, and she put a Brussels sprout in her mouth. Chewing hard because it wasn't completely cooked, she prayed that the evening would proceed uneventfully. But God wasn't listening. Even before she swallowed her food, David made a noise in his throat, spit meat onto his plate and wiped drool with the back of his hand. Her stomach grumbled, hurting with gas. *Nu?* she thought, now it starts.

"The turkey's raw," her grandson said when he could speak again. "It's *bleeding* around the bone."

"Don't touch it, you'll get sick." Libby snatched his plate and moved away from the table.

"Mine's cooked," Chloe said.

"You got the breast meat."

"Why didn't you ask for that?"

"Bubbe always makes it so dry I choke." He clutched his throat.

"So put yours in the microwave."

"Bubbe doesn't have one."

"Why doesn't she have one?"

"Old people don't have new stuff like everyone else. She doesn't own a laptop, a digital camera or a cell."

Chloe nodded thoughtfully, as if Molly weren't there. "Or even have a car," she said.

"Old people don't drive."

Molly felt like banging their heads together and shouting, I have something better than toys! She dared to peek at Saul, who was mopping his plate with bread, and wanted to gently clean his shiny lips with her fingers.

"That's enough, you two." Libby scraped her son's turkey into the garbage under the sink. "Have more vegetables," she said, handing his plate back.

"They're too hard. I'll break my teeth."

"The potatoes are soft. You can fill up on that."

Mel slapped the flat of a knife against the turkey's breast and offered to cut more slices of white meat, but Libby and Renata frowned, Ben shook his head, and the kids made faces. "How about you?" he asked Saul, who was wiping his mouth with a napkin.

Saul put the napkin down and seemed about to make a speech, but Molly interrupted.

"What, you're trying to poison him?"

"There's nothing wrong with the breast meat."

"My father liked the *pulke*," Ben said mournfully, and everyone turned to gaze at Saul sitting in Nathan's chair.

Molly looked harder than the rest. Don't say a word! she transmitted silently to him across the table, pressing her fingers between her breasts to keep her heart from flying out.

"More wine?" Renata asked, topping up her husband's glass, and Mel jumped in with the story of the nose job of a well-known actor. "After the surgery, you could tell a mile off she wasn't born with a schnoz like that. It looked like something Michael Jackson's plastic surgeon dreamed up."

From there the conversation moved awkwardly to Aunt Tilly's most recent facelift, and Molly put her elbows on the table and tented her hands, pretending to be interested. Mel had done the job the last time around and thought the results were good, natural and flattering. Tilly disagreed. For the next one she tried a guy who pulled her skin so tight she couldn't wink or smile anymore.

"Serves her right," Mel said. "I don't care if she comes crawling, I won't have anything to do with that bitch again."

Libby said loudly, "Watch your mouth in front of the kids," and David echoed, "Yeah, watch it."

Then all at once, without warning, to be polite or maybe find a more appropriate subject, Renata turned the conversation away from surgery and asked Saul sweetly if he'd known Molly a long time.

Molly held her breath while Saul thought out loud.

"Fifty-three, fifty-four years," he concluded. "Before Ben was born."

"When Molly was single?"

"She was already married. Ida introduced us, and I knew Nathan Wasserman too. I thought they made a nice couple."

Renata smiled encouragement. "They were your friends?"

"Like family. But finally I got a job elsewhere and had to go."

Ben circled the top of his glass with his finger. "Did you see them a lot?"

"Molly more than Nathan, because I wasn't working yet and had free time during the day when he was busy."

Molly's heart was skipping beats, bubbling and sputtering as if it might come to a halt and suddenly she'd fall over, her face landing in her food. She didn't like the direction the conversation had taken but said as calmly as possible, "I showed him around the neighbourhood and helped him with his English, and Nathan was happy I had someone to talk to besides Ida next door and the two Cohen yentas."

"Why didn't my father offer you work in his factory," Mel asked, "especially if you were friends? He was always giving people jobs."

Saul caught Molly's eye and didn't answer.

"He'd only just got here," she said, "and wanted to look around before settling in one place. Isn't that what happened?"

Her cheeks were hot burners now, her brain boiling over. Ben looked at her with his eyebrows peaked. Was he wondering if she and Saul had ever been more than friends? From there, she thought grimly, it was only a hop and skip to figuring out the rest.

Saul cleared his throat and spoke. "Also I wanted a better job than what I could get in a factory. That's why I moved on."

"And what did you wind up with?" Renata asked.

"A sales job."

"Isn't it nice"—she turned to Ben—"that he knew your parents back then?"

Ben spread his hands on the table like duck feet and levelled his eyes at the man in his father's chair.

Saul leaned toward him, extending a hand. "Let's you and me be friends. I think your mother would like that."

Ben's fingers curled like petals wilting.

"Shake," said Renata, and when her husband didn't move she nudged him closer to Saul.

The old man bobbed forward, scooped up one of Ben's hands and gripped it in his own. "If I had a son," he said, "I'd want him to be like you."

"You have *daughters*," Molly squeaked.

"That's right," Saul agreed, "two lovely daughters. I don't have a bad word to say about my children."

"Sons, daughters," Libby sighed, "every one's a blessing."

Ben's mouth was a thin line, but Saul held on to his hand and wished him a happy life. Then he finally let go and sat back in his seat at the head of the table. "That's all I got to say."

Molly made the sound of a dying motor as she sucked in a mouthful of air and released it, but no one seemed to notice. Saul had nothing more to say? Nothing about their love affair and his *farshtinkener* DNA? So this was the end of it? She widened her eyes at him, and he smiled across the table.

A ball rose in her throat and she wanted to hug him. People were messy, Molly thought, good sometimes and sometimes not and everything possible in between, and every once in a while, in a moment like this one, a person could be more than good. A person could be noble.

Saul was a mentsh! He hadn't told the whole truth but didn't tell a lie either. Only as much as they needed to know.

Soon after, three conversations started up at once. David and Chloe spoke across their mother about computer games, Libby was explaining a yoga pose to Renata, and Ben and Mel discussed the future of heart and lung transplants. Next, the children began tapping cutlery together and stamping their feet rhythmically, while Libby elbowed them to stop and Mel sang parts of songs featuring the word *heart*. Renata joined in, singing to whistles and applause. But Molly barely heard the tumult. Daydreaming about Saul, she'd tuned out her family.

It was Libby who finally got her attention, saying very loudly that the children were getting bored and maybe it was time for dessert.

Molly agreed and stood up.

On her way to the fridge for an apple pie, she accidentally knocked over the bottle of red wine and spilled what was left in it. Renata grabbed a napkin and dabbed at the wet spot, but Molly motioned for her to stop. She was thinking again of her meal with Saul in the restaurant and how, when she spilled wine because he was asking about Ben, a waiter hurried to clean up. This time nobody ran to change the tablecloth, ruined once and for all. But she couldn't help seeing the stain as something beautiful, a dark angel with wide-open wings.

Renata put the kettle on and cleared the dirty table, then Libby hopped up as well and loaded the dishwasher, washed glasses, scrubbed pots and left the roaster in the sink to soak in soapy water. No one was as fast and efficient in the kitchen as Libby, Molly had to admit.

When the kettle whistled, she put a couple of bags in a teapot and filled it. The hum of the lamp over the sink reminded her of bees, and she looked out the small kitchen window at the next house. She had a view of Ida in a red and yellow housedress, sitting on her back step and expertly shelling peas, her eyes looking elsewhere. Roses bloomed close by. Her busy fingers and dreamy look, the green peas and flowers were a picture of summer, and Molly was already thinking of later, when everyone had gone home and she and Saul could sit in the yard and take in the evening. She watched her neighbour working until she finished and went in, then turned away from the glass.

She put out cups and plates, milk, pie, ice cream, the teapot and whatnot, and passed all of it around. Things went quickly after that. They ate their sweets and drank their drinks, and then it was time to go.

Renata was the first to stand. She thanked Molly and winked at Saul. Then Libby bounced up, made David and Chloe say polite things to their bubbe, and swept the children out the door. Mel was next. After hugging Molly, he stepped around the table and stuck out his hand over the last of the apple pie oozing in its aluminum pan. Saul was already standing in place, bent like a hanger, and the men solemnly shook hands.

When it was Ben's turn, he pushed away from the table, said good-night to Molly and Saul and started for the door, where Renata was waiting. He dipped to one side as he walked, Molly noticed, as if he carried a box of bricks on his shoulder. But there was nothing more she could do to help him with his life.

She closed the front door behind her family and sighed.

Alone again with Saul, she opened the back door, walked into the yard with the teapot and mugs, and set everything down on a rusty metal table. She used a rag to wipe clean a couple of lawn chairs, pulled them to the table and flopped down on one of them. *Gott in Himmel*, her feet hurt! Running, running all day long, standing, sitting, up and down: that's how her life went, from luck to troubles, *mazel* to *tsouris*, and back again.

Saul came out and looked around, frowning at the spotty lawn pitted with squirrel holes, overrun with creeping charlie, dandelions and violets, and promised to dig it up, fertilize and plant grass. She smiled to hear him speak about improving the property. This time he might stay.

She waved him into the next chair and filled their mugs. "Don't drink it if it's cold."

He took a sip—"Just right"—reached out and touched her arm. "You're just right too."

Bending forward, she rubbed her face against his. He smelled sweetly of apple pie and faintly of shaving cream. "You surprised me tonight," she said.

"What I said to the family?"

"What you didn't say to them."

"I surprised myself too."

"You made me very happy."

"I have to say," Saul said, "I didn't know when I sat down how things would go."

"I'm glad it went the way it did." She leaned back and sipped tea. "But something still bothers me."

"About Ben?"

"About God." She pinched the handle of her cup. "You think He forgives us?"

"Sure he does. That's His job."

"What if He thinks it's not right that we should be in love again?"

"God doesn't begrudge love."

"How can you know that?"

"Because of what's in my heart. That's how He speaks to us."

With her free hand she patted down the delicate spray of hair on his head, peeking through the wisp at his heart-breakingly pink scalp. Slowly she moved her face up close and kissed his mouth. It wasn't as thrilling as smooching with Nathan in Prospect Park, or even kissing her babies, and it wasn't like kissing Saul when their lips were full, their teeth white and their breath smelled of honey . . . but you had to make allowances. Considering their age now, the pain in their joints and the stiffness of their old bones, it wasn't too bad at all.

Ida came into her yard again and peered through the chain-link fence. When Molly waved and called hello, she raised her arm slowly and wiggled her fingers at them.

"How's it going?" Ida asked, and Saul answered, "Can't complain."

CHAPTER 17

His eyes twitched open and, for a few seconds, he didn't know he was on a train. To his right was a large window and fast-moving scenery in summery shades of green—forest green, lime green, pea green and olive—that registered as *landscape*; to his left was a blurred face coming into focus that seemed at first to be Arthur's but actually wasn't.

Ben was sitting on a train next to someone he didn't know.

He pulled off earphones and dropped his iPod into his bag. Before he dozed off he'd been listening to Beethoven and scrawling lines of melancholy poetry on his ticket stub. Now he looked them over, frowning, tore the stub into pieces and threw it away.

The passenger beside him was eating peanuts, and Ben winced to hear him chomp. Then the sound of static and a speaker braying that Cobourg was the next stop, "Exit at the front of the car." He rubbed his face in his hands to fully awaken and listened again as the message was repeated in

French, as if hearing the words in a foreign tongue might crystallize their meaning.

People were crowding the aisle. The guy next to him jumped up and pushed into line, but Ben waited for the train to stop before getting off.

From the platform he spied Arthur's van in the parking lot, walked over and climbed in. Arthur raised his brow in greeting.

"I was surprised to hear from you today," he said as they drove away from the station.

"I can't explain it." Ben paused. "I just had an urge to come. Hope I'm not disturbing you."

"Not at all."

"I promise not to stay long."

"The garlic's ready. It's a good time to be here."

The van swerved away from town, and suddenly on either side were cornfields and hayfields; apple, poplar and maple trees opening to July's heat; bright dabs of wildflowers edging the roadside. They passed an algae-green pond, sheep, cows and horses, swallows on a wire and a quick, sputtering creek. A seagull and two grackles startled by the car's engine cawed, rose and swooped away as Ben followed them with his eyes. He was happy to be riding through the countryside again, absorbing its colours and sounds.

He swept his arm across the front to take in the windshield and side window. "Nothing's changed," he said, and Arthur chuckled in reply, "Things are always changing. It's a new season, for one thing."

Soon he made another turn and drove past Carol Stanley's tidied-up property—shrubs trimmed, lawn mowed—and finally parked in the driveway of his own home.

Ben hoisted his shoulder bag, swung out of the van and stood hunched beside it, scuffling in place like a boy in a schoolyard waiting to be told where to line up. Now that he'd arrived, he wondered again about his impulse to come here. What was he looking for, and what did Arthur make of his sudden reappearance?

But Arthur was smiling and seemed unbothered. He motioned to him as if he knew what Ben meant to see, and they strode past the house and went directly to the garden.

The garlic stalks stood about three feet tall in the straw-covered beds. Their upper leaves were green, but the lower ones were turning brown and some had flopped over. Ben pointed at the plants and said they looked half dead.

"As they should be. It's time for the harvest."

As Ben stood beside the garden, Arthur entered and walked up and down the rows, touching the tips of dying leaves. From a nearby speaker came the cheerful notes of Beethoven's *Pastoral*.

Stopping at the end of a row, not far from Ben, he raised his chin to the music. "Sixth Symphony, first movement," he nodded at the speaker. His hands began to dance in the air. "It suits your return to the country, doesn't it?"

Ben turned an ear to Beethoven's Sixth, which he knew well. *Allegro ma non troppo.* His fingers played a flute on his thigh in time with the lively piece.

Arthur tipped his head toward the speaker and sang out, "Here comes the next movement! Close your eyes and listen to the sound of the woodwinds. Can you hear birds and a running brook?"

A softer, flowing segment was playing now, and he did indeed hear chirps and the patter of water. He heard the tick of his pulse and the quick, strong rush of blood through his body.

Arthur came out of the garden, halted beside him and turned toward his withering plants. "A wonderful sight," he said.

Ben followed the man's gaze until he too was staring at the garlic. Considering the stalks, he imagined the bulbs below—the fat, juicy cloves that he used to mash with butter and parmesan for garlic bread and put in spaghetti sauce back in his student days—the new life underground. Ripe bulbs and brown leaves: the living and dying of everything. The ever-changing cycle.

Shuffling in the grass, he realized he expected something special to happen now. Something metaphysical, beyond his own tired thoughts. While Arthur looked out across the neat lines of plants, like troops in formation, Ben stopped moving and waited to be transformed.

"What is it?" Arthur turned to him. "What are you feeling?"

Ben glanced at the rows, then down at his feet, solid as bricks. "It's not like the last time," he said, shaking his head. "I don't feel anything."

"Be patient," Arthur said, putting his hand on Ben's back and pushing him gently toward the plants. "Stand in the middle of the beds," he directed him.

Ben dropped his shoulder bag and stepped forward.

Carefully he walked between two rows of dying plants. In his tan shirt, tall and narrow as a spear himself, he blended in with the garlic. Halfway down he rocked back on his heels as if blown by a wind, then righted himself and stood in place.

At first nothing happened. His nose, cheeks and hatless head burned in the hot sun, and sweat ran down his face and neck into his collar. Overhead, the sky was too bright, making him blink, and his forehead contracted in pain.

What a fool I am! he thought.

But in a while there seemed to be a faint disturbance in the air. And, like the time before, Ben started tingling. Squinting at the garlic, he felt the same tickle in his arms and shoulders, a funny sensation that was strangely comforting. His heart was suddenly bulging, as soft as a pudding, and he swung slightly from side to side as though he were being rocked in their green arms.

"You're swaying," Arthur said, and Ben admitted he was feeling peculiar, a little light-headed.

"The plants are excited. You're feeling their vibrations."

"Maybe I should sit down."

"It's nothing to be alarmed about."

Holding his ground, he turned up his palms to the magical sensation. It pushed through his veins, he imagined, and spread within, massaging his bones and organs . . . and he felt the energy of the plants warming and steadying him.

In this way he shared their joy.

He thrust his arms above his head and stretched up his fingers to the brilliant light.

When he came out of the garden he was laughing heart-
ily. He looked around at lilac bushes, bird feeders and wildflowers, then back at the garlic and beyond, to the cedar hedge,
undulating treetops, lake and sky . . . and stayed there for several minutes, taking it all in.

"Beautiful, isn't it," Ben said.

"Peaceful," Arthur answered.

"I could stand here forever."

"But it's time to go in now. Iris wants to say hello."

Ben followed his friend to the house. They wiped their
shoes and went inside.

The kitchen was empty. Iris was seated at one end of the
living room couch, eating a muffin and drinking tea. Sun
brightened the rug and lit up a sculpture on the floor resem-
bling a beaver dam, and the twig furniture smelled green.
Curtains ballooned as a breeze crossed the room, and flies
bumped against the screens of the open windows. The overall
effect was that the outdoors had been let in.

"Come in," Iris waved at them standing in the doorway.
"It's cooler here than outside."

Ben walked into the room and sat on the other end of the
couch. Arthur lowered himself between them, dropping a hand
on his wife's knee, while the symphony played briskly, breath-
lessly, in the background.

"Have a muffin," she said to Ben, pointing at a tray on a
low table by their knees. "I made them myself and they're full
of nutritious things."

He reached for one and took a bite as Iris bent forward

and poured tea into china cups with matching saucers decorated with flowers and vines. When he raised his cup to drink and then set it down again, it tinkled pleasingly against the pretty saucer.

He was sipping tea when all at once waves of deep, rumbling music crashed into the living room. Balanced on his knee, his cup and saucer trembled. After a particularly ominous drum roll, a picture of Renata in the kitchen sprang into his head: standing by a dropped stool, scowling at her teacup.

"Does your wife bake?" Iris asked, as if she understood his thoughts.

"She doesn't have time for that. Our lives are so hectic."

He stiffened as he listened to a thundering crescendo, then put aside his saucer and cup. His heart kaboomed with the music. Suddenly he leaned toward Iris over Arthur's knees.

"We never really *talk* anymore," he burst out.

"Talk's important," she agreed.

"I don't listen well, I guess—my mind's always floating off. Or else I'm running out the door."

"Does she know you're here today?"

"I said I was going out."

"You didn't say where?"

"No."

"Bring her along next time," she said. "We'd like to meet her."

"We have a few things to straighten out first before . . ." He glanced up as if the words he needed were overhead.

"Before you fall in love again," Iris completed his sentence.

Ben didn't answer, though his brain bulged with worried thoughts. No one said anything more. With folded hands they sat unmoving, knees and shoulders lined up as if they were posing for a magazine photographer. Before long, the breeze let up, the curtains flattened and the symphony faded away. Even the flies quieted.

The stillness went on and on.

Ben stopped thinking. He became aware of warm air, murmuring insects, the rich smell of turf and loam. Sadness and harmony.

When snatches of the symphony wafted in again through the screens, Arthur cocked an ear and announced the piece, "Shepherd's Song." Strong and resonant, it swelled toward its last refrain.

The chords played in Ben's chest, widening his rib cage. He shut his eyes and saw Renata's lovely face in the darkness, her brilliant eyes and fine skin. Abruptly her expression changed, tears dribbling down her cheeks, and he became weepy himself, squeezed and released from inside.

Something else was moving in the space around his heart too. A quiver of gratitude. That was it: he was thankful.

Ben looked around the room as the last of the symphony rang out and said he had to go now. He had to get back to his wife.

The Raes nodded in unison, then Arthur smiled and stood up. "Before you run off again, let me give you some garlic."

So Ben followed him outside to a tool shed behind the house and back to where he'd left his bag at the edge of the garden.

Carrying a pitchfork, Arthur walked between rows and came to a stop partway along. Muttering as he worked, he loosened soil around a plant and tugged at its dry stalks. The earth broke apart at once, and a bulb popped to the surface like the head of a white mole. Continuing along the row he pulled up several more, shook dirt from their roots and then tramped out of the patch.

Standing at Ben's side, he stabbed the pitchfork into the ground, braided and knotted the stalks, then handed him the leaves and bulbs.

Ben shoved the bundle into his bag and smiled crookedly. "If I eat enough garlic, will it cure whatever ails me?"

Arthur leaned an arm on the handle of his pitchfork and looked into the distance. "Healing's a mysterious thing," he said solemnly. "I can't say what will happen next."

CHAPTER 18

Awestbound train arrived at the Cobourg station and Ben got on the third car. It wasn't full and he could've sat alone but decided, to his surprise, he'd like some company and thus chose a seat beside a female passenger carrying a baby in a sling-thing.

When she turned his way and grinned at him, he noticed the chip on her front tooth and immediately thought of his wife's dental defects, which he'd always found endearing. And so he was inclined to like the young woman from the start.

Almost at once she began speaking rapidly, not even saying her name, as though he already knew it. Apparently she was travelling to Toronto from Montreal, where she'd gone to visit the baby's grandparents, Kim and James—or was that Cam and Jane? He couldn't hear well because the infant was squawking, but Kim-Cam and Jane-James were the parents of Cary—Gary or Grant—and she didn't like them much because they said the child looked like their son, Cary Grant—if he got that right—which anyone could see was wrong, and she was glad to be away from them and on her way home.

"I didn't catch their son's name."

"*Grant*," she said emphatically. "But don't you think she looks like me?" She pulled aside the upper part of the carrier so he could examine her daughter's dainty, serious face.

"Yes, I think she does. So Grant is her father?"

"Of course he is—*was*, maybe. 'Is,' 'was,' 'knows,' 'knew'—I'm never sure what tense to use."

"I don't follow," Ben said.

"He's dead, I mean. Grant's dead. He died last year in an accident I don't want to talk about except to say that mostly I'm over it now, especially with having to focus on my daughter."

"He died before she was born?"

"Before I even found out I was pregnant," she said, "and maybe if we'd known that, we would've tried harder to get along. Our marriage was sort of up and down, but the birth of a baby is something to look forward to and would've given us good stuff to talk about for a change."

"Talking helps," Ben said.

"I don't understand it, but since she was born I speak to him more than ever and tell him all about her—in my head, I mean, because I'm not one of those people who talks to herself on the street." She drew a few quick, short breaths and her chest jumped. "It's like he's still with me, you know, like he's still here, which doesn't make much sense."

"It makes sense to me," he said.

"I know he won't be back and I can't, like, fix things, and that makes me sad."

"You must miss him very much."

"Well, sure I do . . . but also it's time he was gone already. I want to be free of him."

"That takes a while."

"I'm still pretty young, you know, only in my twenties, so why shouldn't I meet someone new and fall in love again?"

Ben assured her that she would.

"I want to meet someone with a big heart and arms long enough to hold us both"—she clucked at her daughter—"and we'd love him twice as much, wouldn't we, Katrina? We'd be crazy about him. But wanting something doesn't make it happen, does it."

"I think it's a good start."

The infant began to whine more insistently, and the mother smiled down at her as she pulled a shawl from a bag at her feet, covered herself modestly and half opened her shirt. "Meanwhile I have you," she said, putting the child to her breast. The baby bunched her lips and eagerly began to suck, making short smacking sounds like small, wet kisses.

Feeling uncomfortable, Ben looked past them and out the side window at a stream and a veil of trees, a freight car on a siding . . . and then, reflected in the glass, he saw Renata in the kitchen, pouring milk into her tea, and wished the train would speed up.

When the infant gulped and sighed with pleasure, signalling that she was done, the young mother did up her shirt and put the shawl aside. The baby chirped in her arms as she lifted her out of the carrier, put her on her shoulder and rubbed circles on her back.

The child gave a loud belch—enormous, it seemed, for such a delicate creature—as her mother carefully turned her to the window to see out. She grabbed at what she saw in the glass, stretching out her short neck as if she wanted to see more, and hummed with enjoyment.

A short time later, the woman pulled the baby back and settled her on her knee. "Kids are so open and responsive," she said, "and Katrina seems especially in touch with nature."

"Katrina," he repeated, the name skipping on his tongue. He cooed at her and tickled her palm, and the baby cheeped and smiled back.

"She likes that," the woman said. "You must have kids yourself."

Slowly he shook his head, and she said that was too bad, he seemed like the sort of guy who'd make a good father. Lifting her daughter up, she asked if he wanted to hold her.

"She's not afraid of strangers," she insisted, "so go ahead. I need to stretch anyway."

Katrina kicked her legs and moved her arms in a paddling motion, but Ben only blinked at her.

"Take her," she said. "It's okay."

Timidly he raised his arms, and in one fluid motion the baby swam into them and gazed at him with bottomless eyes.

The mother stepped over him, into the aisle, and began walking up and down the rolling car.

Katrina was heavier in his grip than he had imagined and smelled not entirely fresh, her pink sleeper wet in spots, but Ben didn't mind. His fingers closed decisively around the squirmy bundle that was spitting drool along his sleeve. Gently cupping her head, he placed her on his shoulder and hugged her against him as her pudgy legs thrashed about, one of her arms pulled free and five fingers opened and closed. Absorbed and delighted, he nibbled her thumb, but the sound that escaped his throat was more a blubber than a laugh.

He lowered the baby with care, shifted her head to his elbow and smoothed his hand over her scalp, the fine hairs softer than grass.

His elbows swung as he cradled her and watched Katrina resting. She filled the space in his arms as completely as a lake fills the crannies of its basin, her weight a simple and unmistakable fact.

In a whisper he recited "The Owl and the Pussycat," and she moved her head and neck about, wagged her fingers and made splendid warbly sounds as if trying to sing along. He saw them in a wooden boat on a slow, meandering river, with a small guitar and runcible spoon—whatever that was—sailing away, away . . . and chanted to her about dancing by moonlight. "A beautiful, beautiful moon," he sighed.

He stared at her with moist eyes. There were tiny dimples in her cheeks, and her brows were blonde crescents. Her mouth was pursed, her nose blunt, her eyes bright and such a midnight blue they were nearly black. She gazed at him, unblinking, and something puddly rose in his throat as he looked back.

And this is what he was thinking: that the love he felt for a stranger's child had nothing and everything to do with the infant. That his love touched everyone—babies born and unborn; Arthur and Iris; the crew and passengers on the train; families in passing towns; men and women waiting in Toronto for their sweethearts; and especially his wife Renata, sitting on a kitchen stool and smiling at her teacup for no particular reason. He didn't know exactly what to make of his thoughts, but they seemed right.

The baby was suddenly restless and Ben readjusted his arms. "How's that?" he said, and she smiled back at him gummily.

"I'm getting the hang of it now," he laughed, studying her remarkable face.

Katrina burbled in his arms, sounding like a fountain, and he gazed at her shiny lips that seemed to be forming words.

"Who's your daddy?" he asked in the sweetest voice, and she beamed at him with luminous eyes reflecting his pleasure. *You are*, she seemed to say, and his heart caromed against his ribs like a billiard ball.

Abruptly the mother reappeared, standing over him in the aisle, banging his knees as she made her way back to her seat. She reached out, and he passed the baby over reluctantly. His empty fingers fell like pick-up sticks onto his lap.

But as the woman shifted, Katrina turned her head his way and met his eyes with a deep look. And Ben supposed the baby was thinking what he was: that in every moment something grows.

ACKNOWLEDGMENTS

My thanks to Maria E. Subtelny, Professor of Persian & Islamic Studies, Department of Near & Middle Eastern Civilizations, University of Toronto, for her translation of the novel's epigraph, line 2383, Book 1, the *Masnavi* of Jalal al-Din Rumi.

I greatly appreciate the insight and encouragement of those who read various drafts of my manuscript: Jane Finlayson, Jane Finlay-Young, Deborah Levine, Helen McLean, Susan Mockler, Anna Porter and my wise editor Diane Martin. My love and thanks to Bill and Paul, for any number of reasons.

Among the many members of the medical profession who helped me with my research, I wish to thank Dr. Martin M. Antony, Dr. Andy Cheok, Julie Cissell, Linda Wright and Dr. Sandra Yuen. I especially want to acknowledge Dr. David J. Dixon, a psychiatrist in private practice and formerly a staff psychiatrist with the Multi-Organ Transplant Program at Toronto General Hospital, University Health Network. My initial conversations with Dr. Dixon inspired this novel. Over several years, he has answered my questions and read and commented on versions of the book. I am deeply grateful for his time and generosity.

CYNTHIA HOLZ is the author of four previous novels and a collection of short fiction, all widely acclaimed. Born and raised in New York City, she has lived in Toronto since moving here as a journalist in 1976, an occupation she soon set aside in favour of writing fiction and teaching.

www.CynthiaHolz.com